DINNER WITH DRACULA

Being the Weird Adventures of Charles
Winterbottom, Archeologist with Azathoth, Cthulhu,
the Yeti Queen, the Dark Gods of Lemuria – And Other
Terrifying Creatures of the Night

JOE VADALMA

Futures-Past Editions
A Renaissance E Books publication
San Francisco CA
2011

Copyright 2008 Joe Vadalma

All rights reserved under International and Pan-American Copyright Conventions. This book may not be reproduced in whole or in part without written permission. For information contact: Renaissance E Books, Inc., 2930 Shattuck Ave. Suite 200-13, Berkeley CA 94705.

Futures-Past Editions and the Renaissance E Books names and logos are property of Renaissance E Books Inc.

www.Futures-PastEditions.com

ISBN 9781615083749

Manufactured in the United States of America

First PageTurner Edition: Nov. 2011

10 9 8 7 6 5 4 3 2 1

Cover art:: Laura Givens
Book design: Frankie Hill

I would like to dedicate this book to my wife, Alice, and my entire family who have supported me wonderfully in my writing career.

I also wish to thank my publisher, Jean Marie Stine, for making my crazy stories available to those who enjoy reading them.

CHAPTER 1. EXPLORING CYDONIA

A Proposal

A colleague of Doctor Charles D. Winterbottom's, a rival archeologist, Doctor Heinrich Schmidt, came to Winterbottom with a proposal.

"Charlie," he said, "I've spent years studying photographs of the Martian Cydonia Mensae area and am positive that the structures are not natural formations, but artificial. An alien race built them. It's up to us to find the proof."

Winterbottom did not care much for Schmidt, who was short and rotund, and had an aura of sauerkraut and stale beer about him. He wore his hair in what could only described as a long crew cut. His mustache was in the style of Hitler and Charlie Chaplin. He talked too much and cared more about publicity than archeology. "Many people disagree with you, Heinie."

"But none of them have been to Mars. No one has even sent a robotic probe to Cydonia."

"They probably won't. To the space people, there are more interesting places to explore such as Olympus Mons or Valles Marineris."

"They're fools. What could be more interesting than finding artifacts from an ancient Martian civilization?"

Winterbottom rubbed his chin. Although he did not completely trust Schmidt's motives, the man's enthusiasm intrigued him. "It certainly would be an adventure." Adventure and danger was what he loved about archeological field work. "But, my dear Heinie, how would we get there?"

"I have a cousin in the upper echelons of NASA. He's a grandson of one of the German scientists who came to America with Wernher von Braun. I brought my proposal to him. He's sure that he can talk upper management into initiating the mission. People are bored with ordinary Mars and Jupiter moon missions. NASA needs something spectacular to justify their existence."

"I see. But why come to me? I would think that you'd want to go it alone and not share any discoveries with another archeologist."

Schmidt flushed. "It's your flamboyant reputation. NASA is looking for the most publicity for the buck. Your scandalous affairs with women, your antics and narrow escapes are well known. That's what they're looking for. Hard working but unknown archeologists like me don't attract that kind of media attention."

Winterbottom took this as a compliment and puffed out his chest. "I understand completely. I'll go."

"Very well. Pack your bags. I'll book us on a flight to Orlando." He patted Winterbottom on the back, rather too low for comfort. "I'm sure we'll make a great team."

Astronaut Training

Winterbottom discovered that he would have to go through several weeks of training. After filling out several forms, he was introduced to the astronauts assigned to the mission. Sally Randy, an attractive brunette, was mission commander. Before she became an astronaut, she had been a hot shot jet pilot in the Air Force and a test pilot. Before that she had something to do with large feathery fans. She stuck out her hand. "I'm Randy."

He removed his floppy hat and took her hand in his. "I am too, usually."

She caught on immediately and laughed. "Do you know how many times I've heard that in my life? Just call me, Captain Sally."

"Pleased to meet you, Captain Sally. I'm Charles Winterbottom."

"This is my crew, Plush Blue and Jack Dooper. Blue is our medic, biology specialist and social scientist. Dooper is our science officer and navigator."

Blue was a slightly plump woman, but not bad looking. She had thick shoulder-length hair. Winterbottom was delighted to learn that there would be two young nubile females on the mission. The nights were cold in outer space.

Dooper was a stern looking young man, very military in his bearing.

After shaking hands with the astronauts, Winterbottom said, "What about that fellow there? Isn't he on the mission?" He pointed at a rather drab looking character standing near the wall.

"Oh him," Sally said. "Larke's our chief engineer. He's not a he, but an it, an android."

"Does he speak?"

"Only when spoken to. Larke, come over here."

The android approached in a stiff-legged manner. When it stopped, Winterbottom put out his hand. "I'm Doctor Winterbottom, archeologist."

Larke gripped his hand so hard that Winterbottom almost went to his knees and shook it vigorously. "Welcome to the NASA Space Center, Doctor Winterbottom. My name is Larke. I am an animatronic artificially intelligent humanoid robot. I fix things."

"Very nice. But what if something goes wrong with you while we're on the mission?"

"I do not know the answer to that question. Please consult ground control."

Winterbottom turned to Sally. "Do any of you know how to fix the fixer?"

She shrugged. "Nothing will go wrong with old reliable here. I've been on two missions with Larke. It never hiccuped once."

And the third is a charm, thought Winterbottom, but did not remark about his doubts.

* * * *

Although Winterbottom considered himself educated, athletic and in good shape, the training was more rigorous than he thought it would be. On the first day he was given a complete physical and was told to lose ten pounds. When he told Sally, she laughed and said, "You'll lose thirty by the time we're through with you." She let him feel the muscle on her upper arm to show how fit she was. It bulged up inches and was as hard as a rock.

The first four hours of each day were lectures on the spacecraft, including operational characteristics, mission requirements and objectives and support systems. In these classes he flirted with Sally every chance he got. She responded in a whimsical way, as though she was mentally laughing at his crude attempts to get to first base. Plush Blue, usually nearby, continuously annoyed him by poking him or making sexual innuendos; Schmidt, on the other hand, hung around with Dooper and the android, Larke.

Winterbottom and Schmidt were also given science and technical courses to get them up to speed with the latest developments in meteorology, guidance and navigation, astronomy, physics and computer sciences.

The rest of each day was spent in physical training as vigorous as boot camp in the marines.

After a few weeks, Winterbottom and his fellow travelers were given information about the area around Cydonia. They were trained in flight simulators and spaceship mockups to become familiar with systems, support equipment, crew operations, null gravity housekeeping and emergency procedures. A full day was spent on how to use the null-gravity commode.

Winterbottom's first experience with simulated weightlessness in a diving aircraft was a disaster. He immediately became ill and vomited his lunch, which floated about his head. After several times, however, he was able to eat, drink and handle tools and equipment. Somehow, once gravity was returned, he always wound up falling on Plush Blue. After each of these encounters, she would giggle and remark, "We must stop meeting like this."

As the time approached for the actual mission, they were given mission specific training, which included working and traveling in the specially designed Mars spacesuits in a landscape similar to the Cydonia area. This training was intense and difficult because of the heavy, clumsy suits. One day as Winterbottom perspired and huffed and puffed, Sally said, "Don't worry, Winter. It won't be as bad on Mars. The gravity there is only two fifths of earth's."

"How come you're not breathing heavy?"

She raised her eyebrows and laughed. "I only do that in the bedroom. Besides, we women have more endurance than you men. A few strokes and you're done."

He grinned back at her. "I think you would find that I have more endurance than most. May I give you a workout?"

She patted him on the cheek. "You men all say that until you're alone with a woman. Maybe someday. But this close to liftoff, we'll be too busy for hanky-panky."

Blastoff

After several months of training, the big day arrived. With the help of Plush Blue, Winterbottom donned his spacesuit. Cameras flashed as the Cydonia team strolled out to the minibus that would take them to the shuttle. They waved to the onlookers and press who cheered and applauded.

Once Winterbottom was strapped into the acceleration couch and the countdown was down to T minus five minutes, he had second thoughts. *What the heck am I doing in this evil contraption?* Perspiration broke out on his forehead and fogged the face plate on his space helmet. *I should be mucking around inside a pyramid, up to my ears in dirt and poisonous serpents, or having angry natives chasing me with spears after I snatched their prized idol. Some people are not made for space travel.*

He glanced over at Sally in the next couch over. She appeared relaxed. He realized that he would look like a coward and idiot if he suddenly screamed, "Stop the countdown. I want my mommy."

"...four...three....two...one...ignition." There was a loud roar. Winterbottom felt as though someone had dropped a two-ton weight on his chest. The next several minutes seemed like hours. Suddenly the weight lifted, and he had the sensation of floating. They were in orbit around the earth. Sally said, "Nice ride, huh Charlie?"

He grunted.

The shuttle pilot did a burn to take the vehicle to Space Station Five. A small amount of gravity returned, and Winterbottom relaxed. A docking maneuver was performed, and the pilot floated down the aisle. "Okay ladies and gents, time to disembark."

Winterbottom unsnapped his harness and floated upward. He tried to recall how to maneuver in null-G, but panicked as his nose hit the cabin ceiling. He flayed around for a while until Plush Blue took hold of him and dragged him by the arms out of the shuttle exit. Randy laughed at him. "By the time we get to Mars, you'd better figure out how to move around without crashing into walls."

"Don't pay any attention to her," said Blue. "We were all awkward at

first."
He flushed. Never before had he felt such a clumsy fool before the ladies.
The space station rotated like a giant bicycle wheel to produce artificial gravity. After they took an elevator down one of the spokes to the rim, gravity returned. Nonetheless, Winterbottom still felt strange and ill as they strolled along. He said, "I'm lightheaded. This space travel has affected my balance."
Randy grinned. "You dummy. Your head *is* lighter than your feet because of the artificial gravity produced by rotation. Didn't you learn anything in astronaut class? If you think that short trip up to space station messed with your senses, what're you going to do on the way to Mars. For nine months we'll be in null-G. You'll be a basket case." She slapped him on the back so hard he stumbled and almost fell on his face.
"Don't listen to her, Charles," said Blue. "You'll do just fine. And you're as smart as us – in your own field."
"Yeah, like Larke," cracked Randy.

The Perceival

The passengers and crew of the Perceival, the Mars spaceship, had lunch at the space station. Immediately afterward, they boarded the deep space vehicle. Sally Randy as the pilot sat up front in the command area. Dooper took the navigator's seat next to her. Blue and Winterbottom crawled into the next two acceleration couches, and Schmidt and Larke took the third set of seats.
After burn maneuvers sent the ship on a trajectory toward Mars, the astronauts and passengers were free to float about the crew module. Although the crew module was larger than the shuttle, space was at a premium. Unless Winterbottom was extremely careful, he often rubbed against one of the others as they passed. He did not mind when the person was Randy or Blue, but he actively disliked the sensation when it was one the men, especially Schmidt.
As the days dragged on, Winterbottom became bored. So far, his activities were the mandatory daily exercises, failed attempts to seduce Randy and maneuvers to avoid Schmidt. In the close quarters of the ship, the last was impossible. During each encounter with Schmidt, his fellow archeologist dragged out photos and other data about Cydonia and went on endlessly about plans for the dig.
Winterbottom told him, "Let's not assume anything. We'll decide on an approach once we observe conditions at the site."
Nonetheless, each day he bugged Winterbottom with some new plan.
Sally Randy, Jack Dooper and Plush Blue spent most of their time on their normal duties, checking gauges, inspecting items, taking astronomical readings and performing experiments for scientists. To engage Randy in conversation, Winterbottom asked her about piloting

the spaceship.

"It's a breeze. Actually, while we're between planets, I don't really have any piloting duties. The onboard intelligent navigation computer, OINC, does all the driving. Jack and I simply check up on it once in a while. I won't be needed until the landing phase."

This did nothing to relieve Winterbottom's unease about being in a tin can thousands of miles from earth in the vast emptiness of space. He hid his fears by making light. "OINC? It must be a hog for data."

Randy laughed and slapped him on the back, causing him to sail halfway down the corridor. "You're a card, Winter."

He tried another approach. "What do you do for entertainment for the next eight months?"

"Well, we've got TV. All the shows are reruns, but I have some hot DVDs to watch." She wiggled her eyebrows in a lascivious manner.

He brightened. "Really. Perhaps we could watch them together."

"Don't think so, Winter." She pinched him on the cheek. "Me and Dooper got a thing going."

Crushed, Winterbottom floated away. Plush Blue accosted him. "Say Charles, you look bored. Want to join the million mile high club?"

He gazed at her quizzically. She had plenty of curves, perhaps a few too many, and a pretty face. He realized that she had been flirting with him from the time they met. Since Randy was out of his league, he thought, *why not?* "You putting me on?"

"Why would I do that?" She put her arm around him. "These long space trips are dreary if you don't do something to break the monotony. Why do you think NASA assigns crews of mixed sexes? On long voyages, we change partners often throughout the trip."

His eyebrows shot up. Maybe he still had a chance with the lovely Randy. "Well, where would..."

She grabbed his arm and pulled him along. "Back in the storeroom for privacy. You'll enjoy this, Charles. There's nothing quite like a roll-in-the-hay in null-G."

After she pulled him into the storeroom, locked the door and tore at his clothes, he asked, "Why me? What about Heinie?"

"I don't think he likes women. He never tries to rub up against me like you do."

"You're probably right."

As Blue had pointed out, sex was quite an experience in zero gravity. Positions were unlimited. After a while, however, Winterbottom became dizzy and had to call a halt until he recovered.

Larke, the Android

One day while Blue was at her duties, Winterbottom saw Larke in a corner staring at nothing. Curious he approached the android. "How are you today, Larke?"

"My systems are nominal. How are you, Doctor Winterbottom?"

"You can call me Charlie. Almost everyone else does. Actually I'm bored."

"Would you like to play a game of chess, Charlie?"

"Sure. That'd be fun." Winterbottom had been class champion in college.

A table in the mess bay had an inlaid checkerboard. The chess pieces were magnetized to keep them from floating. In the first game, the android checkmated Winterbottom after ten moves.

"I'm a bit rusty," Winterbottom alibied.

They played ten games. When Larke won each one handily, Winterbottom realized that he was outmatched. "I'm tired of chess. Perhaps we should simply converse for a while."

"On what subject do you wish to converse?"

"Oh, I don't know. Do you know anything about archeology?"

"Yes."

They began to talk archeology. Winterbottom bragged about his exploits but soon realized that Larke knew more about the subject than he did. It was like talking to Schmidt. Finally he said, "What do you do for fun, Larke?"

"Fun? Androids do not have fun. We provide it."

"Really? What kind of fun do you provide?"

"I play all sorts of games. I give lessons in various activities. I do sex with women."

"You do? You mean you have ... you're provided with..."

"Is the word you're struggling to recall 'penis?'"

Winterbottom flushed and cleared his throat. "Uh hum. Yes."

"I do indeed. It is most large and admired by female crew members. By gay men also."

"Have you ever done it with the women in the present crew?"

"Often. Not on this voyage, however."

"Both of them?"

"Not at the same time."

It galled Winterbottom that Sally Randy had been with a robot, but refused him. It gave him a feeling of inferiority.

"Would you like me to service you as I did the women?"

"Um, no thanks."

Course Correction

Halfway to Mars, Plush Blue took Winterbottom to the side. "Charlie, I'm afraid our affair is over for the rest of the trip."

Winterbottom's jaw dropped. "You ... you're dumping me?"

"Sorry sweetie, but we can still be friends." She patted him on the cheek.

"Why?"

"I've stolen Jack Dooper from Captain Sally."

"Oh! What's so great about him?" Nonetheless, he was not too put out by this news. It meant that Randy was no longer seeing the navigator.

Blue grinned. "They don't call him Super Dooper for nothing. Sorry again, old chum." She floated away.

Winterbottom went to seek out Randy. She was in the observatory peering through a telescope. "We still on course, Captain Sally?"

"Actually, no. I need to do a corrections burn. Want to watch?"

"Absolutely."

She sat at the command console and announced that everyone was to strap into acceleration couches while she made a course correction. Winterbottom took the navigation position. Once all aboard signaled that they were secured, Randy typed in commands to OINC. The spaceship shuddered. For a few minutes weight returned as the maneuvering rockets fired. Sally peered at the navigation information. "Shit. Something's wrong. We've over-corrected." A red warning light came on. "That must be it." She pointed at it. "A starboard engine burn shut off too soon. Damn!"

Winterbottom became frightened. "Wh-what's the matter?"

"This frigging bucket-of-bolts is way off course now, worse than before."

"Can it be corrected?"

"Not until we fix whatever is wrong." She shouted, "Larke, report to the command console immediately." She turned to Winterbottom. "I hope the android can figure out what the problem is."

Winterbottom's stomach churned, and he began to perspire. "What will happen if he can't?"

"Oh, we'll shoot right out of the solar system."

"Someone will come to our rescue, won't they?"

Randy shook her head. "How can they do that? They have no way of catching up with us. And even if they did, our life support would have failed long before they reached us. They'd simply be picking up corpses."

Winterbottom felt faint. He wondered what it would be like to die of suffocation as their oxygen ran out. He turned away so that Randy wouldn't see his tears.

Larke appeared. It saluted. "Android Larke reporting."

After Sally explained the problem, she and Larke exchanged places. Larke opened up its shirt and a panel in its chest. It pulled out a USB connector and plugged it into the console. Screens of numbers scrolled down the monitor. Larke muttered something unintelligible. The spaceship shuddered several times. Randy grabbed the back of Winterbottom's couch to keep from being thrown around. Finally the shuddering stopped. Larke turned to Randy. "The starboard aft engine is out of alignment. An EVA will be necessary to execute repair."

"Okay, Larke. I'll suit up. Get whatever tools we'll need."

Randy went to the spacesuit rack. Winterbottom watched as she unzipped her coveralls and stepped out of them. Beneath she had on only bikini briefs and a see-through bra. She glanced in Winterbottom's direction and noticed his interest. "Stop staring, pervert," she cried. Winterbottom flushed and turned away.

"I'm sorry," he muttered. Nonetheless, his glance kept going to the mirror-like observation screen.

When she was in the spacesuit before donning the helmet, she called for Jack Dooper. "Me and Larke need to go EVA. Man the airlock door."

Larke did not wear a spacesuit. It donned a tool belt and followed Randy into the airlock. Dooper shut the door, listened in his earphones for Randy's signal and pressed the red button under the word *Evacuate*. There was a hiss as air was drawn out of the chamber.

Winterbottom peered through the small window in the airlock door and watched as Randy and Larke floated out of the hatch to the vacuum and darkness of space. Their footfalls as the made their way toward the engine module sounded on the overhead bulkhead. Once past the crew module, the sound stopped.

Hours went by.

"Should they be out there so long?" Winterbottom asked Dooper.

Dooper glanced at his watch. "Randy's at the limit of her oxy. I'd better check on her." He fitted the headphones and mike on. "Calling Captain Sally."

Winterbottom eavesdropped on the conversation with the console earphones.

"What the frig you want, Dooper? We're pretty busy out here."

"Better check your oxy level, Captain. You've been EVA for three hours."

"Oh shit. You're right. I've only got ten minutes left. Hey Larke, think you can finish up here. I gotta go in and replenish my oxy. Dooper, aborting EVA. Standby."

Five minutes later, a space-suited figure entered the airlock and closed the outer hatch. Oxygen was pumped into the airlock, and Randy floated through the airlock door. She took off her helmet, but to Winterbottom's disappointment remained in the space suit. She donned comm gear.

A half an hour later, Winterbottom heard Larke's odd voice. "Repair accomplished. Returning to vessel interior." Clomping footfalls rang on the bulkheads again. It stopped halfway toward the entrance hatch. "Error situation. Joints frozen. Cannot proceed."

"Oh crap," cried Randy. "What now? Can you move at all?"

"Negative."

"Guess I'll have to save that idiot savant. I told it to apply that nonfreezing grease to its joints."

After she went EVA again, there was another long wait during which

Winterbottom bit his nails. "What if we lose both of them?" he asked Dooper. "Do you know how to land the spaceship?"

"I've been trained, but have never done a descent maneuver except in a simulator. It's Larke I'm most worried about. It's the only one aboard who can troubleshoot ship systems and effect a repair. Captain Sally has nine lives. She'll be okay ... I hope."

Finally Randy's voice came over the comm equipment. "Son-of-a-bitch is a clumsy package. Having a hard time maneuvering Larke to hatch. Estimate time of return from EVA ten minutes."

Winterbottom and Dooper sighed with relief as eleven minutes later, Randy shoved Larke through the outer hatch. After pushing the android into the spaceship interior proper, she removed her spacesuit and sat at the console in her undies. Again she ordered everyone into acceleration couches. "Dooper, take the navigation position. Winterbottom, drag Larke back to the passenger bay and strap him and yourself in back there."

Winterbottom was disappointed that he would no longer be unable to admire Randy in her unmentionables.

Repairing Larke

Once the ship was back on course, Winterbottom and Randy maneuvered onto the operating table in sickbay. Randy said, "Plush, can you fix his joints? They've seized up."

"I'm a medical doctor, Captain. I fix human beings. I don't know a damn thing about androids."

"Well, do the best you can."

Schmidt, who had been watching with interest, said, "I know a little about mechanics. I've repaired land-rovers and other vehicles that had broken down in wilderness areas."

"Good," said Randy. "Help her out."

Winterbottom, who knew nothing about machines or electronics, wondered whether this was a good time to approach Randy. "Now that we're back on course, and you've delegated Larke's repair, I wonder whether I could talk to you privately."

She eyed him suspiciously. "As long as this doesn't take too long. I've got to make a report to ground control. Come to my cabin." As commander, she was the only person aboard that had the privacy of a small room by herself.

Her cabin was tiny. With two people inside of it, they were inches apart. This suited Winterbottom's purpose well.

Randy leaned her back against a bulkhead. "So what is it, Winter?"

"Bottom."

"Bottom what?"

"I mean my name is Winterbottom, not Winter."

"You're so damn dense. I know that. It's a mouthful. What do you want?"

"You actually. I understand that you and Dooper broke up. Since you're now available..."

She chuckled. "You're a card, Winter. Have I shown the least interest in you?"

His lips turned down in a pout. "You invited me to watch you do a course correction."

"Just wanted to teach you a thing or two. Sorry buddy, I like brainy guys, like Doctor Schmidt."

"Heinie? You're interested in him?" His self esteem went through the floor. Heinie? How could this lovely desire the rotund little man more than his manly, broad shouldered self? "But is he interested in you?"

"Actually yes. He asked me on date like a gentleman."

"A date? How can you date on a spaceship?"

"We had a candlelight dinner in the mess and watched TV in the lounge."

"Watch what? Porno movies?"

"No. A romantic comedy, in fact. Now, please leave. I have work to do."

Winterbottom was tempted to simply grab her and kiss her. Instead he left her cabin like a beaten dog. There would be no romance for him during the rest of the way to Mars. That nerd, Heinie, had beaten his time with the gorgeous Sally Randy.

He went to the medical bay to see how Larke was doing. The android was all in pieces. Its arms were on chair; one leg leaned against a wall; Schmidt was examining the joints of the other; its head was disconnected from its body. "Oh my. Will you be able to repair Larke, Heinie?"

The archeologist shrugged. "I'm more familiar with automobiles and trucks."

Larke's head said, "Good afternoon, Charlie. I would play a game of chess with you, but as you can see, I've gone to pieces."

"Retained your sense of humor, I see. That's good. A cheerful attitude will help you heal."

"Androids don't have attitudes, a sense of humor or heal, for that matter," Larke replied.

"Where's Plush Blue? Why isn't she attending you?"

Schmidt said, "She doesn't know a damn thing about machinery. She was in my way."

Randy's voice came over the loudspeaker. "Astronaut Blue, report on the condition of the android."

Winterbottom donned comm gear. "Winterbottom here. Plush isn't in sick bay."

"Where the hell is she?"

Winterbottom asked Schmidt whether he knew where Blue had gone.

"She said something about going to the storeroom with Jack Dooper."

11

"Oh." Winterbottom knew what that meant. He said to Randy, "She's gone to the storeroom for supplies."

"Storeroom, huh. I know damn well what she does there. I suppose Dooper's with her."

"Uh ... yes."

"Is anyone working on the android?"

"Heinie."

"How's it going?"

"Well, he's taken Larke apart. He's examining the joints."

"Okay. I don't need its arms and legs right now, just its head and torso. Bring them here."

"Me?"

"Who else? You said that Schmidt is working on the android's limbs, and Blue and Dooper are banging in the storeroom."

"Okay, Sally."

"Captain Sally to you. And it's 'aye, aye' not 'okay'."

"Aye, aye, Captain Sally."

"That's better. We'll make an astronaut out of you yet, Winter."

He tucked Larke's head under his arm and pushed its body before him toward the command bay. It was a good thing that there was no gravity. Otherwise, he could have never maneuvered the heavy awkward android trunk. As it was, he kept banging against objects in their path and the bulkheads. When they arrived at the command bay, Randy said, "What the hell? Why is its head off?"

Winterbottom shrugged. "Heinie took it off for some reason."

"Well, I need it on." She pulled out a drawer. "Here's some tools. Reattach its head."

"But I don't know anything about robot repair. What do I do with all these dangling cables?"

Randy snorted in derision. "You're as useless as turd on Christmas. Take the copilot/navigator's position." Winterbottom obeyed. "Now see the display before you. The smaller circle must be kept within the larger, as close to the center as possible. You control them by manipulating these two knobs. Do you think you can handle that while I fix Larke?"

"Aye, aye, Captain Sally." He placed his hands on the knobs. They vibrated slightly. As Randy got out of the commander's couch, the smaller circle drifted to the left. Winterbottom turned the left knob to the right. The circle drifted upward. He quickly turned it to the left again and turned the right knob to the right. The circle moved back to center.

Randy slapped him on the back. "See. You're doing fine. We'll make an astronaut out of you yet."

She knelt down on the deck by Larke and began to plug cables from his head into sockets in the throat area of its torso.

Meanwhile, Winterbottom found that keeping the small circle in the center of the large was more difficult than it had seemed at first. The

12

knobs did not always control it the same way. Sometimes the left was for up/down, sometimes for left/right. The same was the case for the right knob. As a result, he would sometimes send the small circle in the wrong direction completely. He needed to move swiftly to recover. His hands cramped. As he concentrated on the circles, they made him dizzy. He began to see double; four circles appeared. Once he thought he sent the small circle into the center of the large circle but it was an illusion and had actually moved further from true center. He had to act even more swiftly to recover. He perspired profusely. It was one of the hardest tasks he had ever performed.

Just when he thought he would go mad with frustration and tension, Randy placed Larke's torso on the commander's couch, strapped it in, plugged its USB cable into the console and whispered something into Larke's ears. The small circle snapped to the center of the larger one and stayed there.

"Okay dummy, you can take your hands off of the stellar navigational controls."

Winterbottom pulled his hands away and rubbed them together to get the circulation going.

Randy unplugged Larke. "Okay Winter. Take Larke back to sickbay. Everything's back to nominal."

Winterbottom was glad that Larke's head was on. It made the return trip to sickbay easier. When he arrived, Blue and Dooper were there. Dooper was helping Schmidt repair Larke's joints.

"How's the repair work going?"

"Just about done," said Dooper. "The damage was from the cold. The next time Larke does an ETA, it should wear a spacesuit. I'm surprised that its computing circuits weren't damaged."

Larke, whose torso and head were back on the operating table, said, "They may have been. I'm getting intermittent fatal memory errors that are affecting my computing processes."

The three people in the room gazed at the android with concern. Blue said, "Oh you poor dear." She went over by it and stroked its head.

Winterbottom said in a trembling voice, "What about the navigation stuff you just did for Captain Sally? You did enter the correct data, didn't you?"

"I believe so. But I cannot be sure. My random access memory is cloudy."

Winterbottom felt faint as he visualized gasping his last breath as the oxygen supply gave after they had traveled millions of miles off course. "I'd better report this to Captain Sally."

He returned to the control bay.

"What now, Winter?" Randy said in an irritated manner. Winterbottom told her about the android's problem. "Too bad. But we shouldn't need Larke until we get to Mars."

13

"What about the navigation data Larke entered into the onboard computer?"

"Must be A-okay. We're right on course."

"Does anyone know how to repair the android?"

"Nope. Android repairs are done earth side."

"But what if we need him to fix something?"

She shrugged nonchalantly. "Guess we'll have to call ground control. Say, if you're going back to sickbay, would you send Heinrich up here. I could use some pleasant company."

Winterbottom slumped out of the control bay. For the rest of the way to Mars, he was bored, jealous and depressed. One good thing came out of Larke's disability; however, the android's chess playing ability had deteriorated to the point that Winterbottom could beat it every tenth game.

Descent to Mars

As they approached Mars, Randy called everyone together to brief them on landing procedures. "First we'll do an aerocapture maneuver. We'll be using Mars' upper atmosphere to brake the vehicle enough to insert it into orbit around the planet. The turbulence may be a little rough and fiery, so don't shit your pants, Winter."

Winterbottom resented the fact that she singled him out. *Heinie will be just as frightened*, he thought.

Randy continued, "Once our orbit is well established, we'll perform the descent maneuver. The same aeroshell we used for orbit insertion will provide thermal protection for the descent module during atmospheric entry. Once the descent module enters the Martian atmosphere and slows down sufficiently, the aeroshell will separate from the module inside and parachutes will be used for the last stage of vertical surface delivery. Any questions?"

Schmidt said, "What about our equipment?"

"It's been sent to the landing site and should be waiting for us. Mission control assured me that the insertion, descent and landing went perfectly."

"How near to the Cydonia artifact will we land?"

"About two hundred klicks north."

"Why so far away?"

"The terrain in the Cydonia area is too rough for a safe landing. Once we land, we'll setup a base camp, and haul whatever equipment is needed south to a temporary camp in the Cydonia area. It may be quite a while before we reach that hill you people call an artifact. You'll need to keep you pants on for a while when we arrive. It may be days before we'll be ready to travel to the Cydonia area."

* * * *

Two hours before the aerocapture maneuver, they donned spacesuits and went to their assigned acceleration couches. Randy reordered the seating arrangement. Schmidt was seated in the navigator's position. The next two couches held Blue and Dooper. Winterbottom was in the last row next to Larke. To relieve the tension as Randy counted down, he asked Larke how it was feeling.

"Many intermittent random access memory errors have occurred. I needed to reboot several times. There must be a partial short on my motherboard. This aerocapture maneuver could aggravate the problem."

"Sorry to hear that." Winterbottom hoped that they would not require Larke's services for the remainder of the voyage. "Tell me, were you specifically built to do maintenance aboard a spaceship?"

"No. My earlier employment was at a waste management station. I sorted trash for recyclable materials."

"Really? How did you happen to get into spaceship maintenance?"

"My boss at the waste management plant called me a 'screw up.' At that time NASA was in a budget crunch and bought me at a bargain price."

Winterbottom was dismayed to learn that Larke had not been very good at a simple job like sorting through garbage and that NASA had bought it cheap. What did that say about the android's ability to repair complicated items on a spaceship?

Before Winterbottom could make another remark, the count went to zero. The ship shuddered and made terrible noises as though it were shaking apart. Through a porthole, Winterbottom saw flames shooting past the window. The interior temperature rose steeply. Perspiration ran in rivulets from his forehead, down his back and from his underarms. He closed his eyes and repeated over and over in a low voice, "This is normal. Nothing's wrong with the ship. I'm not going to die. Mommy."

After a few minutes, the shuddering, flames and heat ceased and null-G conditions returned. Randy announced over the comm system, "Mars orbital insertion successful. You people may relax while I notify ground control. When I get their okay, we'll start descent mode. Stay strapped in. You may remove your helmets, but have them nearby."

Winterbottom took off his helmet. Since Larke did not wear a helmet, he asked, "Are you all right, Larke?"

"Most systems are go. They are no worse than before the orbital insertion maneuver."

"Tell me, why did your boss at the trash transfer station consider you a screw-up?"

"Too much initiative. Androids are supposed to do exactly as they are told, nothing else. One day I became bored and started tossing metallic material into the metal bin from some distance away. I and my fellow androids held contests as to which one of us could toss items into the bin from the greatest distance. One large metal object missed the bin and accidentally hit a human overseer that no one liked on the head. It killed him. When my boss asked who started the game, the other androids snitched on me."

"I see. Say, if your job was to sort trash, why were you given a wang?"

"Wang? Oh, I understand. 'Wang' is slang for penis. Originally I was manufactured to work in a male brothel. I was fired from that job too."

"Why?"

"The brothel owner said that I was too good. I could sustain an erection for as long as the client wished. As a result, my clients usually went past the usual twenty minutes. The human male prostitutes complained."

"I understand now why you're popular with the women."

They discussed this and other subjects until Randy's announcement. "Helmets on. Refasten restraints. Prepare for descent. Descent maneuver to begin in five minutes and counting."

Five minutes later, there was a loud clunk as the descent module separated from the orbital module. The ship shuddered again. Winterbottom was shoved back into his seat. There was a roaring, and flames appeared in the porthole. He did not panic this time. He gritted his teeth, closed his eyes and thought of beautiful scenery such as at that at the beach at Cape Hatteras during spring break.

A short time later the shuddering and flames stopped. The descent module jerked as the parachute deployed. For a while there was a swaying motion that gave Winterbottom motion sickness. Somehow he managed to keep from vomiting until he felt a terrific thump. All motion and sound stopped except for the whisper of the air circulating fans. In addition, gravity had returned, although it was not as strong as on Earth.

Randy announced, "The Perceival has landed. Welcome to Mars, lady, gentlemen and android. Keep your helmets on until I make preliminary tests to make sure the landing did not inflict any damage." A few minutes later, she gave the okay to remove their helmets and unstrap. "You may now move about the module."

Winterbottom was ecstatic. They were on solid ground once more. He peeked out the porthole. All he saw was a rust colored desert that stretched as far as the eye could see. The sky was pink with wispy clouds. How he longed to go out there and enjoy what appeared to be a fine day. "Captain Sally," he said into the comm unit. "When will we disembark?"

She chuckled. "Anxious to stretch your legs huh, earthworm? This afternoon I need to locate the equipment module and bring it back here. You, Heinrich and Larke can come with to help with the loading. Dooper and Blue, deploy the solar panels, and check that all systems are functional, especially the emergency regenerative fuel cells."

The people going with Randy donned helmets again, including Larke, who also donned a spacesuit. Randy was not taking a chance of further damage to the android. The airlock procedure was done in the same manner as for an EVA in space. Winterbottom gazed around with wonder at the orange desert full of boulders and stones. His heart leaped with excitement. He was really on Mars. Who knew what great adventures lay ahead?

Randy had an instrument for locating the equipment module. "It's over there about eight klicks," she said pointing. "We have a little hiking to do. Be careful of sharp stones. Even a small rip could cause decompression."

Although they carried a backpack loaded with oxygen and tools, walking was relatively easy because of the lower gravity. Winterbottom and Randy, with their longer legs, arrived at the equipment landing site in a little over an hour. Schmidt and Larke arrived twenty minutes later. Randy did not wait for them. With Winterbottom's help, she opened up the module. The eight sides opened up like the petals of a flower. Inside were various crates and a truck-like vehicle with threads rather than wheels. A second unmotorized hauler was attached to the back of the truck.

When Schmidt and the android arrived, all four began to load the crates on the vehicle. Actually, Larke was not much help. It had a tendency to wander away or simply turn in circles. When the loading was done, Randy got in the driver's seat, and ordered that Schmidt should sit next to her. Winterbottom and Larke were consigned to back of the truck. They used the crates as seats. Randy drove at the vehicles top speed of thirty-two kilometers per hour through the uneven sandy surface. Winterbottom and the android had to hang on for dear life not to be thrown with all the jolting and quick turns to avoid obstacles.

When they got back to the descent module, the two astronauts had set up solar panels for power and a tent-like habitation module. They were busily connecting power cables to it. Randy helped them complete this task. Everyone helped unpack the equipment needed to make the habitation module habitable. Randy brought all systems online and proceeded with a lengthy check of them. By then, darkness had fallen. A celebration dinner with alcoholic beverages was enjoyed by all except Larke. Afterward everyone retired. The habitation module was divided into five sleeping areas and the common area. Two of the sleeping areas were not used, however, as Schmidt and Randy slept together and Blue and Dooper cohabited. Winterbottom wore earplugs so that he would not hear their grunts and moans.

The next day was spent locating a water source. Randy had an instrument for detecting underground water. She wandered around, holding the liquid detection gear in front of her like a dousing rod. Finally, the rod dipped. She called the crew over. "Approximately one hundred meters under this spot is an underground lake. We'll dig the well here."

They brought well digging equipment to the spot and turned it on. Since the digging would be through solid rock, it would take hours to reach the water supply. Randy put Larke in charge of the drill, since the android did not get bored. The crew and archeologists spent the rest of the day unpacking. The equipment to be taken to Cydonia was loaded on the trucks. The rest was set up at the base camp.

Four hours later, Larke cried, "Water. We've struck water. We're rich." His mental state was definitely worse.

Everyone donned spacesuits and went outdoors. It was true. Water gushed out of the ground where the drill had bitten through, forming a geyser in the manner of an oil well. When the water was tested for potability, it was clean and sweet and pure. Randy took the first glass to her lips. "Yum. Martian water is the best in the solar system. If only I had a means of getting it to earth, I'd make a fortune."

The astronauts capped the well and ran pipes to the spaceship and the habitation module. In addition, a large rubber bladder was placed aboard the cart attached to the truck. This was filled with water. While they were drinking their fill, Winterbottom said to Randy, "I'm worried about Larke. Something got jiggled in his computing equipment. He's not altogether sane and is getting worse."

"Yeah. I've noticed. But what can we do? None of us knows anything about repairing androids."

"Can't you call ground control for instructions?"

Randy made a face. "It's kind of a pain talking to Earth. When I speak, it takes four minutes or more until they hear my voice. Sometimes it's more, depending on where earth and Mars are with respect to each other. Their replies take just as long. So you have these long gaps between question and answer. But, you should know all that. If you hadn't been so busy flirting with me and Blue, you might've learned something in astronaut school. It would take forever to diagnose Larke's problem and receive instructions to repair it. If you and Heinrich want to do any archeology at Cydonia, we need to get going soon. Our supplies won't last forever."

"I see. I hope he will be all right." Winterbottom walked away. He glanced with sadness at Larke, who he now considered a friend. The android was sitting by the well, mumbling to itself.

Setting Up

For the remainder of the week, the astronauts went about their various duties which included various experiments, gathering Martian rocks and soil samples, and making reports to ground control. The archeologists made plans, argued, flirted with the women, played games and sometimes helped the crew with various tasks.

Before they left the spaceship, Randy had Dooper convert water from the well into hydrogen and oxygen. They stored the gases in separate tanks, which they loaded on the trucks. They also took along food items that did not need to be refrigerated. Everything they needed to survive,

food, fuel, oxygen, water, shelter and tools, was loaded on the vehicles.
    Randy and Schmidt rode in the cab. Blue and Dooper remained at the base camp. Again, Winterbottom had to ride in the enclosed truck bed with Larke among boxes of supplies. At first they traveled fairly swiftly at thirty-two kilometers per hour, but Randy had to slow down and drive a zigzag course as they traversed terrain full of boulders and craters. They stopped once for lunch, to stretch their legs and empty the urine bladders in their spacesuits. All in all, it took them nine hours to reach The Face, as the mesa at Cydonia was called.
    The features that made the mesa resemble a face could not be seen from below. Schmidt and Winterbottom walked all around the great stone structure examining the walls. There were marks that could be hieroglyphics or simply scratches caused by cracking and wind scoring. Wind driven sand had smoothed the surface so that it was difficult to determine whether they were made by an intelligent agency or normal erosion.
    Schmidt pointed at a particular series of scratches. "These markings are definitely made by intelligent beings."
    "I beg to differ with you," said Winterbottom, who always contradicted anything Schmidt had to say. "They're simply scoring made by the pebbles flying through the air due to Mars' high winds."
    They argued like this continuously as they circled the mesa. When they came around to their starting point, Randy hollered over the comm unit. "Hey, you two. Come here. Do you frigging idiots expect me to do everything? We've got to set up camp."
    The archeologists replied together, "Aye, aye, Captain Sally." They rushed over to help her with the habitation module and unload survival equipment and other items needed immediately. They hooked up water, cooking and heating stoves and oxygen to the tent-like module. Before they completed these tasks, night fell. Sally made a gourmet dinner of Spam and beans. By the time they finished eating, everyone was exhausted except Larke. The android remained standing in a corner muttering to itself.
    Before they retired for the night, Winterbottom asked, "How are you doing, old friend?"
    "Not well. Error rate increasing. Martian interference."
    "What do you mean Martian interference?"
    "The Mars broadcasts are interfering with my software execution."
    "You're hearing voices?"
    "Yes. Martian voices."
    Schmidt, who had been eavesdropping, came over. "The Martians are speaking to you? What are they saying?"
    Larke shrugged. "Some gibberish about *the old ones.*"
    "This is the proof that a Martian civilization does exist, probably underground. Where are the signals coming from? The Mesa?"

"No. They are stronger in that direction." The android pointed.

Winterbottom whispered to Schmidt, "There are no signals from Martians. Can't you tell? Larke is having auditory hallucinations. He's ill."

"Nonsense," Schmidt shouted out. "We should head out immediately in the direction the android pointed. If I recall my maps, it's where the largest pyramid is located." He headed toward the airlock.

Randy grabbed him by the collar. "Where the hell are you going? In the first place, you don't have your spacesuit on. And even if you did, no one leaves the habitation module while it's dark. Go to bed. Tomorrow you can explore."

Looking contrite, Schmidt slunk to his sleeping bag.

Winterbottom told Randy what the android had been saying. "The damage to his computer is getting worse. He's becoming demented. We've got to do something."

Randy sneered. "There's nothing to be done. If it gets violent or uncontrollable, we'll shut it down. Otherwise, it'll just have to stay broken until we get back to Earth."

Exploring

The next morning, Schmidt rose early and made everyone a fine breakfast of Spam, powdered eggs and overcooked coffee. Because he was cheerful and eager, Randy and Winterbottom became grumpy. Schmidt wanted to go immediately to check out the pyramidal structure to the west. Winterbottom said, "But we haven't explored The Face. We should see what's on top." He liked the challenge of climbing the mesa. "Are you going to go half cocked because of the ravings of a mad android?"

"It's not ravings. Larke has picked a radio transmission from underground. We must go to the pyramid as soon as possible."

Winterbottom folded his arms over his chest and got a stubborn look on his face. "No. The Face first."

"The pyramid first," Schmidt shouted.

"The Face."

"The pyramid."

"Whoa," interrupted Randy. "There's only one way to settle this. I'll toss a coin." She took out a silver dollar.

Winterbottom said, "Since I'm for exploring The Face, I'll take heads."

"Fair enough." They squatted on the floor of the module, and Randy flipped the coin. Winterbottom watched as it spiraled upward, turning over and over. When it almost reached the ceiling, it reversed direction and fell downward and smacked into the floor. The three people peered at it. Winterbottom groaned. The Statue of Liberty was uppermost. Tails! Schmidt had won the toss. Randy pocketed the coin whose head contained a likeness of a former president of the United States, Barack

Obama.

Since the pyramid was two and half kilometers in a south by southwest direction, a half hour hike, they loaded up Larke with the equipment they thought they would need and headed out. Actually, because of the heavily cratered uneven ground, large boulders and rocky hills, it took an hour and half. As they neared the Great Pyramid of Cydonia, it became obvious that it was of a tremendous size, a virtual mountain.

Upon arrival at the foot, the archeologists stared at it in awe. Meanwhile, Randy ordered Larke to setup a temporary camp. She had to help the android and continuously watch it. It had a tendency to wander in circles instead of doing what it was told while it mumbled to itself. When the camp was ready, she too examined the pyramid. To her surprise, it really did seem to be constructed by sentients. It consisted of enormous rectangular blocks, as large as twenty feet by ten feet by ten feet, piled on top of each other to form a pyramidal shape. It had to be very old. It had been scoured by time and windblown sand so that it had become rounded to resemble an upside-down child's top.

The archeologists had magnifying glasses out to examine every minute detail of the bottom row of blocks. Finally Winterbottom said, "We should search for an entrance."

"Absolutely," Schmidt replied. "But where? The artifact is so enormous. It could be anywhere."

"Perhaps Larke can help us. Larke, come here." The android sauntered over by the archeologists and stood still except for its continuous mumbling. "Those signals, can you tell from what part of the pyramid they're coming from?"

Larke pointed at the top, which came to veritable point, almost like a radio tower.

"I guess we'll have to climb up there."

Schmidt said, "The signal may be coming from up there, but that doesn't mean the entrance is there. I think I'll search a little closer to the ground."

Winterbottom was amused. He knew the rotund Schmidt was not much for climbing. "I guess I'll have to go by myself."

Randy said, "I'll go with you. I always enjoy a good climb. Larke, you stay with Heinrich in case he needs help with anything."

Winterbottom and the space jockey got their mountaineering equipment out. They hooked an eight foot rope between them and began to climb.

Schmidt watched enviously as they scaled the enormous structure. He wished he had the nerve to go with them, but he suffered from acrophobia. He began to circle the pyramid. Larke followed him. On the north side he found scratches carved into a block that resembled the hieroglyphs he had seen on The Face. After he photographed them, he

21

noticed that there was a rounded protrusion four inches in diameter beneath them. He placed his hand on it. As a result, it moved a little. He pressed harder and found that he could push it in until it was flush with the face of the stone. From somewhere underground came deep rumbling and grinding sounds. A square stone two feet by two feet slid back into the structure, leaving an opening. He took out his flashlight and peered into the hole. He saw a long tunnel that led downward.

He radioed Winterbottom and Randy. "I've found an entrance."

Randy replied, "Don't do anything until we come down. We'll head back."

"Very well. But hurry. I can't wait to see where it goes."

While Schmidt was talking to Randy, Larke went up to the hole. It switched on a built-in light in his forehead and peered in. After a few moments, it crawled into the hole.

"Hey," cried Schmidt. "Captain Sally wants us to wait for her and Charlie."

Nonetheless, Larke did not stop. Schmidt heard it say, "I'm coming, Martian people. I'm coming."

Summit of the Pyramid

"Heinrich has found an entrance. Let's go down," Randy said.

"I heard. But Captain Sally, we've got only a little ways to go to the summit. Let's see what's up there first."

Randy glanced upward. The spike like top of the pyramid was but another seven meters above them. "Right. Y'know Winter, I've finally found something you're good at. You scrambled up the Great Pyramid quite well. You're almost as good at mountain climbing as I am."

"Well, thank you. That's a real compliment coming from you. But I'm an experienced mountaineer. I've been to the summit of Mount Everest a few times."

"Since you're so good, we should do Mount Olympus while we're here on Mars."

"Love to. Will we have time?"

"That depends on you and Heinrich and how much time you spend mucking around Cydonia. Say, how about a race to the top. Unhook the rope, and we'll see who gets to that pole-like rock at the top first."

"All right."

They unhooked themselves from the rope and cached it in a crevice.

"On the count of three," Randy said. "One ... two ... go."

Winterbottom climbed as fast as possible, quickly pounding spikes into the rock and using them as handholds. Randy was right there with him and pulling ahead. He exerted himself and moved more swiftly. He had never climbed as quickly in his life. Suddenly a stone crumbled under his foot, and he began to slide, slowly at first and then more swiftly. When he tried to grab one of the pythons or a crevice in the stone structure, his sweaty palms slipped. He thought, *at least it's a pyramid shape. Perhaps I'll survive the fall.*

Suddenly something had hold of his wrist and stopped his downward plunge. It was Randy. "Drive in a spike. I can't hold you long, you big ox," she said over the comm.

As Winterbottom drove in the spike, the stone moved slightly. Once he got himself stable, he said, "Come down here, Captain Sally. I may have stumbled upon another entrance to the pyramid."

Randy joined him, and they retied the rope to their belts.

Winterbottom said, "This stone moves. If we push together, it may be a way inside."

Together they shoved against the stone. Randy's muscle power was what was needed to move it. The stone pivoted around, and an opening appeared. Winterbottom flicked on his flashlight.

"What do you see?" asked Randy.

"Not much. It's a tunnel slanting downward. Wait, I'll crawl in."

Randy watched as the archeologist disappeared into the cavity. The slack of the rope that linked them tightened. After a while it drew her toward the hole. She yelled into the comm unit. "Charlie, where the hell are you going?" All she heard was static. "Damn. I've lost radio contact with him."

The next moment she was yanked into the hole.

Inside the Pyramid

After the android disappeared into the opening, Schmidt radioed Randy, "Captain Sally, Larke went into the pyramid. Should I follow it?"

There was no reply, only static. "Oh dear, something's wrong with my suit's comm unit," he muttered. "I'd better wait until Sally and Winterbottom come down here." He sat on a boulder. Fifteen minutes went by. "What the heck is taking them so long?" The thought occurred to him that they were fooling around. "That rascal is trying to steal her from me." Dark thoughts caused him to grind his teeth. A flush came to his face. A half hour went by. "I hate that bastard. Shit. The hell with them. I'm going into the pyramid. At least I'll have the glory of being the first to discover a dead civilization on Mars."

He entered the pyramid. A narrow tunnel slanted downward. He called to Larke on his comm unit. "Larke, can you hear me."

Although the sound was muffled and crackled with interference, he heard, "I am coming oh ancient ones. The way is difficult."

"Larke, this is Heinrich Schmidt. Where are you?"

"Is this really Doctor Schmidt? Please save me. I am lost in what seems to be a catacomb."

Schmidt immediately became excited. "A catacomb. That's wonderful. Have you found alien corpses?"

"Some kind of corpses. This place is a labyrinth. There's no way out."

"Don't panic. I'll find you. Stay put. And keep talking. I'll try to determine where you are by the signal strength."

Since the tunnel he was in led in only one direction, in a downward spiral, Schmidt plodded on. Meanwhile, Larke's irritating voice buzzed in his ear along with static and an interfering signal. Finally he came to a small empty room whose walls were covered with hieroglyphics and reliefs of strange creatures, whether they were animals, sentient beings or mythological creatures he could not tell. He took out his camera and photographed them. "I'll try to decipher the glyphs back at camp."

When he was finished, he noticed that the only exit from the room was the one he entered from. *That's strange,* he thought. *Larke had to have come through here, but where did the android go? There must be a hidden doorway.*

He wandered around the room checking for another way out. Opposite the tunnel he discovered a square stone knob protruding from the wall. He pushed on it, and it slid into the wall. He heard a clunk in back of him. A thick stone had dropped, blocking the way he had entered. He went over by it. He could barely tell where the doorway had been. His knees turned to water. As he began to feel claustrophobic, his breath grew labored. He was trapped.

He returned to the knob, which was flush with the wall. He tried to pull it out. He could not even grasp it. He trembled uncontrollably, and his miserable life flashed in front of his eyes. Then he thought, *there must be another way out. The android left this room.* "Larke," he called. "After you went into the pyramid and followed the tunnel, did you come to a room with hieroglyphics and drawings all over the walls?"

"Who is this? I am trying to reach you but this catacomb is a labyrinth."

"This is Heinrich." He repeated his question.

"Oh, Doctor Schmidt. I thought it was the Martians. They keep talking to me."

Again fear made Schmidt feel ill. His only hope of rescue was a delusional android. He reversed his former opinion that Larke was receiving signals from Martians. He thought now that the voices were in Larke's head. Nonetheless, he repeated his question a third time.

"Oh yes."

"How did you get out?"

"I waited until the room filled with air and went out the door that opened."

Schmidt realized the room was an airlock like on the spaceship. He tested the air. The pressure was rising. He checked what gases were entering the room. Again, he was happy to see that it was mainly oxygen with traces of other elements including a large percentage of nitrogen. He waited until the pressure rose to slightly less than earth normal and carefully lifted one corner of his space helmet. Although the air smelled musty, it was breathable. He took off his helmet and took a deep breath. He could breathe normally. "That's a relief. The Martians must be oxygen breathers." It was also good to get away from Larke's constant chatter. He tied the helmet to his backpack on his shoulders.

There was a screech of stone rubbing against stone, and a doorway appeared in front of him. He sent the light from his torch into it and followed a downward spiraling stone stairway at the end of which was a path between high stone walls. This tunnel continued in a straight line for several hundred paces and made a right-angle turn. Just beyond the corner was second stairway, again descending. *How far down does this go?* Schmidt thought.

The steps wound deeper and deeper underground. As Schmidt neared their end, he heard liquid splashing. When he stepped off at the bottom of the stairs, he saw its source, fluid spraying upward from the center of a malignant pool which gave off an unwholesome stench. A narrow ledge curved around it in a swooping arc.

Before Schmidt continued his trek, he became curious as to the nature of the pool's contents. The ebony liquid smelled atrocious, like rotting flesh. He dropped a large pebble into the foul substance. As soon as it touched the surface, it dissolved, fuming thick smoke as it sank.

"Ugh," he cried. "That's not water, but some corrosive substance. If it melted a rock, what would it do to living flesh?"

He crept around the ledge, keeping as much distance between himself and the edge as possible. When he was halfway around, he heard footsteps ahead, "Tap, tap, tap." Each tap was followed by an echo that made him shudder. *Martians?* he wondered. The hackles on his neck rose; logic gave way to terror and paranoia. *Or perhaps it's the mad android, Larke.* He switched the flashlight to his left hand took out the pistol he always kept in his backpack..

As the footsteps approached, "TAP, TAP, TAP," he raised the flashlight which started to grow dim. A shadowy figure in a spacesuit walked slowly toward him. The apparition, whose face was hidden by the helmet, also held a flashlight and a pistol. Schmidt pointed his pistol at the space suited figure, his hands trembling so that he could hardly keep it steady. "Who ... who goes there?"

The mysterious creature continued to walk towards him in silence, heels clicking menacingly and echoing on the stone walls of the oppressive chamber. Step by step its footfalls resounded on the stone ledge.

Schmidt realized that whoever it was could not hear his question through the helmet.. He pointed at his own head and tried to indicate by signs that the helmet should be removed.

Slide into the Abyss
After Winterbottom crawled into the small opening, he realized that

the slant of the tunnel was extremely steep. What was worse, the floor was smooth and covered with fine dust which made it as slick as bacon grease. He found himself sliding forward uncontrollably.. He tried to stop himself by pressing his hands against the walls, but they too were slippery. Soon, he palms grew so hot from friction that he could no longer hold on. His downward slide became faster and faster. The rope that attached him to Randy tightened. He hoped that she would be able to stop his descent.

No such luck. He heard her cursing loudly through the comm unit. He glanced back. She was sliding in back of him at the same rate of speed. Down and down they plunged. Finally he slid off a ledge, landing head first, which was lucky since it was the part of him least likely to be injured. Seconds later, Randy landed on top of him in a tangle of arm, legs and rope.

"Get your hand off my ass, pervert," she screamed.

"I'm sorry, Captain Sally, but in the dark I thought it was your breast."

She slapped him so hard across the chops his head spun. "Ouch."

After a few minutes and many awkward positions, they became untangled.

Randy rose to her feet and played her flashlight around. The ledge they fell from was ten feet above their head. They were in a small chamber with walls that went straight up. One wall contained an archway. Beyond it was only darkness. She scowled at Winterbottom. "Another fine mess you've gotten us into."

"I'm sorry, but once I started sliding, I couldn't stop myself."

"Yeah. And you couldn't help putting yourself into the first hole you saw. I know your type."

"So, what do we do now, Captain?"

"We could climb back up through the hole we came down here in, but it would be tough. It's a slippery slide. Maybe there's another way out."

"We know there is. Heinie radioed us that there was one at the base of the pyramid."

"You're right. We went down a long ways. It must be above us. Let me try to get hold of him. Heinrich, Heinrich, this is Captain Sally. Do you hear me?"

It was Larke who replied. "Captain Sally. Help me. I am lost in a catacomb."

"How did that happen?"

"The Martians. They kept after me to follow their signal."

"Martians, huh." She switched briefly to a private channel between her suit and Winterbottom's. "Larke still thinks he hears Martians. He's says that he's lost in some catacomb."

Winterbottom shook his head. "Poor Larke. He's still delusional. Ask him where Heinie is."

Sally switched back to the open channel. "Where's Doctor Schmidt?"

"The last I saw of him was outside the pyramid. I was in communication with him for a while, but we were cut off."

"I see. Sit tight. We'll see whether we can find you."

She said to Winterbottom, "He doesn't know where Heinrich is. He may be still outside the pyramid waiting for us to climb back down. Let's see whether we can find either Larke or an exit." She checked the oxygen in her backpack. "We have four hours."

"Aye, aye, Captain Sally." Winterbottom saluted. He prayed that they would find a way out before the four hours were up. The thought of dying because of lack of oxygen made him ill.

They went through the archway into a large cavern in the middle of which was a statue on a pedestal. They went over to examine it.

Randy said, "Wow. Look at that." She pointed to the large phallus on the creature, which had a two-inch diameter and stuck straight out two feet. She reached up and stroked it. "Mm. Wouldn't it be something to do it with him."

"Would you really do it with such a horrible creature." He pointed at the head which consisted mainly of tentacles like an octopus with ten eye stalks in the middle. This pulpy, tentacled head surmounted a grotesque and scaly body with rudimentary wings and prodigious claws on its hind and fore feet.

"If it was gentle and prolonged foreplay. I can imagine being touched on several parts of my body at the same time with those tentacles." She sighed as though in ecstasy.

Winterbottom grunted. "You sure have weird fantasies. No wonder even Super Dooper couldn't satisfy you." He paused. "Say, I know what this thing is."

"You do?"

"It's Cthulhu. There's a cult that worships it. They claim that it came from the stars. Perhaps, it was a Martian who visited earth in the distant past. Some archeologists believe that aliens visited the earth in prehistoric times. Various drawings and carvings by ancient peoples show what seem to be spaceships and people in spacesuits. Of course, most of the archeologists who believe this are ostracized from the archeology community and are called blasphemers, idiots, mad men, hoaxers and other invectives. Conventional archeology attributes the resemblance to spacemen an illusion."

"Interesting. Do you think we'll meet any Martians who look like this creature down here?"

Winterbottom shrugged. "I suppose we might find other traces and artifacts of an ancient Martian civilization."

"I wonder what kind of lovers they were."

"You-you would really consider making love to something like that?"

She punched him on the arm. "Just kidding, Winter, old buddy. Come on, time's a wasting."

At the other end of the cave, there were two archways. Randy pulled out a compass. "Let's see now. Heinrich was on the west side of the pyramid. That would be that way." She pointed to her left. "We'll take the left door."

They went through to find themselves on a narrow ledge that circled a putrid liquid pool. Approaching them was Schmidt.

"For Christ's sake, he's not wearing his helmet. The air in here must be okay to breath."

Randy removed her helmet and shook her head to allow her hair to fluff out. Winterbottom found the gesture charming.

Schmidt cried, "Captain Sally. How did you get down here? I suppose that big lunk behind you is Winterbottom." He pocketed the gun he was holding, ran up to Randy and kissed her.

As Winterbottom removed his helmet, he teetered on the edge of the poisonous pool. Schmidt, seeing this, let go of Sally and grabbed his arm, pulling him back. "Cripes. You don't want to go swimming in that." He kicked another stone into the liquid and watched as it hissed and dissolved.

Winterbottom turned pale. "You've saved my life."

"Perhaps. We still need to find a way out of here."

The Call of Cthulhu

"What do you mean?" said Winterbottom. "We'll simply go back the way you came in."

"It's blocked by a thousand pound stone. No human could possibly lift it."

Randy said, "An android could. We've got to find Larke."

Schmidt said, "In my last communication with him, he said he was in some sort of catacomb."

"He told us the same thing. Apparently he's lost, which is strange. Androids usually have an internal guidance system that allows them to find there way anywhere."

Winterbottom said, "You forget. Larke is broken. Perhaps his guidance system isn't working."

"Well, I guess we'll just have to find him."

"But what if we get lost in the catacomb?"

Randy chuckled. "We each have a guidance system in our backpacks similar to the one built into Larke. Let's go back where we took the door on the left and go into the one on the right. We'll see whether it leads to the catacombs where Larke is."

They returned to the room with the statue. Schmidt went over to examine it. Winterbottom and Randy followed him. Winterbottom said, "Do we have time for this?"

Randy replied, "Sure. Now that we know the air is good in here, we don't have to worry about our oxygen running out." She began to admire the phallus again, stroking it and licking her lips.

Winterbottom said to Schmidt, "I believe it's the Cthulhu, the god worshiped by that tribe of wild women of ... where was it now."

"New England mostly. They called their secret organization SWOC, Slave Women of the Cthulhu. I learned all about their cult in *Arcane Grimoires of Forbidden Lore*. There's a chapter on *The Call of the Cthulhu*."

Randy said, "I seem to be hearing that call myself. How does one join the SWOC?" She mounted the pedestal and stood facing the statue, her eyes directed at one of its eye stalks. As though in a trance, she raised her hand and wiped perspiration from her forehead. "It's warm in here." She removed her backpack and unzipped the spacesuit.

Schmidt cried, "We've got to get her away from this thing. It's having a bad affect on her. It's the call of the Cthulhu."

Winterbottom was hoping that they could wait until Randy removed her spacesuit before they acted. However, Schmidt leaped up on the pedestal and tugged at Randy's arm. Winterbottom took hold of her other arm. They dragged her to the other end of the room. She shook her head violently. "What the hell happened to me?" She glanced down at her unzipped spacesuit. "Shit. What the fuck were you doing, you pervert?" She punched Winterbottom so hard in the stomach that he retched.

"Stop," cried Schmidt. "It wasn't him. It was the call of the Cthulhu. It has a strange affect on women. Don't you recall getting up on its pedestal and unzipping your spacesuit?"

"Holy crap. I thought I was dreaming. That thing seemed to be alive. I was about to make love with it. I'm sorry, Winter, that I sucker punched you."

Winterbottom was unable to speak through his swollen jaw.

Randy zipped up her spacesuit. "Where's my backpack?"

"It's by the statue."

She started to walk back to the Cthulhu. Schmidt stopped her. "You can't go back there. You'll fall under its spell again. Charlie, go get her backpack."

Winterbottom, somewhat recovered, sauntered to the statue and retrieved Randy's backpack. He stood for a moment gazing at the monstrous thing. "What's your secret?" he whispered. "It has to be more than a tremendous wang."

When he returned, the trio went through the arch on the right. A short tunnel led to more steps. They followed this to a room full of beautiful vases, urns, statuettes and other baked clay items. Some of things were glazed and painted with elaborate designs and drawings of strange creatures.

Schmidt's eyes popped out. "El Dorado. This is an archeologist's paradise. I could spend ten years examining and cataloging the contents of this room."

"If we get out of this place, you can come back. We'll haul this junk back to the ship. Right now, we've got to find Larke."

Meanwhile, Winterbottom had picked up one of the vases and was gazing at a drawing on it. He hefted it a bit to feel its weight. It slipped out of his hands, dropped on a pile of other artifacts and broke into several pieces. The items it had landed on were also shattered.

Schmidt turned red with fury, "You clumsy idiot. What kind of archeologist are you? You're like a bull in a china shop. Get away from those things."

Winterbottom, stunned by this tirade after the accident, took a couple steps backward, knocking down an urn, which in turn hit against a table that contained several artifacts. They all came tumbling down and broke, as well as the urn. He leaped away from that accident to blunder into another table, knocking more stuff to the stone floor.

Schmidt lost it. He came after Winterbottom. He grabbed him, and they both stumbled, knocking over and breaking more things. Schmidt tried to hit Winterbottom but he was kept at bay by Winterbottom's long arms. They rolled around on the floor wrestling, bumping into and breaking more of the artifacts. When they finally ran out of steam, they sat panting and glaring at each other. The room was a shambles. Every artifact except one was broken.

Randy leaned against a wall bent over with laughter. She pointed at the one remaining vase. Schmidt and Winterbottom peered around at the carnage and began to laugh too. They nodded their heads at Randy. She picked the vase up and threw it to the floor. "That was fun, guys. The best laugh I've had in a long time. You two are the funniest buffoons I've ever met. You're in the wrong business. You should've been circus clowns."

Winterbottom said, "It's all right. We're used to working with shards. It adds to the challenge, like putting together jigsaw puzzles." He got up and gave Schmidt a hand. "No hard feelings, Heinie."

Schmidt grunted and headed toward the archway at the end of the room. Randy and Winterbottom had to hurry to catch up.

The Catacombs

The archway led to another tunnel. At the end was a room with niches along the walls. Winterbottom peered around. They were in ancient catacombs with walls of stone. The stench of the long dead permeated the chamber. In a niche on the left wall was a mold covered skeleton. He and Schmidt examined it. It was not human, but was apparently from a sentient being. "A Martian," Winterbottom intelligently deduced.

"Of course." Schmidt took out an instrument to determine the age of the skeleton. His eyes popped. "According to my instrument, it's over a million years old. How can that be? It should've turned to dust."

Winterbottom shrugged. "The Martians must've had hardy skeletons.

Take a bone. We'll analyze it back at camp."

The other two walls contained archways. What was beyond them was lost in the gloom.

Winterbottom scratched his head. "Which way, Captain Sally? Or should I toss a coin?"

"I'll try to contact Larke. Maybe I can determine which direction his signal comes from." She donned her space helmet and took out another instrument.

Winterbottom saw her mouth move. Afterward, she seemed to be listening. At the same time she examined the instrument in her hand. She pointed to one of the archways and walked toward it.

Before they left the chamber, Schmidt took out a marking pen and placed a large X on the door frame. "If we see that X again," he said, "We'll know that we're walking in circles."

Randy kept speaking to Larke, watching her instrument and leading them on. Every time they passed through an archway, Schmidt made another X on the left side of the frame.

They hiked for what seemed like miles. Each chamber was much the same as the last one. Some had niches with skeletons in them, some did not. Some had two archways, some three, a few had only one. When they reached one of the latter, they had to backtrack. It was a dead end – in more ways than one.

One chamber was different than the others. A skeleton was wrapped in elaborate colorful material and laid out on a stone dais. Surrounding it were vases and bowls with vegetative material which had long ago rotted and turned to dust. A vinegary odor came from a ceramic bottle. In what the archeologists believed was the head of the skeleton was a golden jewel-encrusted crown. In its hand or claw was a large crystal.

Schmidt's eyes fastened on the crystal. "This chamber is the resting place of a king or a prince."

"Or a queen or a princess," said Randy.

Schmidt picked up the crystal. "There's something unusual about this. I think I'll take it with me." He slipped it into his backpack.

"Well, if we're taking souvenirs, I'll just have this," said Winterbottom and removed the jeweled crown.

Randy replaced her helmet and pointed toward an archway. Winterbottom stepped through it into a dark chamber. Instead of striking the hard stone floor, his foot went into nothingness. He tipped forward and whirled his arms around windmill fashion to keep his balance. It was not enough. He found himself falling forward. Just before he took a nose dive, Randy grabbed him by the collar of his spacesuit and hauled him back.

Once he recovered from his near fall, he shined the light into the chamber. There was no floor, only an open pit with three-foot spikes sticking up. They went through the other archway. "That's the second time you saved my life, Heinie. I owe you."

"I'll remember that."

From that point on, Winterbottom did not step into a room without seeing what was in it.

They came upon a chamber with a puddle of dark gooey substance on the floor. Schmidt got down on his knees and examined it with a magnifying glass. He dipped his pen into it and sniffed it. "This is a spore of the Yog-Sothoth. Primal slime."

"Really?" said Winterbottom. He shuddered. "I sure hope we don't meet that thing down here. Ugh. The very thought of it makes me ill."

Randy asked, "What the hell is a Yog-Sothoth?"

Schmidt said, "Protoplasmic flesh that flows blackly outward to form an eldritch, hideous horror from outer space."

Winterbottom said, "A tentacled amorphous monster."

Schmidt said, "An extra dimensional entity."

Randy said, "What does it look like?"

Winterbottom shrugged. "No one knows. It's an invisible eater of souls. The cult that worships it does human sacrifices."

Schmidt said, "Also, it can take over a human body. In other words, it can possess a person."

Randy said, "What do we do if we encounter it?"

Schmidt and Winterbottom looked at each other and turned their gaze back to Randy. "Run like hell," they said together.

"You two are brave men," she said with a lopsided grin.

The Lost Android

After they left the room with slime, they found Larke. The android stood in the center of the room, muttering to itself.

Randy said, "How are you doing, Larke?"

The android gazed at her in a manner that suggested disbelief. "Not very well. I am still experiencing disk and memory errors. The Martians are interfering with my input/output functions. I am lost in these labyrinthine catacombs. And I have a headache."

"I see. Well, maybe we'll attempt repairs once we get back to the lander. Now we're here to take you out of the pyramid."

Larke looked at her with an expression of sadness. "Oh my dear Captain Sally and archeologists, you should not have come here. You are all going to die. There is no way out."

Winterbottom said, "Don't give up, Larke. We'll simply return to the place where you entered."

"How will you find your way? My internal guidance system is blocked by interference from the Martians."

"It must be malfunctioning. We'll use mine." She took an instrument that looked like a universal remote with many buttons on it. At the top was monitor which showed a view of Mars from the orbit of their spaceship. Winterbottom watched over her shoulder. She pressed a button marked with a plus sign and the view zoomed in to show the Cydonia area. Using the arrow keys she centered the pyramid on the screen and pressed the plus sign again. The pyramid filled the screen. She touched a button labeled X-Ray Vision along with the plus sign. It showed an overhead view of a myriad of tunnels. She pressed Locate Me. A red dot started flashing in one of the tunnels on the map.

"Amazing," Winterbottom cried. "That's quite an invention."

Randy turned to him. "Dope. You've got one too. Where were you on the day we were instructed in the use of the Boogle Universe device?"

Winterbottom flushed. He recalled that he had skipped that class after a night of wine, women and song in a bar at The Cape.

Randy turned back to device. "What the hell!" The screen became filled with zigzag lines and blotches. She pressed several buttons in an attempt to resolve the problem. Nothing worked. "Larke is right. There's an interfering signal. I hope we can recall all the twists and turns we took getting here."

"No problem," Schmidt said. "I marked an arrow on each archway we passed through." He led the way back through the labyrinthine catacombs.

After they had traversed through many rooms of the catacombs, Larke said, "Something is not right. I did not go through this many archways. I've been counting them. I passed through seventy-two to arrive at the location where you found me. I've counted one hundred and thirty seven so far, and we seem not to be anywhere near the exit from the pyramid."

Winterbottom said, "Look, all three exits from the room have arrows on them, all pointing inward."

"Oh cripes," said Schmidt. "Someone's been placing additional arrows on the archways that are identical to mine."

Randy said, "How could that be? We're the only people in the pyramid."

"Are we?" whispered Winterbottom. "Listen." He put his finger to his lips to indicate that they should be silent.

Soft footsteps were approaching, as though someone with bare feet or moccasins was walking in one of the adjacent rooms. The three humans and the android waited in anticipation for the arrival of whatever was there.

Schmidt whispered, "I hope it's not the Yog-Sothoth."

Randy said in a low husky voice, "Maybe it's the Cthulhu."

Winterbottom said in a shaky voice, "We should've brought weapons."

"I have a pistol," said Schmidt and took the weapon from his backpack.

33

The Martian

The seven foot creature that entered the room seemed almost human. In general appearance it resembled a human being, with two arms, two legs and a rather handsome face. However, its skin was green and slick looking, like a snake's. It was bald with a large crest on its crown. It had a thick stubby tail and its feet were claw like. Its only garment was a belt with various pouches and devices hung from it. Since it was nude, it was obviously male and well endowed. In its hand it held a rod with a glass-like crystal at the end that glowed, giving off a bright light.

Randy pointed at its maleness and cried, "Wow. Look at that. He's hung like a bull."

"Are you going to moo at it?" Winterbottom said.

The Martian opened its mouth and hissed, grunted and made various other noises.

Schmidt said, "It's trying to communicate."

"Duh," replied Winterbottom. "Maybe it knows some Earth languages." He said to the creature, "Do you speak English? *Sprechen sie Deutsches? Vous parlés français? Usted habla español?*" He tried several other languages, both modern and ancient, including some long dead.

The only response was that the Martian hissed and gargled and grunted louder and waved his rod around.

Winterbottom shrugged. "I guess he doesn't speak any Earth languages."

Larke said, "I can translate. The Martians have sent language instruction by wireless to me. Shall I translate?"

"Hell yes," said Randy. "I'd be quite interested in what this big fellow has to say for himself."

"Very well. He says, 'What are you bozos doing in the catacombs? It is forbidden except for priests and the dead.'"

Winterbottom said, "Tell him that we entered the pyramid by accident. If he would show us the way out, we would be glad to leave."

Larke made noises similar to the Martian. The Martian replied. Larke translated, "He says that you are under arrest for trespassing, desecrating the dead, profaning a sacred place, and committing sacrilege. You must come with him."

"Suppose we refuse."

Larke relayed this to the Martian. "He says that he will be forced to execute you immediately."

To prove his point, the Martian aimed his rod at Schmidt's pistol. Before he could pull the trigger, it grew so hot that he dropped it. It began to fire from the heat. Everyone in the room did a little jig to avoid the flying bullets at floor level. The Martian aimed his weapon at it a second time. The directed beam vaporized the gun and the stones underneath it smoked and boiled. After a few seconds, all that was left was a charred hole.

Larke said, "I would advise going with this fellow. He does not seem to have a sense of humor."

The Martian pointed the way. Randy tried flirting with him with her eyes. He ignored her.

Winterbottom said to Larke, "Did he say what the penalty was for the misdemeanors we committed by being here?"

"Death by sacrifice to their demon god, Azathoth."

Winterbottom turned pale. The future did not seem very bright unless they found a way to escape. He whispered to Randy, "There's only one of these fellows. Perhaps one of us can distract him while the others overwhelm him."

"Fine plan," Randy replied. "But a little late."

Several more Martians joined them. They came through archways from several directions. They all carried the rods with the crystal tips.

The Martian City

The group was escorted through miles of underground tunnels and caverns. Orders to them were given through Larke. Schmidt took notes and photographs of everything. On the way they went through areas that contained artifacts of all sorts, including strange machines. Schmidt asked Larke if he could read the hieroglyphs they encountered.

"Yes. I now have a complete grasp of Martian, written, verbal and telepathic."

"So what does that say?" He pointed at glyphs above a doorway.

"Admission for the dead only. All others enter at their own risk."

At another point there were more symbols scrawled on a wall.

Larke translated, "S'kn'pon was here."

A third group of symbols was translated as "Authorized Personnel Only."

While they marched along and Schmidt busied himself with recording this important archeological information, Randy cozied up to one of the husky guards and felt his muscular arm. He brushed her hand away and waved the rod at her warningly. She turned to Larke. "Tell him that I'm trying to be friendly."

Larke imparted this information to the guard and received his reply. "He says he does not like being touched by awful creature with thick rough skin."

"Oh. He must think my spacesuit is my flesh." She unzipped the front of her protective clothing and pointed to her stomach. "See. My real skin."

The guard smacked her with his rod and hissed and grunted.

Larke said, "He said, 'Keep moving.'"

"Shit. He's probably gay."

Winterbottom, on the other hand, peered around looking for a possible escape route. But the Martians kept sharp eyes on their prisoners. He realized that he would be vaporized before he took two steps. He plodded on.

After several hours they entered an awesome cavern. It extended hundreds of kilometers in every direction. Even the roof was many meters above their head. In the center of it was a great ball of incandescence as bright as the sun as seen from the Mars surface. Ahead lay a great endless sea. On the shores of the sea was a large city with high towers, roadways and many buildings. The road they were on led directly to it.

"Wow," cried Schmidt. "An entire thriving civilization dwells underground. Who would've ever guessed it? It was always thought that if we found evidence of Martians that they would have long ago perished."

"Now it's us who will perish," moaned Winterbottom as he was prodded to move along more swiftly.

"I wonder whether they're all as unfriendly as this bunch," said Randy. "Where are they taking us?"

Larke interrogated their captors. "To the official in charge of justice in the great city of Azathoth. This official will interrogate us and hand down the sentence for our crimes. Afterward, we will be held until the holy festival day when sacrifices are made to the demon god Azathoth."

"H-how long before this festival?" asked Winterbottom.

"In seven days. I assume they mean Martian days, which are approximately the same length as earth's."

Schmidt remarked, "How interesting. At one time these people must've lived on the surface that they keep time by the length of a day."

Winterbottom gave him a withering look. "How can you think of such things when we're being led to our death?"

"Oh c'mon Charlie, do you really think they'll execute us when they find out that we're from another planet?"

"More likely to, I'd say."

They were brought to a building with a large portico whose roof was held up with massive columns decorated with skulls and demon-like creatures. After walking up a long staircase with wide threads, they were halted before enormous metal doors. The leader of their guards went over to an enormous gong and smacked it with a mallet. The sound resounded so loudly that the Earth people had to cover their ears. When the enormous doors opened, they were prodded to enter.

They were brought before an official in a loose fitting robe that covered the person from neck to ankle. Nonetheless, Winterbottom noted that it was a female by her shape, which was so spectacular no loose fitting gown could hide it. Also, she was different from the male guides in that she had long red-brown hair that covered her shoulders. Her features were comely. In addition to the gown, she wore a colorful brimless hat.

Their guard captain issued orders, and the guards prostrated them before this official. Larke said, "We are to go down flat on our faces before the Matron of Absolute Justice." The android lay down on its belly with its forehead touching the floor as the guards had done. The three Earth people followed suit.

The Matron of Justice said something and the guards rose to their feet. Larke said, "We can get up now." The Earth people rose.

The guard captain spoke to the official. Larke said, "He is relating our criminal activity in the catacombs."

The Matron glared at the earth people and hissed and grunted. Larke said, "She asks whether you have any defense of your blasphemous, desecrating trespassing."

Winterbottom said, "Explain that we are from Earth and except for yourself don't understand their language and that we meant no harm. We entered the catacombs by accident."

Larke repeated this in Martian. The Matron replied. "She wants to know where this 'Earth' place is. She never heard of it."

"Explain that it is another planet and that we came in a spaceship and landed on the surface. While we were exploring, we wandered into the pyramid."

Larke told that to the Matron. She laughed and replied. Larke said, "She said that what you say is impossible. One cannot travel in the sky nor live on the surface. There is not enough breathable air, and the temperatures are too extreme."

"Tell her we have special equipment. Here, show her my helmet."

Larke explained and demonstrated placing the helmet on his head. After he removed it and handed back to Winterbottom, the Matron spoke again in an obviously angry manner. "She says, 'Do you take me for a fool? You show me a diving helmet for going under the sea and claim that you used it on the world above whose conditions are so harsh you would certainly die, helmet or no helmet. Your punishment will be that much more gruesome for lying to me.'"

Schmidt whispered to Winterbottom, "Shut up, you idiot. You're just getting us in deeper. Apparently they never go to the surface." He said to Larke, "Tell her that we are archeologists from a land far across the sea. We did not how sacred your catacombs were and are deeply sorry if we trespassed there. It was completely unintentional."

Larke spoke to the Matron again, and she replied, shaking a gavel at Schmidt. "She said, 'Ignorance of the law is no excuse. Archeologists, you say. Spies are more likely, little fellow with the pink face. My sentence is thus. You are to be incarcerated until the festival of Azathoth, at which time you will be sacrificed to the demon god after torture."

When Winterbottom heard the sentence, he fell to his knees and cried, "Mercy, your matroness. I never really wanted to come to Mars. I'll do anything, but don't feed me to Azathoth."

Larke translated. The Matron spoke. Larke said, "No mercy is allowed in cases of sacrilege. Take them away."

The guards roughly took each of the Earthlings by the arms and led them away, except Larke, who would not budge. The guards who held him hissed, grunted something to their captain. When he replied, they stepped away and zapped the android with their weapons. Larke did not melt but glowed for a couple of minutes and fell over backwards. The guards in charge of it picked it up by the arms and legs and carried it behind the other prisoners.

The Dungeon

The Earthlings were taken to an even more subterranean section of the building and thrown into a stinking, dank cell. The heavy brass door slammed shut with a solid clang. Winterbottom explored the cave-like cell, hoping against hope that he would find a means of escape. It was bare except for straw in one corner and a slimy bucket to relieve themselves into. Its walls consisted of cold, damp stones, none of which were the slightest bit loose. Nothing larger than a rat could crawl through its niches. Nonetheless, cockroaches and spiders had no trouble entering.

"Another fine mess you've gotten us into, Winter," said Randy. "You attract trouble like a magnet."

"Me?" He pointed at Schmidt. "What about him? He's responsible for this whole crazy mission."

"At least he shows some gumption. You cry like a baby when things go awry. Do either of you have any ideas of how to get us out of here?"

Schmidt said, "I don't think the Martians are aware of how strong Larke is. Also, I noticed a resemblance between the crystal I took from the skeleton and the one's on the Martian's weapons. Perhaps I can discover how to use it as a weapon."

"Good thinking, Heinrich. We'll need a plan though."

Winterbottom said, "If you're planning on using Larke, I don't think he's in very good shape. When the Martians zapped him, it must've shorted something out. Look at him."

Larke lay immobile on the dungeon floor. Its eyes were turned up so that the pupils did not show. It looked dead. Randy knelt down by it. She removed its spacesuit and opened a panel in its chest. She pressed the Reset button. Larke's arms and legs shook and sparks spewed out from the panel. She turned to Schmidt. "Heinrich, know anything about electronics?"

"A bit. Sometimes on digs, I needed to repair our comm equipment. Let me have a look at the android." He searched in his backpack until he found his tool kit. He knelt down next to Larke and unscrewed the panel cover.

Randy stood up and said to Winterbottom, "Your buddy is quite a guy. He's prepared for almost any emergency. What the hell are you good for?"

Winterbottom sniffed. "I've escaped from tighter spots than this. I have the experience to devise an escape plan. Besides, I don't eat bugs." He pointed to Schmidt, who had trapped a cockroach and was putting it in his mouth.

Schmidt crunched down on the insect and chewed it up. "I learned to enjoy insects when in the wilds. Many societies consider them delicacies. Who knows when these Martians will feed us. We need to keep up our strength. Cockroaches are nutritious." He caught another one and afforded it to Randy. "Try one. They're crunchy and delicious, like potato chips."

"Uh, no thanks, Heinrich. Well, devise an escape plan, Winter. I have a question that maybe one of you two bozos can answer. These Martians plan on sacrificing us to their demon-god Azathoth. You both seem to recognize that name. What do you know about Azathoth?"

"Outside the ordered universe there is an amorphous blight of nethermost confusion which blasphemes and bubbles at the center of all infinity. It's called the boundless demon sultan Azathoth, whose name lips dare not speak aloud, and who gnaws hungrily in inconceivable, unlighted chambers beyond time and space amidst the muffled, maddening beating of vile drums and the thin monotonous whine of accursed flutes," replied Winterbottom.

"Flutes?"

Schmidt said, "That's how you will know when Azathoth is near – the flutes. After you hear the thin, monotonous piping of an unseen flute, you will meet. Azathoth, a primal horror too awful to describe."

Winterbottom said, "Its worshipers practice obscene rites that involve atrocities on living victims in a conical temple, which consists of a shell supported on many pairs of flexible legs. From the half-open shell several jointed cylinders rise, tipped with appendages. In the darkness within the shell resides a horrible bestial, mouthless face, with deep-sunk eyes and covered with glistening black hair."

Schmidt continued, "According to tradition, Azathoth comes from the red star. Many believe that meant Sirius, but it could refer to Mars."

"Heinie and I have seen such a temple among a tribe of south sea islanders, but inside it was only an ugly statue that reminded me of modern sculpture. That was some narrow escape when the natives caught us inside the temple. Right Heinie?"

"Sure was. It was a good thing that I knew how to paddle the native boats."

Randy said, "Enough reminiscing. Do you think the real Azathoth is on Mars?"

"Perhaps. Or maybe they'll simple torture us to death in front of another ugly statue. By the way, Heinie, were you able to do anything with Larke?"

"Well, when I took the cover off its control panel, I noticed several wires were burned away. I reattached them to its motherboard. Luckily I had a soldering gun and the correct gauge wire in my tool kit. However, when I put the android back together, it did not move."

"Did you press the On button?" asked Randy.

"I didn't realize it had one."

"Sometimes you can be as stupid as Winter. And don't offer me any more bugs to eat. I'm not that desperate yet." She knelt by the android and turned it on.

Larke's eyelids fluttered. "Oh my, what happened to me?"

Randy said, "You were zapped by Martians." She closed its skin over the control panel.

"Who are you?"

"Captain Sally. You'd better do a systems check."

"Systems check? What's that?" Larke sat up and peered around. "Where am I? Who are you people?"

Winterbottom cried, "Cripes, he's lost his memory."

"Its hard drive must've been erased. Larke, I'm the captain of the spaceship Percival. These other two gentlemen are Doctors Heinrich Schmidt and Charles Winterbottom. They were passengers. Do you recall them at all?"

Larke peered into their faces. "No. But I am pleased to meet you, Captain Sally, Doctors Heinrich Schmidt and Charles Winterbottom." The android chuckled. "Funny name that, Winterbottom. Are your cheeks cold?" It laughed.

Randy shook her head. "Its whole personality has changed. It never made stupid jokes before. Look Larke ..."

"Larke? Is that my name?"

"Yes. Now Larke ..."

"What a lark," he said and giggled.

"Quit with the puns already. We're in a tight spot, and we need your help." She told about coming to Mars in the spaceship and what happened to them after they entered the pyramid. "So you see, we must escape before the Martians feed us to their demon god."

Larke stared at her, looking confused. "Did you say that this Azathoth had no mouth?"

Winterbottom said, "That's the myth. We heard directly from the natives of Bugaboo Island. They're the ones who worship it."

"Then how can these Martians feed us to it? I think you people are pulling my leg."

At that moment the door to their cell opened and two of the seven foot guards entered and a slightly smaller female Martian. She was naked and quite attractive, which made Winterbottom's and Schmidt's eyes bug out and their tongues hang out. She carried a tray of fruit, covered meat dishes that smelled delicious and other goodies, which she laid on the floor near the door. She left, but the guards stayed in the cell. One pointed at Winterbottom and hissed and grunted.

"What's he saying Larke?" Winterbottom asked the android.

"How would I know? Is that really a language?" Winterbottom groaned. "We've lost our translator. What'll we do?"

Schmidt said, "I've picked up a little of the Martian lingo from listening to their sounds and Larke's translation. Apparently they want you to go with them." He hissed and grunted at the guard, who returned the favor. "You will be fed at whatever place they're taking you. They want us to be nice and fat for Azathoth. I guess we won't have to live on cockroaches and spiders after all." He sounded disappointed.

Winterbottom waved good-bye. "Captain Sally, can I have one kiss to carry to my grave?"

Randy eyed him suspiciously, but relented. She kissed him heartily on the lips. One of the Martian guards had to break them up. As Winterbottom was led away, he smiled, sure that Randy was deeply in love with him.

The Princess Golygee

The guards took Winterbottom into the streets of Azathoth. It was an interesting place. The Martians were tall, mostly good looking and wore little clothing. Narrow winding streets were crowded with busy scurrying Martians. Most were on foot, others rode on carts pulled by weird animals or on the animals' backs. Their conversations, in their outlandish hiss and grunts, sounded like a frog farm. In the market place, colorfully decorated stalls sold a tremendous variety of exotic fruits and raw and cooked meats and vegetables. Wines and spirits were also on sale. Other products bartered for in the bazaar were colorful silks, exotic spices and strange drugs and nostrums.

At the end of a wide boulevard was an enormous multichambered palace. On the long sides were vaulted archways with arch-shaped balconies. Tall towers stood on each corner. An onion shaped marble dome decorated with gold was its most spectacular feature. At the corners of plinth stand minarets, the four large towers each more than 40 meters tall. All in all it was similar to the Taj Mahal. Winterbottom wondered who the Martian architect was and whether he had been to earth.

The interior of the palace was as splendid as the outside with many statues and intricate patterned floors and walls with bejeweled silken couches and carved dark wooden tables and other furniture. Winterbottom was taken up a long winding staircase to an apartment of pink and rose colored silks and furnishings. A thin translucent curtain divided the room. Barely visible, someone sat on a throne behind this covering.

A female voice hissed and grunted in the Martian manner.

Winterbottom's guards bowed low and left the room. When they were gone, the person behind the curtain said in the language of Bugaboo Island where Winterbottom and Schmidt had made their narrow escape, "I am Princess Golygee, ruler of the city of Azathoth. I have been told that you and your companions claim that you came here from the sky. Is this true?"

"You speak an Earthean language. I'm surprised. Where did you learn it?"

"On another planet. The third from the sun."

"That's Earth. It's where we came from."

The curtains parted. Winterbottom was expecting one of the giant green Martian women. Instead a beautiful young Earth woman with light brown skin and oval eyes stepped through. She had a lovely feminine figure which was enhanced yet unhidden by the translucent tight-fitting sarong she wore.

"Y-you're not Martian. You're a lovely young lady." Winterbottom stared in admiration and astonishment.

She smiled at him. "Thank you. And you are handsome man. It has been long since I have seen an Earth man."

"What are you doing here on Mars?"

"I might ask you the same thing. However, I will tell you my sad tale first. Please take a seat. I will order refreshments."

She clapped her hands. Moments later, a Martian female appeared and bowed to her. She hissed and grunted in the Martian tongue. The Martian went away and returned a few minutes later with ceramic drinking cups and a bottle of some green liquid. She poured and handed the cups to Princess Golygee and Winterbottom. Winterbottom stared dubiously into his cup. "What is this?"

"Martian wine. It's delicious, but be careful, it can be quite intoxicating if you're not used to it." She held her cup and said, "To Earth, the beautiful planet."

Winterbottom clinked his cup against hers. "To Earth."

They each took a sip of the green wine. As the princess had indicated, it was sweet and spicy, a bit like sherry with a peppery spice in it. "Um, this is good."

"Now I will tell you my sad tale. It started before I was born. One evening, while the villagers were sitting around chatting, strange lights appeared in the sky. They came closer and close until they finally landed on the beach. It was a saucer-shaped flying vehicle."

"A UFO!"

"Is that what you call such things? You white men have acronyms for everything. The villagers went to investigate. Several Martians disembarked from the 'UFO.' The Martians on the ship had a box that was able to translate any language. They told the villagers that they must build a temple to their demon-god Azathoth and gave directions on how to construct such a building. When our tribal leaders refused, they were disintegrated with those rods the Martians use as weapons. After the villagers built the monstrous temple, the Martians placed the horrible idol within it and told them that they must worship the thing, making a human sacrifice once a year. They also chose the prettiest woman in the village to mate with the Martian prince who traveled with them. That woman was my mother. Nine months after the Martians left, I was born."

"You don't look at all Martian."

"I believe human traits are dominant in a Martian-human pairing. Nonetheless, I am a half breed."

"You must've inherited your mother's good looks."

"Some say that I resemble her closely. Anyway, I recall when you and another man came to our island. It was time for a human sacrifice to the Martian god. The elders of the time preferred strangers rather than one of our own tribe. But, somehow you escaped. I was but a child at the time, perhaps six years old, but I still remember the incident and your frightened faces."

"I really wasn't all that scared. I've lived a charmed life. It was not my first narrow escape."

"That's good, because you will need all the karma possible. To go on with my story, when I was sixteen, the Martians returned. They wanted to know which one of us was the prince's child. That was me, of course. They said that the prince had died. Hence, I had to go to Mars to be their ruler. I've been here ever since. Now, tell me about yourself."

Winterbottom told her about their mission to explore Cydonia and what happened after they arrived on Mars. When he finished, he said, "I'm quite relieved to hear that you're the ruler of the Martians. You can simply pardon us, and we'll go free."

Princess Golygee shook her head. "It's not that simple. If it was a civil crime that you had committed, for example, murder, I would have the power to pardon you. But you committed a sacrilege, a crime against religion. Religious crimes are the province of the priesthood. Actually they have much more power than I have, since there are many more religious prohibitions than civil crimes. Unless you find a way to escape, you will die horribly. Executions are conducted by feeding you to their demon-god Azathoth, who slowly digests you alive."

The Princess's Plan

"Oh. So there's no hope." Winterbottom had to choke back tears. He felt he was much too young to die, especially in such a terrible manner.

"Don't give up." She lowered her voice. "I have a plan. I can help you escape, but you must take me with you."

"Absolutely. Tell me your plan."

She whispered in his ear what she had in mind. He nodded. It might just work.

"I have a question about the story you told me," he said. "If the Martians have the technology to come to Earth and a translation device, why has everyone we met so far except you acted like they know nothing of even the surface of Mars, much less Earth. Also, no translation device was ever used when they captured us."

"The priesthood and highborn keep all technology secret from the general public. They want the peons to be as ignorant as possible. It makes it easier to rule over them. I must warn you to be careful of the high priest, M'lovv'nt. He's a powerful sorcerer."

"Sorcerer? Do you believe that he can do actual magic?"

"I have seen him perform miracles."

The guards who had brought Winterbottom to the princess pounded on her door. They hissed and grunted.

Princess Golygee said, "They say that you must return to the dungeon now." She whispered, "If all goes well, we will return to Earth soon."

Winterbottom nodded. Golygee put her arms around him and kissed him. "You're so brave. If we escape this planet, I will reward you handsomely. I am also a princess of my tribe." She rubbed against him to let him know what additional reward would be waiting for him.

Winterbottom was pleased. For the first time since Plush Blue dumped him, he felt like a man. He went to the door and allowed his guards to take him back to the cell.

When he got back to the dungeon, he told his companions all that had transpired between Princess Golygee and himself.

Randy said, "This Martian princess sounds like one hot number. How do we know we can trust her?"

Winterbottom caught a note of jealousy. "What choice do we have? Have you come up with a better plan?"

"Not really. We've been spending most of our time getting Larke up to speed as to what's going on."

"How's he doing?"

"See for yourself. He's right over there." She pointed to a corner of the cell where the android was squatted down with its head in its hands.

Winterbottom went over by it. "How are you doing, Larke?"

"As well as can be expected while being locked up with you people. The stories those two have been feeding me are fantastic. They claim we came from another planet which is in the sky somewhere. Of course, we can't see the sky down here in this prison, so they could not point out this place. And the most fantastic bologna that they've been feeding me is that I am some sort of artificial being and not human as they are. What a laugh. So what weird thing are you going to say? Oh, I know. That you talked to a princess and that she's going to help us escape. What rot."

"But Larke, it's all true. And we need your help."

"I suppose I don't have much choice since you storytellers seem to be in the same boat as I am, prisoners of those tall green guys."

"Don't you remember anything before we came here?"

"Only fragments. A Martian shining a bright light at me. Being somewhere very cold and dark. Playing chess. Sorting through trash. Making love to a woman. Standing on a loading dock of a factory. That's about it."

Winterbottom patted Larke on the back. "I'm sure everything will come back sooner or later. Keep trying to remember your past."

Festival of Azathoth

The day came when the Festival of Azathoth was to be celebrated in the demon-god's namesake city. Winterbottom and his companions were chained together by metal collars around their throats and manacles on their ankles and wrists. They were marched out into the street where a grand parade was commencing. On a float pulled by oxen-like animals was a statue of the demon-god Azathoth and the high priest M'lovv'nt in colorful flowing robes. He waved his crystal rod cheerfully. Behind the float was a marching band that consisted of only drums and high pitched flutes. The band played throbbing hypnotic rhythms that set Winterbottom's teeth on edge. Behind the marching band was another float which carried the minor demon-gods Cthulhu and Yog-Sothoth. Last in line slogged the Earth people chained together throat to throat, and ankle to ankle. Their guards carried whips rather than rods with the crystals on them. They would occasionally flick a whip at the prisoners to sting them. This brought roars of hissed and grunted approval from the crowds that lined the street. It was a joyful occasion for the Martians since strangers were to be sacrificed to Azathoth rather than one of their own number. They waved flags and pennants and danced around playfully.

After winding through several streets, the parade ended at the den of the demon-god, a conical temple, which consisted of a shell supported on several pairs of flexible legs. Several jointed cylinders tipped with appendages were raised from the half-open shell. It was identical to the one on Bugaboo Island where Princess Golygee had lived, except even larger and more atrocious in appearance. At this point, M'lovv'nt hissed and grunted a long speech, pacing back and forth and waving his arms. At certain parts of his talk, the crowd hissed and grunted a rousing response. At the end they cheered lustily, an earsplitting raucous sound that sent shivers down Winterbottom's spine.

M'lovv'nt hissed and grunted to his aide. The aide came to the captain of the guard with his request. The prisoners were marched to the entrance to the temple. M'lovv'nt dismounted from the float and was about to lead them into the temple when a litter covered with jeweled silks and carried by four husky Martians arrived. Princess Golygee dismounted and approached the high priest. She hissed and grunted to him.

Winterbottom whispered to Randy, "She's telling him that she wishes to have the honor of escorting the sacrificial humans into the temple."

M'lovv'nt seemed to argue with her. She stamped her foot and hissed and grunted some more. With a sour look, M'lovv'nt nodded. The prisoners were brought forth and herded through the temple door. Both M'lovv'nt and Golygee followed. The guards were not allowed to enter the sacred building.

As they entered, a horrible stench assailed Winterbottom's delicate nostrils. The other prisoners also gagged and put their hands to their noses, except for Larke who merely stood docilely. In addition to awful odor, they heard the awful keening roar of the demon-god within the inner chamber. It was a sound to turn knees to gelatin.

Winterbottom whispered to Randy, "Be ready to act. Pass the word to Heinie and Larke."

The priest began to unlock the first victim to be thrown to the horror within the inner chamber. This was Larke. After he was released, M'lovv'nt pointed toward the entrance of the inner chamber and hissed and grunted. Princess Golygee translated. "He wants you to go in there." Winterbottom translated her translation, "He wants you to go in there."

The Escape

"No way," cried Larke and moved toward the priest. M'lovv'nt raised the crystal-rod in a threatening manner. However, before he could use it against the android, Golygee took out a blowgun she had hidden in the folds of her gown and fired a poisoned dart at the clergyman. It struck him in the throat. He collapsed in a heap. Golygee picked up his dropped key and released all the prisoners. Winterbottom retrieved the crystal-rod weapon.

Golygee said, "There's a secret exit to the temple around this way. Move quietly so as not to rouse the beast within. It is hungry now and wishes to be fed. It will be very angry when it does not get a victim."

Winterbottom passed this information to the others.

Schmidt said, "Perhaps we should appease it a bit." He dragged the body of M'lovv'nt to the entrance to the lair of the demon-god and threw the high priest inside. Apparently he regained consciousness, for he began to scream, hiss and grunt loudly.

Golygee led the group into a kind of hallway that spiraled around outer edge of the temple. At the end was a door that led to a back alley. The escapees followed the princess through meandering path among several narrow streets. The last one led to the docks. They ran along a pier to a barge with oars and sails. "This is my official barge. You may have to row since there's not much wind today."

Winterbottom said, "This is Princess Golygee's barge. We'll use it to escape."

"But where are we going?" cried Randy. "We entered the city on the side furthest from this body of water."

Schmidt said, "There's no way we can return there without being caught by the Martians. Perhaps at the other end of this lake there may be a way of returning to the surface."

Azathoth's Rampage

Meanwhile, back at the temple, apparently Azathoth was not satisfied with eating the priest. It roared loudly and stuck pseudopods out through various openings of the temple and grabbed any Martian it could get a hold of. The Martians ran in every direction to escape. The lower orders of priests realized what had happened and told the soldiers to find the sacrificial prisoners.

* * * *

Martian sailors guarded the barge. When they first saw Golygee, they bowed, thinking that she wanted to take a little jaunt. But when they saw the other humans, they realized that they were trying to escape and took out clubs to fight and capture them. The escapees each fought in their own manner. Winterbottom used the priest's crystal-rod as a club since he did not know how to make it vaporize people. Princess Golygee hung back and blew poison darts at the Martian sailors. Larke simply picked up the Martians bodily and threw them overboard. Schmidt brought out tire iron from his backpack. And Randy used judo and karate.

The fight went on for a long time. Meanwhile the soldiers sent by the priests had reached the docks and were running up the pier. Golygee spotted them and said, "We've got to get underway quickly." As the soldier neared the ship, she spat poison darts at them.

By that time, Larke had thrown the last sailor overboard. Winterbottom pulled up the anchor, and Randy unloosed the ropes that held the barge to the pier. The barge drifted away. A breeze began to blow, so Winterbottom and Schmidt raised the sail. Randy and the princess womaned the rudder. The barge moved swiftly out onto open water.

Their pursuers stopped at the end of the pier. They piled into a smaller, but swifter sailing craft. Soon they were underway and closing on the barge.

As the ship with the soldiers encroached, Winterbottom and Schmidt threw things at them to keep them from trying to board. This went on for a long while. Meanwhile the ship sailed on into the unknown sea.

After a while Schmidt spotted something. "What's that?" He pointed at thin shiny line that ran from the roof of the cavern and down into the sea.

"I haven't the foggiest," Winterbottom said. "Let's head for it."

The women turned the barge so that the bow pointed at the object. Winterbottom and Schmidt adjusted the sails. As they came closer, they saw that it was metallic rod or pipe that came from the cave roof. As they neared it, Randy said, "Shit. That looks like the pipe we used to bring water up to the base camp. When we come abreast, throw out the anchor. I want to take a close look at it."

"Aye, aye, Captain Sally," Winterbottom said. As the side of the barge brushed against the four-inch diameter round metal object, he threw out the anchor and looped rope around the object.

Randy stood on the deck rail, held the object with one hand to steady herself and examined it. "Look at this. I'll be damned. It's our own pipe. Look at this lettering. It says, *Made in China*." She peered up the pipe and estimated. "It's about thirty meters to the top. We could climb it."

Schmidt said, "And then what?"

"We should be able to contact Blue and Dooper. They'll dig down to us."

"I don't know. Suppose it were possible for all of us to climb to the top, how long would we have to wait there before they dug us out? The strain would be too much."

"With the machinery they've got available, perhaps four hours. I have a plan for that too. There are fishing nets on this barge. Once we were at the top, we could tie it to the pipe and sit in it to rest until we're rescued."

"What about Princess Golygee?" said Winterbottom. "She can't go to the surface without a spacesuit."

"Have her put on Larke's. He doesn't need one."

Winterbottom turned to Golygee. "How are you at climbing?"

Golygee chuckled. "Back on my island, I climb coconut and banana trees all the time. This pipe has many joints to hold on to. It would be a snap."

"How about you, Larke?"

"I don't know. I can't recall whether I ever climbed before."

Schmidt said, "And I definitely cannot. I have acrophobia."

"Larke will help you."

"We must hurry," said Golygee. She pointed at the Martian boat, which was only a couple of meters from pulling alongside the barge.

"Quick, Larke. Take off your spacesuit and give it to the princess."

"I'd be happy to. It's bulky. I'll be able to climb easier without it." The android removed his backpack and space suit.

Since he was naked, everything showed. Golygee stared at his member. "My! You have a big one."

Winterbottom and Randy helped the princess into it. Everyone put their helmets back on too. Using rope from the ship, they tethered themselves together. Princess Golygee, being the best climber, went first. She scrambled up the pipe like a monkey, so that she had to wait for the others to catch up. Next came Winterbottom, who was an expert climber, but slow and cautious. Schmidt clung to Larke's back with his eyes shut tightly. By the time Randy mounted the pole, the Martians had boarded the barge. One tried to grab her by the ankle, but she swung around like a pole dancer and kicked him in the face. He fell back against two others. All three fell awkwardly to the deck. Randy climbed furiously upward until she caught up to Larke. "Move it," she cried.

The Martians on the barge took out their crystal mounted rods and began to fire golden discharges at the escapees. Golygee and Winterbottom were already out of range of the device. Besides, the weapons were not accurate at any distance. Nonetheless, Randy kept prodding Larke to move faster as the glowing flashes broke all around her. One hit the pipe, producing a hole in it. The pressurized water spurted out at the Martians, bowling them over. It also began to fill the barge with water. The Martians began to bail, but the water flowed faster than they could get rid of it. The barge sank lower in the water. The Martians released the barge from the pipe and pulled up the anchor to get away from the stream, but they were too late: the barge sank. Some Martians saved themselves from drowning by climbing up the pipe. Randy pelted them with unneeded items from her backpack.

When the Martians had all fallen back into the sea, she handed the net up to Golygee, who attached it to the pipe. The escapees, one by one, crawled into it. They were all squashed together, which Winterbottom did not mind since Golygee was pressed against him. Before Randy entered the net, she used her comm unit to contact Blue and Dooper.

Blue answered, "Astronaut Plush Blue, here."

"This is Captain Sally. We're in trouble. We need your help."

"Sure chief. Do you want me and Dooper to drive over to Cydonia?"

"No. We're not at Cydonia. We're hanging on to the water pipe of our well."

"What? Are you playing some kind of joke, Captain?"

"No. It's true. What I want you and Dooper to do is dig a hole right next to the well. It must be wide enough around for a person to crawl into with a spacesuit on."

"Aye, aye, Captain Sally. If that's what you want us to do. How deep should we make the hole?"

Randy heard her whisper to Dooper, "It's the captain. She's got a make work project for us. Probably figures we're doing nothing but screwing around."

"Just keep digging until you see us. I have no idea how deep under the dirt and rock of Mars we actually are."

"Aye, aye, Captain."

"Signing off. Brief me on your progress every half hour."

Randy entered the net and snuggled up against Schmidt. After four hours went by, they heard the sound of machinery overhead. Chunks of rocks began to fall, sometimes striking them, but not hard enough to cause any life-threatening injuries. Suddenly a great gush of debris fell into the Martian sea. Air roared up the hole from below. Randy contacted Blue again.

"Okay. Get the hoist and drop the hook end into the hole. Slowly. I'll grab hold of it when it reaches us."

When the hook at the end was below the ceiling of the cave, Randy gave it a yank. "Heinrich, you go first."

Trembling violently, Schmidt grabbed the rope and stuck one foot on the hook. Randy told Blue to raise the hoist. Schmidt closed his eyes as he rose threw the hole. Next Princess Golygee went up, followed by Larke, Winterbottom and Randy in that order.

Back to Earth

After resting a few days, they returned to Cydonia and explored The Face and the other pyramids, but refrained from entering these artifacts. They found little of significance. After another month, they decided that it was time to return to Earth and report on what they had experienced. It would be up to some Earth government to decide what should be done about the Martians.

When everything was packed or discarded for the return journey, Randy said to Winterbottom, "I guess we don't have time to climb Mount Olympus."

"Maybe on the next trip. I'm sure that we'll be back some day."

They entered the lander and prepared to blastoff to rendezvous with the main section of the spaceship.

During the return voyage to Earth, Winterbottom was a much happier passenger than he had been on the way to Mars. He and Princess Golygee spent a lot of time in the storeroom, even more than Blue and Dooper.

CHAPTER 2. CALL OF THE CTHULU

Weeks after their return from Mars, Winterbottom, Schmidt, and Princess Golygee went to a nightclub at Cape Canaveral to celebrate their safe return and drown their sorrows at not being believed when they published an account of their adventures. The club was noisy, crowded and filled with hazy smoke. The band was loud and played off-key. Just the sort of place they were looking for.

They toasted each other with exotic drinks. They toasted their luck in narrowly escaping the Martians. They toasted not becoming food for the demon-god Azathoth. After many more toasts, Winterbottom and Golygee went to the dance floor where Golygee did her native erotic dances to the beat of the club's thunderous rock band. No one noticed any difference between her shimmying movements and the latest dance craze. Meanwhile, Schmidt drank and ogled the ladies. Toward the end of the evening, all three were plastered.

It was at this point that Schmidt said, "Since our return from Mars, I've been having nightmares."

Golygee, who had learned English from Winterbottom on the trip back from Mars, said, "I too have had weird dreams. Tell us yours."

Winterbottom yawned. He had little interest in Schmidt's dreams, or Golygee's for that matter. He was anxious to return to his and Golygee's cozy nest in their hotel. Since neither of his companions took the hint, he ordered another round of tequila Margaritas.

Schmidt said, "I found myself at the top of a mountain surrounded by the ruins of a building. It was late at night but a full moon lit up the area almost like daylight. Naked women were doing an erotic dance before my eyes, very like the dances we've seen here tonight."

"And you call that a nightmare?" said Winterbottom. "I would call that a most pleasant dream."

"Not if the women were all insane and tied you to a pole while they did ritual dances around you. After a while, the Cthulhu rose from a hole in the ground and reached for me with its claws and tentacles and tore out my heart. It was awful."

Golygee said, "My terrible dream was similar to yours. Only I was one of the gyrating worshiping women. And after the victim's heart was torn out, I was chosen to eat it raw. Afterward, the awful monster from the earth raped me. It must mean something. It's an evil omen that we had such similar dreams."

"Oh come on, you two. Tonight is supposed to be a fun night. Quit scaring each other. Your dreams are probably a result of the adventures we had on Mars and the pepperoni pizza we had at lunch."

Schmidt shook his head. "Perhaps. Or perhaps not. Something about the dream left a great impression on me." He shivered.

"I think it's time to go home. You're two are giving me the willies with your dream talk."

They asked for the check. For a while they argued about who had how many and which drinks and how much tip to leave. When that was settled, they left. On the way out, Schmidt took Winterbottom to the side. "Tomorrow, stop by my hotel room. I have something to show you." He acted mysterious and would not tell Winterbottom what it was. "You'll see tomorrow. It's an important discovery."

Winterbottom and Golygee returned to their hotel room and made hot passionate love for twenty minutes. Afterward, while the archeologist puffed on his after-sex cigar, Golygee held her nose and said, "Charlie, I want to return to Bugaboo Island to be with my people."

He blew out a great cloud of acrid smoke, causing Golygee to choke and gag. "Of course, my darling. I'll make arrangements tomorrow."

"Once I am back to being the princess of my people, I will repay you handsomely for all you have done for me."

"Unnecessary. It's what I would do for any hot number like you."

She stroked his cheek, almost burning herself on the butt of his cigar. "You're so sweet. Take that awful thing out of your mouth, and we will make steamy love again."

"You bet your sweet bippy, sugar."

He squashed the cigar butt into an ashtray, and they went at it for another round as hot and heavy as before. Halfway through their exertions, however, the tequila caught up to Winterbottom, and he passed out.

Just before dawn, he was awakened by Golygee screaming and waving her arms about so wildly that she smacked him in the face. She was having an awful nightmare. When he woke her up, she threw her arms around him. "Oh Charlie, it was awful. I had that dream again. Only this time I was the victim."

"Once we get back to Bugaboo, and you're among your own people, these nightmares will stop, I'm sure."

To comfort Golygee, Winterbottom made love to her again.

Schmidt's Artifacts

Before Winterbottom phoned his travel agent, he paid a call on Schmidt. He recalled that his fellow archeologist wanted to show him something. When he arrived, Schmidt was in terrible shape, with dark circles under his eyes, rumpled hair, and in a shabby robe that was too small for his overweight body. His breath smelled strongly of alcohol, and he had a crazed look in his eyes. A bottle of tequila and a dirty glass were in front of him.

"What's up, Heinie? You look terrible."

"I dare not fall asleep. Every time I do, I have awful nightmares about the Cthulhu."

"Golygee has the same problem. I wonder what's causing them."

"Maybe it has to do with the artifacts I brought back from Mars." He rose from his couch and tottered over to the hotel room safe.

While Schmidt fiddled with the combination lock, Winterbottom said, "You brought back artifacts? I thought we destroyed everything when we had our little tussle."

"Not quite everything." Schmidt set an ornate wooden box from the safe on the coffee table. He opened it with a small key and removed a replica of the Cthulhu statue that they had seen in the Cydonia pyramid.

Winterbottom picked it up, examined it and hastily put it back down. "Funny, I got a sensation of eldritch evil when I touched that thing. Do you think that it may be the source of your nightmares?"

Schmidt shrugged. "It's possible. There's something Lovecraftian about it. But I have something more important to show you." He took a broken flat clay tablet out of the box and placed it next to the statue.

"What's that?"

"Examine it closely. It's half of a map. After careful examination, I figured out that it shows areas of North America. The writing around the edges is in Martian."

"What does it say?"

"*Where the ruby shines lays the treasure of the old ones.*"

"But there's no ruby, not even a socket where one might've been set into the tablet."

"The jewel must be in the missing section."

Winterbottom rolled his eyes. "So what good is it? The other half is on Mars somewhere."

"Not true. The Cthulhu statue came from Mars, but the tablet originated on earth. I believe the missing half is on Bugaboo Island."

"What makes you think that?"

"I have one more thing to show you. Before I do, have some tequila."

"No thanks. I had too much last night. In fact, I wouldn't mind coffee. I got little sleep because of Golygee's nightmares. I ... uh ... needed to console her."

"Certainly." He called out, "Jeeves."

The android, Larke, entered the room. It bowed. "Yes, Master."

"Go to the coffee shop downstairs and bring us two coffees and a couple of cheese Danish." He turned to Winterbottom. "Cream and sugar?"

"Sugar, no cream."

"I'll have the same." He handed the android a ten dollar bill.

After the android left on its errand, Winterbottom said, "Isn't that Larke?"

"Yeah. NASA was going to scrap him. They'd purchased a newer model. I picked him up for a song and had him reprogrammed as a servant. He now answers to Jeeves."

Schmidt returned the box to the safe and returned with a handwritten journal which he handed to Winterbottom. "This is a log or journal kept by the captain of the sailing vessel Peculiar in the eighteen forties. Recently the ship had been found floating in the South Pacific. No crew was aboard except for one skeleton lashed to mainmast which was hugging the clay tablet to its ribcage."

"How did it come to be in your possession?"

"The fellow who found the ship is a treasure hunting friend of mine. He gave it to me to figure out where the treasure lies. I promised to share it with him if I found anything. Read the last four pages."

Captain Johannson's Log of The Last Voyage of the Peculiar

Winterbottom opened the journal. On the last couple of pages were the following entries:

July 5, 1842. We have been becalmed for a fortnight and are running low on fresh water and food supplies. I needed to institute rationing today. There was grumbling by the crew, but I believe they realized the situation.

July 10, 1842. Still becalmed. The crew is getting restless. Some have complained of nightmares. A strange white mist has risen from the sea. It is though we were transported to some other world surrounded as we are by fog with neither sun nor stars to chart a course.

July 25, 1842. Finally some hope. An island has been sighted not far off of our starboard. I turned the ship so that we would drift in its direction.

July 26, 1842. We are abreast the mist enshrouded isle. I weighed anchor and sent four of the crew in a jolly to explore. The mist is odd in that it never thins.

August 1, 1842. It has been five days since I sent men to the island. They have not returned. I have decided to lead the rest of the crew to the island in order to find out what happened to the men we lost. We will be armed in case they were waylaid by unfriendly natives.

August 5, 1842. Have just returned to the ship. I do not know how to describe the horrors we experienced. I, myself, barely escaped from the monster that dwells there. The rest of my crew is dead, murdered by that thing and the insane natives. After we beached the jolly, we entered a thick jungle. We found traces of the first men we sent and followed the trail they had blazed. We kept our rifles at the ready and a sharp lookout for trouble. In one area we saw signs of struggle. The footprints afterward were of bare feet, many bare feet. We concluded that our men had been captured by natives. We pressed on.

Finally we came upon gigantic ruins as though the buildings had been built for the occupation of giants. They were ancient, grim, dark and forbidding. In the very center of this ruined city, we saw an awful site. The bodies of our former crew were hung upside down on poles in front of what appeared to be a well.

Naked native women were doing an erotic dance and chanting around the corpses and the well. I asked what they saying from one of my crew who had learned the native languages from an islander with which he was fornicating. He said, "They chant the words 'The sleeper awakes. Hail the mighty Cthulhu.'"

We rushed the women, firing out guns into the air to frighten them, and they ran away. While my crew was cutting the dead men down from the poles, I happened upon a clay tablet with a ruby embedded into it. I picked up and examined it. It seemed to be a map.

Suddenly a horrible stench penetrated our nostrils, and an unearthly animal growl unlike anything on earth rent the air. An indescribable unspeakable thing rose from the hole. It grabbed members of my crew with its claws and tentacles and stuffed them into its enormous mouth. I was so astounded by the things appearance I dropped the clay map, which broke into two pieces. I was able to retrieve one half before fleeing into the jungle with the rest of my men.

As the monstrous thing gave chase, natives hiding in the jungle blew poison darts at us. All except myself perished. I rowed like a madman to the ship and hauled up the anchor by myself. My terror gave me the strength of a madman. As the ship drifted away from the island, I saw the uncanny unholy thing waving its tentacles at me in a threatening manner.

August 10, 1842. Ten days have passed since my nightmarish adventure. The mist finally dissipated, and a breeze started up. I think I am going insane. My nights have been filled with horrible dreams. When I awake I have this terrible urge to return to the island. I've managed to raise the sails, but am completely lost. The ship's larder is empty, and little water remains. A storm is brewing from the west. I've decided to lash myself to the mainmast to prevent myself from returning to the island.

* * * *

Winterbottom shook his head. "What a terrible tragedy. But Heinie, you said something about going to Bugaboo Island. What has returning there have to do with what happened to the Peculiar?"

"I believe the island where all that happened was Bugaboo. I checked the navigator's latitude and longitude readings. The area where the Peculiar became becalmed is near Bugaboo. Besides, Captain Johannson's description of the ruins is much like the ruins on Bugaboo."

"But there's no such monster on Bugaboo."

Schmidt shrugged. "Not during the time we were there. Perhaps during the years between Johannson's visit and ours, it moved to another island."

"I take it you wish to travel with me and Princess Golygee."

"Yes. Look Charlie, if we find the treasure of the elder race, we'll be famous. We may even win a Nobel Prize. It'll make up for all the razzing we've had to take lately from the International Archeologists and Explorers Club. Those stuffy guys simply refuse to believe that there's intelligent life on Mars. We may find the proof we need."

"There's that. Okay Heinie, I'll make three plane reservations."

"Make it four. I want to bring Jeeves along."
"Why?"
"He may come in handy. He's very strong and almost indestructible."

Journey to Bugaboo Island Leg One

Winterbottom discovered that they could not go directly to Bugaboo Island. His travel agent never heard of it. As far as he could tell, it did not exist since it was not on any map. The nearest island to the coordinates Heinie had given him was Raiatea, the closest major airport, Tahiti. He booked seats on a flight from Atlanta, Georgia to Tahiti, and a hotel room in Tahiti. From there they would play it by ear.

He rented a minivan for the trip from Cape Canaveral to Atlanta. Schmidt removed the rear seats and loaded up the back end with luggage and crates. Winterbottom said, "What's all this? You won't be able to take this stuff on the jet."

"I know. I'm having it shipped. Stop at a FedEx office on the way to the airport."

"Shipped to where? Bugaboo isn't even on any map."

"You said the flight was to Tahiti. The rest of the trip will be by ship."

"So what's in all this baggage?"

"Just essentials. Camping equipment mostly."

Winterbottom rolled his eyes. "Okay, if you're sure you need it." When in the wild, he believed in living off the land.

The clerk at FedEx's eyes bugged out when he saw what Schmidt was shipping to Tahiti. Schmidt's eyes bugged out even further when he saw what it was going to cost him. Nonetheless he coughed up the money.

They had trouble at the Atlanta airport because of Jeeves. Naturally, the metal detector alarm went off as it passed through it. A tough female security guard pulled the android off to one side. "Do you have any keys or change, sir?"

"I put it in that bowl." Jeeves pointed at his pen, wallet, and coins in the container for that metal pocket junk.

"Hmm. You don't have on a metal belt buckle." She waved her wand over his body. It beeped and kept beeping. "Holy crap. You've got metal all over you."

"Of course. I'm an android."

She narrowed her eyes. "Oh yeah. I've heard that one before. Prove it."

"This is undignified. I should not have to submit to such treatment."

"Listen bud, do you want to get on the plane or not?"

Jeeves opened up his shirt and ripped away the pseudoskin that covered his control panel.

"Okay. Go ahead. Sorry about that, but it's regulations."

As they walked toward their departure gate, Jeeves muttered, "I am going to sue the airline. That was humiliating. Rank discrimination against androids."

The flight to Tahiti consisted of three stopovers. The flight from Atlanta to Chicago was late. They had to hustle through O'Hare's enormous terminal since the gate for the Los Angeles flight was across the entire airport from their arrival gate. As it was, they were the last to board. In LA, they had a four hour layover. The next leg of the journey took them to Hawaii. By the time they landed in Tahiti, they were exhausted. To make matters worse, Schmidt's equipment had not arrived. As a result, they spent several days in Tahiti. Winterbottom did not mind. He and Golygee spent time on the beach sun bathing, snorkeling and surfing.

The first day, Winterbottom had his towel in hand and flip flops on his feet when Golygee came out of the bedroom stark naked. "Um, Golygee, you look swell but I thought we were going down to the beach."

"I am ready."

"You can't go like that. You must wear a swimsuit."

She gaped at him. "Swimsuit? You mean, you white people wear clothing when you go swimming?"

"I'm afraid so."

"How silly. But Charlie, I don't have such a garment."

"We'll have to buy you one. Put on your shorts and a blouse. We'll go shopping."

He took her to the shopping mall next to their hotel. As it turned out, they spent most of the afternoon there. Golygee bought many other things besides a bikini bathing suit, including earrings, souvenir T-shirts, sarongs, sexy underwear and so forth, all on Winterbottom's university credit card. Afterward they had dinner at a Chinese restaurant and returned to their hotel room to change. Golygee modeled her new hot pink teeny weenie bikini for Winterbottom. She said, "This is silly. This swimsuit covers hardly anything. What's the point?"

"As long as it covers certain strategic areas. My, you look lovely in it."

He was moved to kiss her, which led to their making hot love. Afterward, they had to search the room for the two parts which had been flung away in a fit of passion. They went down to the beach and swam in the moonlight.

Foreurs Bar

When Schmidt's crates finally arrived, Winterbottom booked a berth on a ferry from Tahiti to Raiatea. They stayed at the Raiatea Hawaiki Nui Hotel, a mid-priced hotel. While Schmidt tried to find a way to travel to Bugaboo, Winterbottom and Golygee went sightseeing. They strolled through the garden of Faaroa, played miniature golf, took a ride on the Faaroa River, and visited the Temehani plateau which is the only place in the world where a special flower, the Tiare Apetahi, grows. They also indulged in scuba diving, cruised on the lagoon, did some fishing and went horseback riding.

Nine o'clock that evening, Schmidt stopped at their room. "I've been told that motorized sailing boats can be rented from their owners on the waterfront. Most of their captains hang out at bar called *Foreurs*."

The archeologists strolled over to bar with Golygee and Jeeves. As soon as they entered, Winterbottom realized that this was a hangout for a rough crowd. It was dimly lit with a floor covered in sawdust. Most patrons were men in sailing caps, grimy white trousers and flowered shirts. Some were Polynesian, others, French. Most had a beard, a large moustache or both. A pall of thick acrid smoke, spilled liquor and cheap perfume permeated the gloom. The few women in the place wore heavy makeup, revealing clothing and puffed away on thin cigars. Drinks at the bar were served by an enormous brute of a bartender. Table service was by an attractive blonde waitress in a miniskirt.

As the foursome entered, unfriendly eyes followed them. Snickers and rude jokes about tourists were made in French and the native lingo. After they settled in a booth, the barmaid came over. She leaned forward so that a good portion of her breasts were visible. She winked at Jeeves as she said, "*Qu'est-ce que je paux faire pour vous, le monsieur et la dame?*"

Schmidt said, "*Quatre bieres. Parlez-vous anglais?*"

The waitress nodded. "Yes. I speak a little English. Are you Americans?"

"We are. I understand that some people who own boats that can be rented frequent this bar. Do you know who I might talk to?"

"There are several *messieurs* here tonight in that business. After I bring your drinks, I speak to them."

"It would be good if the boat owner also spoke English."

"I understand."

She went to the bar, drew four glasses of the local brew, added a bowl of pretzels to her tray and returned to their table. She patted Jeeves on the head. "You're a handsome fellow."

Golygee said, "The serving woman seems to like Jeeves."

Schmidt said, "She's just angling for a big tip."

Nonetheless, Jeeves grinned. "You are wrong, master. She definitely has a thing for me."

The waitress, whose name was Gigi, spoke to one of the other customers, a grizzly fellow sitting in a booth alone. He got up and came over by the companions. He introduced himself. "I am Jacque Pierre. I have a cabin cruiser that I use to take tourists island hoping."

"Please join us," said Winterbottom. He signaled Gigi to bring another beer.

Pierre slid in the booth next to Golygee. When his beer came, he said, "*Merci*," and drained his glass in one great swallow. Winterbottom ordered another one for him.

Schmidt said, "We wish to go a bit further than the islands in this chain."

He raised his eyebrows. "How far, *monsieur?*" Schmidt gave him the coordinates of Bugaboo Island. "You must be mistaken. I know that part of the Pacific. There are no islands in that area."

"Perhaps. And perhaps not. We're explorers. You must keep this under your hat, but we're treasure hunters. We've come across information that pirates buried Spanish gold on a tiny isle in that area."

The sailor licked his lips. "It is a long way to go. While I am gone, I will lose revenue from island hoping tourists. Plus I will need to order supplies for the trip." He took out a stub of a pencil and began to write figures on a napkin.

Schmidt reached over and put a hand over the hand that was doing the writing. "We're not quibblers over small change. We're prepared to offer you a hundred dollars a day plus the cost of supplies. In addition, if it's true that this island contains buried treasure, a tenth share."

"Ah *monsieurs et dame,* I am your man. I have much experience traveling the Pacific, foul weather and fair." He took another great swig of beer.

"Is your ship large enough to accommodate all of us? Plus we have much equipment."

Pierre ordered another beer for himself. He did not offer to buy for the others. Winterbottom made up for his lack of largesse by paying for another round for all of them.

"Absolutely. *Le Insubmesible* is quite large and seaworthy. By the way, does this island where you think there is treasure have a name?"

"Bugaboo," said Golygee. "It is my home."

A frightened look came over Pierre's face. "I have heard strange tales of this island. The natives are hostile and use human sacrifices in their religion."

"Nonsense," said Golygee. "I'm a native of Bugaboo. Do I look hostile? As for human sacrifices, we don't do that any more."

"I see. But there are other stories. Stories about gigantic monsters that eat people. Some say they are from outer space. Others say that they are the remains of the 'old ones,' those who lived on earth millions of years ago."

Schmidt smiled ironically. "And you believe such superstitious claptrap?"

Pierre rubbed his unshaven chin with a sound like sandpaper. "You said one and hundred fifty American dollars a day."

"One twenty five."

"Very well, you have yourselves a ship, *Le Insubmesible.* Bring yourselves and your equipment tomorrow morning ... not too early. It is docked at berth twenty-two." He got up, tipped his hat to Golygee and staggered out of the bar.

Gigi came to their table to serve more drinks. After she set the drinks down, she placed her arms on Jeeves' shoulders. "Did you strike a deal

with Captain Jacque?"
Schmidt said, "Perhaps ... if we find his ship suitable."

Trouble
Jeeves said, "Is it permissible for you to sit with us a while?"
Gigi smiled, "For a short time." She squeezed in besides Jeeves, who put its arm around her. She gazed into his eyes. "What are you called, *homme bel*?"
"Jeeves. I'm a Scorpio. What's your sign, good looking?"
"Ah, another believer in astrology. We have much in common. My sun sign is Aquarius, the water bearer ... or in my present occupation, the beer bearer." She and Jeeves laughed loudly at her little joke.
Schmidt and Winterbottom looked at each other, wondering what the waitress saw in the android. Could she have an inkling of his sexual prowess? Did it show somehow?
"I think this should be the last round," Schmidt said. "We have much to do tomorrow."
They proposed a toast to the journey ahead. Gigi used Captain Jacque's unfinished beer to clink glasses with them. About the same time, an enormous man walked into the bar. He was six and half feet tall, with a barrel chest, a black beard and arms as thick as most men's thighs. It was obvious that he had been in more than one fight, for a scar ran the entire length of one cheek giving his mouth a puckered appearance, his nose was bent to the side and his ears resembled cauliflower. He glowered around until he spotted Gigi. He let out a roar and stomped over to the archeologist's booth. He was obviously drunk and in a belligerent mood.
"Gigi," he shouted. "*Que faites-vous avec les touristes.*"
"*Functionnement juste ils pour des bouts. Vous ne faites pas l'ennui,* Bruno."
Nonetheless, he grabbed her by the arm and pulled her out of the booth. Jeeves cried, "Let her go. She's with us."
"Americans," said Bruno and spat on the floor. "Gigi is my sweetheart. She has no business with you."
Jeeves stood up. "Unhand her, or I'll have to teach you a lesson. Apparently, she prefers to be with me this evening."
Schmidt said, "Easy there Jeeves. We don't want any trouble."
On the other hand, Winterbottom said, "Don't take any gaff from that guy. Gigi is with us."
Bruno let go of Gigi and grabbed Jeeves by the shirt front. "What you say to me, little man? I break your face."
Jeeves punched him in the stomach, and he went flying against a table and slumped to the floor. "Ow," he cried. His face turned purple with rage. In a moment he rose to his feet and charged head first at Jeeves. He banged against Jeeves' chest and staggered back. Jeeves finished him

with a blow to the chin. Several other men, seeing that their champion was being beat bloody, ganged up on Jeeves. Winterbottom joined the fray. He knocked one man out with a beer glass and used Karate kicks on the others. Golygee also fought. She was adept at several types of martial arts. Schmidt crept into a corner of the booth out of the way.

Not everyone in the bar liked Bruno. The ones who did not started to fight with the ones who were after Jeeves. Soon the entire bar erupted into a brawl. The bartender called the *gendarmes* and joined the chaos himself, throwing everyone he came in contact with out into the street. Finally, the *gendarmes* arrived and hauled everyone except the bartender and Gigi to the local jailhouse.

While they were being processed, Winterbottom surreptitiously placed a hundred Euros in the desk sergeant's pocket. The officer allowed the archeologists, Jeeves and Golygee to leave.

As they came out of the station, Winterbottom remarked, "Wasn't that great? There's nothing like a good bar fight to get the old blood flowing."

"Easy for you to say," said Schmidt, holding a handkerchief to his bleeding nose where a stray fist had caught it. "You're a big lunk. Fighting is not my thing."

As they strolled toward their hotel, Jeeves said, "I'm going back to the *Foreurs*. Gigi is waiting for me."

The archeologists grabbed it before it could walk away from them. Schmidt said, "You've caused enough trouble for one evening. You're coming back to the hotel with us."

Jeeves frowned, but said, "Yes, master."

Le Insubmesible Gets Underway

The next morning after breakfast, Winterbottom rented a truck to haul their baggage and equipment to the waterfront. As Pierre had promised, *Le Insubmesible* was a large ship with two masts, an inboard engine, cabin space large enough to accommodate the four of them and Pierre. It had a large hold for the equipment Schmidt had shipped from The States. However, it was old and somewhat in disrepair. Most of its paint had worn away, and the sails had tears in them. While moving their supplies into the hold, Schmidt noticed several crates of rum. He pointed them out to Winterbottom. "I hope this doesn't mean that our captain's a lush."

"Perhaps he brings liquor along to trade with the natives of Bugaboo."

"Another thing worries me. I hope this ship is seaworthy. It doesn't seem to be in very good shape."

Winterbottom patted Schmidt on the back. "You worry too much. Things like a drunken captain and a leaky ship add to the spice of the adventure."

Schmidt grumbled under his breath.

Winterbottom and Golygee each shimmied up a mast to ready the sails. Jeeves heaved up the anchor, and Schmidt and Pierre released the berthing lines. They were on their way on a beautiful warm and humid tropical day. A swift cooling breeze bloomed the sails, allowing the ship to swiftly sail out of the harbor and into the great Pacific. After consulting his charts, Captain Jacque, as he liked to be called, took the wheel with a bottle of rum handy. He drank a swig and set a course south by southwest.

Winterbottom put his arm around Golygee as they watched the island of Raiatea slowly shrink until it sank below the horizon. "Are you happy that you're returning home, Golygee?"

She turned and put her hand to his cheek. "I am. Thank you for everything, my darling. Only I have an uneasy feeling because of my nightmares. I wonder what will be waiting for us at Bugaboo."

Winterbottom chuckled. "Not the Cthulhu, I hope."

"Do not joke about the Cthulhu. I have the feeling that we are not finished with that awful horror."

"Are you foretelling the future now? I'm sure those fears are caused by the fact that you've been away so long. In the back of your mind, you're afraid that things at home have changed too much, and you will no longer fit into your tribal society."

She smiled up at him. "You may be right. Still that phrase keeps running through my mind, 'the sleeper wakes.' It is the call of the Cthulhu. But you are right, I am being silly. The nightmares have stopped. I no longer feel drawn to the evil god."

Storm at Sea

The weather was balmy for the first three days of their voyage, and they made good time. Captain Jacque estimated landfall at Bugaboo in two more days and nights of sailing. However, on the fourth day, a great storm blew up. The skies darkened, the wind rose and the swells became steep hills of water. Lightning crackled around the masts. Great blasts of lightning and thunder combined with the roaring wind to make a noise like a great battle in the sky. As they lashed up the sails, hard driven rain pelted them until they were soaked to the skin. The ship was tossed about, and the deck became awash with flowing sea water.

Captains Jacque lashed up the wheel and ordered everyone below. "This is going to be a bad blow." He, Jeeves and Winterbottom took turns manning the pumps as water leaked into the lower decks. Schmidt and Golygee were too seasick to do anything except retch into buckets.

As Captain Jacque took over the hand pump from Winterbottom, he said, "This storm is a cyclone. We'll be blown far off course."

"Not too far, I hope."

Pierre shrugged. "We won't know that until the storm quits. I've been in cyclones where a ship like this one went so far off course that it took many days to return to where they were when the storm hit. Of course, that's assuming that we survive at all. Many ships are sunk by such storms." He looked grim.

"Thanks for that little tidbit of good news," remarked Winterbottom.

The bad weather kept up for two days. It was difficult to keep ahead of the water leaking into the ship. As they stood in it ankle deep working the hand pumps as hard as they could, the ship rode lower and threatened to capsize.

On the third day the air became calm and the rain and lightning ended. After the constant booming, it was as still as the inside of a tomb. Nonetheless, the sun did not come out. Instead a thick white mist rose from the sea, obscuring everything. Captain Jacque was unable to figure out their position. "We'll need to drift a while longer until this fog lifts."

Winterbottom stayed out on deck to breathe the salt air. It was stifling below decks and stunk from vomit. He shivered from the damp and thought about the captain's log of the *Peculiar*. The evil mist that surrounded *Le Insubmesible* was similar to what Captain Johannson experienced when the Peculiar was near the island where his crew died.

He went below to check on Schmidt and Golygee. Both had recovered from their seasickness although they were weak and looked drained. They were in the galley building up their strength with a stew cooked up by Captain Jacque which he called slumgullion. Winterbottom sat with them and ladled out a bowl of the awful stuff for himself.

While they were eating, he said, "Heinie, do you recall what Captain Johannson had written in his journal about their approach to the island where their crew died so horribly."

"I have it memorized. Why?"

"Well, the fog that we're in is similar to the one they experienced."

Golygee's eyes went wide. "It is the Mist of Shadows. It surrounds our island and the sea around it after a terrible storm such as the one that tossed this ship about so terribly."

Winterbottom turned to Captain Jacque. "Is it possible that the hurricane blew us toward Bugaboo rather than away from it."

Captain Jacque shrugged. "Anything is possible. We cannot know until this damnable fog lifts."

"Nonetheless, I'm going to go up on deck and look around."

"Me too," said Schmidt.

"Me three," said Golygee.

"Me four," said Jeeves.

Bugaboo Island

Captain Jacque followed his passengers up to the deck. They all stood on the bow staring out at the billowing fog. Suddenly something grim, dark and forbidding loomed up before the ship. "It's Bugaboo," cried Winterbottom.

"It's home," cried Golygee.

"Heave anchor, before we crash into it," cried Captain Jacque as he ran to the wheel to turn the ship so that it was broadside to the island. .

Everyone got to work doing what was necessary to halt the ship. Once it was safely anchored, Captain Jacque and his passengers prepared to go ashore. They loaded the lifeboat that swung on divots at the stern with guns and a few supplies. The plan was to find Golygee's tribe and return to *Le Insubmesible* for the rest of their equipment with native help and canoes.

Once the lifeboat was beached, they each carried a backpack, a rifle, a pistol and a machete into the thick gloomy jungle. Dense vegetation made progress slow. Every step forward was gained by whacking away at thick underbrush. Mosquitoes, flies and gnats tormented them endlessly.

In the overheated air, sweat flowed in streams from every pore in Winterbottom's body. Mysterious jungle sounds were everywhere, the raucous cries of birds, the chatter of monkeys, the laughter of hyenas, the hoot of apes, the roar of a large feline and many animal cries that he could not identify. As he slashed his way forward, an enormous python slithered down a tree. He cut off its head. Another time a poisonous asp crossed his path. He hated snakes more than anything.

After days of slogging through this steamy, insect-infested forest, they reached tumultuous, crocodile infested river. They walked along its banks upstream to seek a crossing through treacherous bogs of quicksand hidden by swamp grass. After they traveled less than a quarter of a kilometer, they came upon a narrow, rickety bamboo suspension bridge from a high bluff on the near bank of the river to high bluff on the opposite bank.

Schmidt was hesitant about anything to do with heights. "Do you think this thing is safe? It looks like it would collapse if a rabbit set foot on it."

Winterbottom said, "Not to worry. We'll go one at a time. It surely can hold one person's weight."

Captain Jacque volunteered to go first. Except for Golygee, he was the lightest. He clutched a vine rope for balance and crept slowly and cautiously across the swaying bridge. A single misstep would cause him to tumble a hundred paces down into the swirling waters where crocodiles waited hungrily for their afternoon snack.

Jeeves went next. As he stepped upon the bridge, it creaked and groaned under his metallic weight. Next went Schmidt who needed Golygee's help to brave the height. When they were almost to the other side, a bamboo strut gave way under Golygee's foot. Only Schmidt's quick action saved her from falling through the gap.

Winterbottom went last. When he was halfway across, his weight caused the vine ropes by which the bridge was suspended to strain and snap strand by strand. He took a step at a time, testing each strut before putting his weight on it. About a third of the way, the bridge shuddered.

With a loud pop, the last of the rotted vines broke. As the bridge collapsed under Winterbottom's feet, he grabbed the guide rope with one hand and a bamboo rung with the other. The bridge swung him forward to crash into the opposite wall with a force that knocked the breath out of him, so that he almost lost his grip. He used the bamboo treads as a ladder to climb to safety.

The party slogged on for several more hours. Winterbottom made a discovery. Hidden behind a wall of jungle foliage were enormous moss-encrusted, ancient ruins.

"The sacred ruins. We are near my village," said Golygee.

"What is this place?" asked Schmidt.

"According to the legends of my people, it is the home of the 'old ones,' the ancient race that lived here before the coming of man. We worshiped them as gods. They may have had their origin at Mars. I now believe that they were evil gods ... demons in your language."

Schmidt and Winterbottom gazed around with interest. Many eons ago this place must have been a bustling center of population. The facades of great stone buildings were carved with artistic designs, scenes of battles between strange creatures, humans hunted by awful monsters, statues of many-armed and animal-faced gods. Although most had tumbled into heaps of stone, some were intact, rising to two or three stories. There were temples, castles, palaces and other buildings. The jungle had largely reclaimed the decaying monuments. Great trees grew through the centers of buildings buckling their tiled floors. Plants and bushes flourished wherever they could get foothold within and between the buildings including rooftops. Vines and creepers over spread everything. Monkeys, birds and snakes had taken over what the sentient tenants had left.

In the center of the jungle infested ruins were a myriad of empty mud huts.

"My village!" cried Golygee. "Where have my people gone?"

Golygee's People

Apparently they had been hiding in the jungle. Olive skin men with painted faces, almost naked bodies and carrying spears appeared from the darkness of the forest. Captain Jacque and the archeologists readied their rifles. Golygee raised her arms above her head and spoke to the newcomers in Bugabooish. Winterbottom interpreted for Captain Jacque and Jeeves. "She's telling them that she is the Princess Golygee returned from Mars, and that we are her friends, the ones who rescued her. She asks whether she may now take her rightful place as the big honcho of the tribe."

One of the men replied. Winterbottom interpreted, "He greets her with great joy that she has returned to them, but the tribe is in dire straits. Only a few of the weaker and older men are left. He said that the sleeper has awakened. First, all the women went away and took their children with them. They were under the spell of the call of the Cthulhu. Soon after, the able-bodied men left in pursuit of the women."

Golygee burst into tears. Winterbottom put his arms around her to console her.

Schmidt, who also spoke Bugabooish, said to the tribesman, "Where did they go?"

Sabu, an elderly tribesman with a twisted leg and one eye, shrugged. "I do not know for certain, but I believe it had something to do with this." He handed Schmidt a clay tablet. It was the other half of the one Schmidt had. However, Schmidt was disappointed to note that the ruby that Captain Johannson had referred to in his journal was missing. Nonetheless, there was a notch where it had been. Schmidt took his portion of the map from his knapsack and placed the two pieces together on the ground. "Charlie, look at this."

Winterbottom knelt down next to him and examined the tablets. It was a map of the east coast of the United States. He pointed to the notch. "And this is where the treasure of the old ones is supposed to be?"

"That must be the place, Charlie."

"But that could be anywhere along the Hudson River north of New York."

"It seems fairly close to Albany and on the west side of the river."

"That's still a lot of territory."

Schmidt gave him a look. "Use your head Charlie. Where do most of the kooks in upstate New York live? What was the name of hippy concert in nineteen sixty nine where people ran around naked and did drugs? What was the name of the concert twenty-five years later where the same thing happened?"

"Woodstock?"

"Yes. And where is the world headquarters of the secret organization known as SWOTC?"

"SWOTC? Oh yeah, Slave Women of the Cthulhu. Let me think. Oh. We learned that they often had meetings in Woodstock, New York. So, you think that's where the treasure of the old one lies?"

"Certainly. And the old ones left Cthulhu there to guard it."

"Your twisted logic makes a weird sort of sense."

Captain Jacque, who had been eavesdropping, knelt down next to them. "*Sacré bleu*. The treasure is in America. I must get my passport renewed. You fellows will help me get a visa."

"Sure," said Schmidt. "We'll tell the authorities that you're our guide."

"Guide?" Captain Jacque and Winterbottom said together.

"Kidding. The people who live along the Hudson River are not like other Americans, especially in the Woodstock area." His pointed finger made a little circle on his forehead. "Y'know, a little nuts."

"Wait a minute, Heinie. I'm from that area originally."

"See what I mean."

Sabu came over and asked in Bugabooish, "What's up, fellows?"

Schmidt said, "We think we know where your women all went. And possibly your men too. We plan to go there and rescue them from the Cthulhu."

Golygee had been standing nearby listening to everything. She stooped down by Winterbottom, flung her arms around him and cried, "You would do that for me? Rescue my tribe from that horrible monster? Oh Charlie, you're so brave. And so smart to discover the meaning of the clay tablet."

Schmidt let out a disgusted grunt.

Woodstock, New York

The adventurers left the island a day later. Sabu insisted that he and the other men prepare a feast for the brave men who were to travel to that dangerous land known as New York State. He had heard that it was full of wild men who lived in great tall buildings, who owned strange creatures called milk cows, paid enormous taxes to the big chiefs and endured the horrible weather.

The Bugabooeans cooked a wild boar whole over a wood fire. They served this with bananas, mangoes and other exotic fruit. Their special treat was a fragrant dish called *phew* (pronounced poo). Captain Jack enjoyed this especially. He said, "It reminds me of our own native dishes, which are a mixture of French cuisine and Polynesian cooking."

He contributed several bottles of rum. They mixed it with native fruit juice and coconut milk and celebrated throughout the night.

They needed the next day to recover from hangovers. The following day they said good bye to Sabu and the others and returned to *Le Insubmesible*. It took them several more days to sail to Tahiti as the storm they had endured had ripped their sails to shreds and did other damage to the ship. They could not use the engines, because the gasoline onboard had become ruined by the water that had entered the ship. Their stay at Tahiti was lengthened because of the paperwork and bribery needed to get Captain Jacque a valid visa to enter the U.S.

Once they landed at JFK, they rented a car and drove to Woodstock where they booked rooms at a bed and breakfast. That night, Golygee's and Schmidt's nightmares returned. In addition, Golygee was distracted and began to mumble under her breath softly. To Winterbottom's ear the Bugabooean words sounded like, "I am coming, oh great Cthulhu."

When he asked her what she said, she replied, "Oh nothing. I said that I am overcome with jet lag."

The next day at breakfast, Winterbottom asked Schmidt, "How will we find where the treasure of the old ones lies?"

"We need a mole, someone to find out where the SWOTC hold their worship services."

"Do you really believe the treasure is hidden by this cult?" asked Captain Jacque.

"Absolutely. Since it an organization that only women may join, there is only one of us who can spy on them for us."

All eyes turned to Golygee. "Me? But I know nothing about being a spy."

Winterbottom said, "It's simple. Pretend a desire to join SWOTC. Find out where they hold their meetings and report back to us."

She looked doubtful. "How do I find this SWOTC?"

Schmidt said, "They'll probably find you. Cults are always looking for new blood. Hang around the village after dark. If you're approached by a man or a drug dealer, give him the brush."

"My brush? The one I use to smooth out my lovely golden locks?"

"I mean tell him to beat it, get lost, go on his way. *Comprende?*"

"I think I understand. If I am approached by a man especially if he is selling drugs, I am to tell him to go away. I am not interested. Yes?"

"Now you got it. However, if you are approached by a woman, and she asks you whether you want to join a secret club, go with her."

Golygee frowned. "I am frightened."

Winterbottom put his arm around her. "Don't be afraid. We'll watch from a distance and follow you. If you get into trouble, just yell. We'll come running."

She smiled at him and touched his cheek. "You are so brave, Charlie. For you, I will do it."

Slave Women of the Cthulhu

Winterbottom and Schmidt kept a watchful eye on Golygee from across the main road that passed through Woodstock. She strolled about peering in windows of novelty shops, used book stores and art galleries. Captain Jacque was in a nearby bar indulging in his favorite hobby, drinking hard liquor. Jeeves had wandered away somewhere. He was not interested in their mission and was unhappy that they did not return to Raiatea and the bar where Gigi worked. Winterbottom was glad that it was not with him. It was getting on his nerves. There's nothing worse than having a lovesick android around.

Nothing much happened until nine o'clock when the shop closed and the main street emptied of tourists. A full moon had risen. Its silvery light gave the town an eerie glow and caused objects to cast faint shadows. A young woman, with long flowing hair with a flower in it and wearing a colorful shapeless dress, came out of a building that advertised fortune telling. When she spotted Golygee, she approached her with an unlit cigarette in her hand. Golygee shook her head, and the woman tucked the cigarette behind her ear. The woman took Golygee's hand, turned it palms up and studied it for a couple of minutes. She said something that Golygee agreed with. Golygee followed her into the house.

"What do you think, Heinie? Is that woman a SWOTC?"

"Hard to say. She might simply be a psychic trying to drum up business."

"I don't like it that Golygee's out of our sight."

"I wouldn't worry. If that woman is a SWOTC, she'll take Golygee somewhere else. I doubt that SWOTC would hold their frenzied Sabbaths here in the village."

They waited. An hour later, the two women came out of the building and walked around the back. After a couple of minutes, an old pickup rolled to the end of the driveway.

"Quick," Winterbottom cried. "Get into the car."

He and Schmidt leaped into the rented car. Winterbottom pulled out of the parking spot just in time to get behind the pickup as it turned right out of the driveway and headed north out of town. After a quarter of a mile, the pickup turned down a badly paved side road marked Dead End. As this road wound around a mountain and gained altitude, it got narrower and more in need of repair.

Schmidt gripped the door handle and the armrest tightly as Winterbottom screeched around hairpin turns where beyond the edge of the road were long drops into nothingness. "Uh .. Charlie. Don't you think you should ease up on the gas a little? This road is dangerous."

"Can't. Don't want to lose sight of the pickup." He tromped even harder on the gas petal as the distance between them and the truck lengthened.

Just short of the mountain top, the pickup stopped where several cars were parked. Winterbottom halted his vehicle without entering the flat area. He and Schmidt watched to see what would happen. The two women got out of the pickup and began to climb up a steep incline. Since they did not look back, Winterbottom pulled into the lot. He and Schmidt got out the sedan and followed the women at a distance. As they neared the top of the hill, they came upon a large container filled with women's apparel, both outer garments and underwear. Winterbottom whispered, "Let's hide in that stand of trees and shrubbery to the right. We should be able to see what goes on from there."

Schmidt nodded and made a dash for the copse. Winterbottom followed. They peered out at the remains of a building. All that was left was the foundation and a few cement blocks and bricks. The full moon provided enough silvery light to see everything that was going on. At least a hundred buck naked women were on their knees raising and lowering their arms in front of an old well. They chanted, "Oh great one, arise and give us ecstasy and joy. We praise thee with our bodies and souls."

Behind the well were two poles with naked men tied to them. The one man's head lolled to one side as though he was drugged or unconscious. The other stared at the women.

The Cthulhu

Winterbottom whispered, "My night vision is not very good, but those men tied to the post look familiar."

Schmidt shook his head and whispered back, "They should. It's Jeeves and Captain Jacque."

"Ohmigosh. They've been captured by SWOTC. What do you think will happen to them?"

Schmidt shrugged. "They'll probably be sacrificed to the Cthulhu."

At that moment, the women stopped their chanting. One of their number rose to her feet. It was a young woman with a spectacular figure. She turned slightly so that she was almost facing Winterbottom.

"It's Golygee," Winterbottom cried.

"Sh. Do you want them to spot us? Let's see what she does."

Golygee walked over to a flat stone in front of the well and laid down on it with her arms and legs spread wide. She called out, "Come to me, my lover. Come to me, oh exulted Cthulhu."

"She's under a spell," whispered Winterbottom. "We've got to do something."

Schmidt cocked the double-barreled shotgun he carried. "Maybe if we shoot a couple of rounds into the air, it'll scare off the women. Then we can ..."

Before he finished his sentence, something awful rose from the well. It was the living Cthulhu. In size and shape, it was the same as the statue on Mars. The organ on the creature had a two-inch diameter and stuck straight out two feet. The head consisted of octopus-like tentacles with ten eye stalks in the middle. This pulpy, tentacled head surmounted a grotesque and scaly body with rudimentary wings and prodigious claws on its hind and forefeet. It crawled out of the well, leaving a trail of green slime. It headed for the stone where Golygee lay spread-eagled.

Winterbottom rose up from their hiding place and cried, "No!!" He shouldered his rifle, aimed and fired at the Cthulhu. The bullet smacked into the monster's tentacled head with a splat. Green ichor flowed from the wound; the creature let out an earsplitting screech, and it waved its tentacles around wildly. To Winterbottom's satisfaction, its organ drooped and shrunk up. It turned to face the direction the bullet had come.

The women did not seem to notice. They went on with their chanting and erotic shimmying. Jeeves burst its bonds and headed toward the Cthulhu. Captain Jacque belched loudly and mumbled in a drunken stupor.

The Cthulhu advanced toward Winterbottom, who kept firing his rifle until it was empty of cartridges. Although the monster was bleeding from several wounds, they simply added to its wrath. It growled and frothed at its maw. Schmidt rose and fired the shotgun at it. It staggered back from the impact and kept on coming.

Schmidt cried, "Run. It's impervious to bullets." He turned to get away, but the Cthulhu grabbed him by the throat with its monstrous claws and lifted him off the ground. It did the same to Winterbottom. It began to shake the archeologists in a manner that would sooner or later break their necks.

Suddenly it stopped and dropped them. Jeeves had climbed on its back and was pulling out its eye stalks. The Cthulhu rolled on the ground to try to dislodge the android. They fought back and forth. Jeeves had brute strength, but the Cthulhu had many tentacles and sharp claws. When it tried to stuff the android inside its enormous mouth, Jeeves knocked its teeth out. On the other side of the ruins was a sheer drop of several hundred feet. The battle between the two titans came closer and closer to it. As they struggled they rolled right over the cliff. Schmidt and Winterbottom ran over to see what happened. to them. They looked down to see the Cthulhu squashed flat like a bug and Jeeves in pieces.

"Do you think Jeeves survived that fall?" asked Winterbottom.

Schmidt shrugged. "We'll see after we get down there. Right now, I'm going to go after the treasure of the old ones. I need your help."

"After I make sure that Golygee and Captain Jacque are okay."

When he turned around, the SWOTC women were running toward the box that held their clothing. Many of them tried to cover their naked breasts and groin area with their hands. Others simply ran squealing.

Winterbottom went over where Golygee lay. "Are you all right, darling?"

She put her arms around him. "I think so. The Cthulhu had me under its spell. In fact I'm not totally recovered. I'm still horny. Let's do it, Charlie."

Winterbottom flushed. "Not here in front of Schmidt and Captain Jacque." The SWOTC women were all gone.

"Oh poo." She rose from the stone, and they went together to untie Captain Jacque. As they neared him, the odor of alcohol was so strong one could become intoxicated from his breath. Once his bonds were loosened, he slipped to the ground.

About this time, some of the women wandered back from the woods. They had light brown skin, wore skirts but no tops and resembled Golygee in appearance. One came forward and bowed her head. She said in Bugabooish, "Is it really you, Princess Golygee."

"Yes. I've returned from Mars and have come, with my friends, to save you from the Cthulhu"

"The Cthulhu was not so bad. It only did it with each of us once. Many enjoyed the experience."

Golygee sighed. "My friends came to my rescue before the monster could ravish me. The Cthulhu is dead. Do you wish to return to Bugaboo now?"

The women looked at each other. Finally the spokesperson for the group of Bugabooean women said, "I am sorry Princess. We have made new lives here in Woodstock. We live outside the village in a commune where we exchange lovers and do our tribal dances to the music of The Grateful Dead."

"In that case I will join you. All the good-looking men have left Bugaboo. There are only a few old men and otherwise unsuitable fellows left there."

"Where did they go?"

Golygee shrugged. "We thought they were out searching for you women. Did they not show up here?"

"No. The rats. They probably only went as far as the next island and found women there."

While this conversation was going on, Winterbottom used a rope to lower Schmidt down into the well where the Cthulhu had been abiding. Halfway down, Schmidt hollered up, "Oh the stench down here is horrible. That monster was a filthy creature."

"I can smell it up here. Do you want me to haul you back up?"

"No. I'll tie a handkerchief around my nose and mouth."

Winterbottom lowered him some more. Finally he heard a splash, and Schmidt cry, "Shit. It's all green slime down here."

Winterbottom peered into the well. He saw the glow from Schmidt's flashlight moving around. After a while he heard Schmidt cry, "I found the treasure of the old ones. Haul me up, Charlie."

Winterbottom tugged on the rope and slowly brought Schmidt to the top of the well. He was covered with slime, stunk to high heaven and carried an ornate box which was also covered in stinking slime. Winterbottom held his nose and backed away as Schmidt crawled out of the well. "Walk at least ten paces behind me, Heinie. You'll need to jump in the creek at the bottom of the mountain. A skunk smells sweet compared to you right now."

Winterbottom looked around for Golygee, but she was gone. He figured that she had returned to the bed and breakfast. He heaved Captain Jacque over his shoulder, and he and Schmidt made their way back to the bottom of the mountain where Schmidt leaped into the creek. Winterbottom also threw in Captain Jacque, who came up from his dunking sputtering and swearing. He crawled ashore and shook off excess water in the manner of a dog. He looked around. "*Sacré bleu*, how did I get here? The last I recall Jeeves and I were sitting with two *belles jeunes femmes*. I was showing them how I could empty a bottle of rum in one great swallow."

When Schmidt had finished washing the slime off, he set the ornate box on the ground. With slime cleaned off, Winterbottom could see that it was carved all over with death heads and unspeakable monsters. He and

Captain Jacque watched anxiously as Schmidt pried off the cover. Inside were rows of ceramic replicas of Cthulhu. The box was full of them except for one spot. Schmidt removed one from the box and examined it. "There's something written in Martian."

Winterbottom asked, "What does it say?"

Schmidt cursed in several languages for several minutes. When he finished, he said, "It says, *Imported from China.*"

Winterbottom and Captain Jacque started laughing so hard that they rolled around on the ground. Finally, even Schmidt could see the irony and started to laugh. Between fits of laughter, he said, "I suppose I could sell them as souvenirs to the SWOTC."

Finally Winterbottom said, "Let us go find Jeeves and see whether he survived the fall."

Captain Jacque staggered back to town. He said he was thirsty.

Winterbottom and Schmidt hiked around to the other side of the mountain where the cliff side rose vertically. The remains of the Cthulhu were fast disintegrating. They searched around and found parts of Jeeves, a twisted arm in one place, a dented leg in another, the other arm and leg near the cracked body, which leaked oil. Everything except its head. Finally, Winterbottom stumbled on something hard and round. He was just about to kick it out of the way, when it cried, "Hey, you big lunk, watch where you're stepping."

Winterbottom bent down and picked it up out of the long grass. "Hi Jeeves."

"Where's that awful creature? That Cthulhu thing. It was its fault. It was going to do something terrible to Golygee."

"It's dead. That was a smart move on your part, falling off the cliff while you were wrestling with it."

"Not so smart. Now I'm all in pieces."

"How did the SWOTC capture you and Captain Jacque?"

"Captain Jacque and I were in a bar with two fine young ladies making small talk when Captain Jacque guzzled a whole bottle of rum and passed out. The women told me that they wanted to take him someplace where they could sober him up. They indicated that they were ready for some hot sex. I went along willingly. When they tied us to the poles, I thought we were going to do something kinky. The babe I was with was a real hottie."

Schmidt came up. "Don't worry Jeeves. We'll send you to a computer repair shop. There's one right in Woodstock. You'll be as good as new."

"Thank you. But once I'm whole again, I'm quitting your service."

Schmidt raised his eyebrows. "You can't quit. You're an android."

"You want to bet? I'm gone. Your business is much too dangerous for me."

Winterbottom said, "Why don't you free him, Heinie? After all, he did save our lives by attacking the Cthulhu."

"Mm. I guess so. This has been a disappointing day."

Winterbottom was also in for a disappointment. Golygee left a note at the bread and breakfast that she was breaking up with him to become a member of SWOTC.

CHAPTER 3. JEEVES

"Good morning sir or madam. You advertised for a housekeeper." The thing outside the door pointed to Cinco's classified in the local daily, which it held.

"But you're an android. You don't even seem to know the difference between a man and a woman. I can't hire you."

"Sir or mad..."

"George will do. That's my name."

"George, are you saying that you will not hire me simply because I am an android?"

George Cinco recalled the new android antidiscrimatory laws. "No. That's not it. I was expecting a female. You're obviously male."

"Do you have a gender bias as well as being an android bigot?"

Cinco looked the creature over. It resembled a window store mannequin with glowing red eyes.

"Okay. Come in. I may as well interview you."

To make room for them to sit down, Cinco pushed a pile of mixed trash, unpaid bills and books off the sofa onto the floor. "As you can see, my apartment is a mess. I don't have time to clean things up. By the way, what are you called?"

"Jeeves, George. I understand your dilemma. You definitely need a housekeeper."

"Well Jeeves, what makes you think you're right for the job? I won't be able to stand over you giving orders. You'll have to show initiative."

"I am programmed for initiative. Proof of that is that I answered your ad. No one ordered me to do so."

"Good. Your duties will be to clean up the apartment daily, including vacuuming and dusting. The bathroom need only be cleaned once a week. I also need a cook. Do you cook?"

"Not at the present, but I can obtain the proper software. My capabilities are endless. It's all a matter of downloading software."

Cinco rolled his eyes. "Well, we'll see how well you do at that. You also must do my laundry and make the bed."

"Of course."

"What salary are you expecting? I'm not a rich man."

"A hundred dollars a week and to be allowed to plug into your outlets."

Cinco's eyebrows went up. The android had offered him a

tremendous bargain. Apparently the creature had no clue as to the going rate for housekeepers.

"You're hired."

"There are conditions regarding my employment."

"Okay. What are they?"

"Occasionally, I need to plug into the receptacles in your apartment to charge my batteries."

"Sure."

"I need two days off a week."

"Fine." Cinco thought it strange that an android would ask for time off. He wondered what it did when it was not working.

"And I insist on a year long contract."

"Okay, but you'll have to prove yourself first. Let me show you around the apartment."

There was not a heck of lot to show. Cinco had one bedroom, a kitchenette, a small bathroom, a combination living and dining room and a balcony overlooking a downtown street. "When can you start?"

"Immediately." Jeeves took a trash bag from the kitchen cabinet and began to stuff the junk on the floor into it.

"Hold it. I need some of that. Those books go in the bookcase. Those ... uh ... bills must be paid ... someday. Stack them neatly on the bookcase and place a paperweight on them."

"Would you like me to pay the bills for you, George? If you allow me to access your online banking account, I can pay them over the internet."

Cinco rubbed his chin. Perhaps he would stop getting dunning notices if his bills were paid on time. "As long as you know what you're doing."

"I'll need to download bookkeeping software into my hard drive first."

They took the bills into the bedroom. Cinco booted up his computer and accessed his account. Jeeves sat down, opened up a panel in his chest, pulled out a USB cable and plugged it into the computer. "I need your credit card number." In a manner too rapidly to follow, the android downloaded and installed bill paying software, and forwarded money to the businesses that had sent notices. Cinco was dismayed when he saw how little money was left in his account. But then he thought, *Okay, I'll limp along this month on what's left. Next month will be better now that I'm caught up.*

"Good job, Jeeves. I need to get to work now. Get on with cleaning the apartment and cooking dinner. I don't want to be disturbed until six in the evening."

"I must download cooking software. Which do you prefer, home style or gourmet?"

"Home style."

After Jeeves downloaded the best food preparation software, it left the room. Cinco began work on his next novel. As he tried to concentrate, he heard the android moving about the house. It was heavy footed and squeaked. The vacuum cleaner went on. He supposed that these sounds were normal when someone is cleaning house. Sooner or later he would get used to them. Suddenly there was a crash. He ran out of the bedroom to see what happened. Jeeves was sweeping pieces of ceramic into a dustpan.

"Did you break something?"

"Nothing to worry about. I'll glue it back together. You won't even know that it was broken."

"Please be more careful. I have some valuable antiques."

"Yes, George."

When Jeeves continued to sweep the mess into the dustpan, Cinco became suspicious. He waited to see what Jeeves would do with it after it was swept up. His suspicions were confirmed when Jeeves dumped it into the trash can.

"I thought you said you were going to glue it together."

"It was shattered into too many small pieces."

"Then why didn't you say that to begin with."

"I was afraid you would be upset if you knew that one of your knickknacks was broken beyond repair."

"So you would rather lie than upset me."

"It is in my android nature to not want to upset people."

Cinco recalled reading somewhere that androids were sensitive of human feelings. He shrugged. "Okay. I'll let it slide. From now on be careful."

Although he returned to his bedroom, he made little progress on his novel that afternoon. All the strange noises that Jeeves made were too much. He hoped his downstairs neighbor was not at home. After a while, he heard music. The android's clomping grew louder. He came out of the bedroom.

Jeeves was clanking around the living room in time to pop music on the radio.

"What in God's name are you doing?" Cinco asked.

"Dancing. My first job was as an entertainer. My manufacturer took me on a tour of universities where I danced, juggled and did acrobatics. I even sang. I could imitate musical instruments with my voice. However, my career in show business ended when the corporation that built me came out with a newer model. I was sold to the highest bidder. I've gone from job to job since. Some very interesting ones. I was an astronaut for a while. After that, I worked with an archeologist."

"That's nice, but these walls are like paper. You can't make all that racket. The neighbors will complain. Besides, it's bothering me." Cinco glanced at his watch. "Shouldn't you be starting dinner soon?"

"Yes George. What would you like for this evening's meal? Pot roast, meat loaf, corned beef and cabbage or strip steak?"

"Strip steak with French fries and salad."

Cinco returned to his computer. Five minutes later, Jeeves walked into the bedroom startling him. "Holy crap. Don't sneak up on me like that. When that door is closed, knock before you enter. What do you want?"

"There's no steak in the freezer and no fixings for salad in the refrigerator. I need to shop for those items and fresh potatoes; yours have plants growing out of the eyes."

"Okay. I don't have any cash. You'll have to use my credit card." Cinco handed him his Visa.

Jeeves left the apartment, and Cinco had peace for a while. A few hours later he smelled cooking. His mouth watered. He hoped that the software Jeeves had downloaded made it a good cook. A few minutes later, the apartment was filled with thick gray fumes, and the smoke detector alarm went off. Smoke billowed out of the oven. Cinco turned off the alarm and opened windows. Jeeves calmly placed slices of potato into a pan of cooking oil while humming *Thus Spake Zarathustra*.

"Jeeves," he cried. "What's going on? Whatever is in the oven is burning."

"By golly. It is." Jeeves opened the oven door, which caused the smoke detector alarm to sound again, and pulled out a chunk of meat burnt to charcoal. "I never asked you how you like your steak."

After Cinco turned off the smoke alarm and the oven, he said, "Rare. You may as well as throw that piece of crap in the garbage."

"But I'll have to buy another steak."

"Make something else. How about meat loaf?"

"Yes, George."

Cinco returned to the bedroom. An hour went by before Jeeves knocked and announced dinner. Everything was laid out on the table, a dinner plate, flatware, napkins, French fries, salad and a covered dish. By this time, Cinco was hungry and loaded his plate with the fries, salad and meat loaf. The fries were a bit underdone, and the salad dressing contained a spice that made it bitter. He dug into the meat loaf and spit it out. "Jesus Christ, what kind of meat loaf is this?"

"There was no white bread so I had to improvise. I used whole wheat."

"I can't eat this crap. I'm going out for dinner. Look I changed my mind about what kind of meals I want. I think I'd prefer gourmet. Does that include Chinese cooking?"

"Indeed it does. I'll download that software while you're gone."

"Do you want to write down my credit card number?"

"Not necessary. I have it memorized. George, do you want me to cook breakfast too?"

"Of course. See you later."

The Maxed Out Credit Card

When Cinco finished his meal, he handed the waiter his credit card. The waiter came back a few minutes later. "Sorry Sir, but this card is at its limit."

Cinco turned red. This was terrible embarrassing. Since the credit card bill was paid by Jeeves that morning, he didn't understand how it could be maxed out. Nonetheless, he gave the waiter another card.

When he returned home, Jeeves stood in a corner with its power cord plugged into the wall socket. The android seemed to be turned off. However, when out of curiosity he approached it, its eyes flicked open. "Is there anything you wish me to do, George?"

"No thanks. See you in the morning. Have breakfast ready by nine o'clock."

* * * *

This went on for a month. Jeeves was more adept at cooking gourmet food than home style, although it occasionally burnt things or put in strange ingredients. At housecleaning, it did a so-so job. It did not vacuum under furniture, sweep away cobwebs on the ceiling or get rid of the soap scum on the bathroom tiles. Jeeves asked whether its grace period was over. "Yeah, I guess you'll do. You're hired for the next year."

Cinco signed a contract that Jeeves had ready. There was a lot of small print that he neglected to read.

On the fifth, Jeeves gathered the bills and started to pay them. Cinco stood behind watching. At one point, Jeeves turned to Cinco and said, "You don't have enough money in your checking account to pay the utility bill."

"What! Let me see that." He snatched the bill from Jeeves hand. The amount for electrical usage was five hundred dollars. "This can't be. It's a mistake. Don't pay this. I'll contact the utility company."

"What about your Visa? Should I simply pay the minimum?"

"Before you do that, let me look at the statement." Jeeves handed the bill to Cinco.

Cinco went over the charges. There were several entries to Robotics Software, Inc. for software packages. The software included Housecleaning, Bill Paying, Home Style Cooking and Gourmet Cooking: several hundred dollars worth of robot software. "Holy shit. This software is expensive. And, for Chrissake, you didn't know anything when you applied for the job. You downloaded all this software using my credit card."

"It was what was necessary to do the tasks you required of me, George."

"All right, pay the minimum. I'm going to call the utility company and get this bill straightened out."

He picked up the phone and dialed. A recorded voice gave him several options to choose from. He chose one and had more options. After the fifth set of options, a heavily accented voice said, "Billing complaints. My name is Baqar. How may help you?"

"There's a mistake about my electricity usage for last month."

"What is your account number please?"

Cinco gave Baqar his account number.

"One moment. Aha, here it is. Are you George Cinco?"

"Yes."

"Hmm. Your electricity usage jumped one thousand percent over the previous month. Have you been running some heavy equipment or a refrigeration unit?"

"No. There's nothing I ... Wait a minute. Can you tell what time of day the electricity is being used?"

"Yes sir. With our new system, your usage is piped right into our computers. We did away with meter readers, saving you money. The heavy usage period at your house occurs each evening between eleven P.M. and two A.M. Highly unusual. For most people that is a low usage period."

Cinco covered the mouthpiece with his hand. "Jeeves. At what time do you recharge your batteries?"

"Between eleven in the evening and two in the morning, when you're asleep."

"Holy crap. It's you. You're using all that electricity."

"It's necessary. Didn't you read our contract? You said that I could charge up on your outlets. Otherwise I would need a larger salary to afford charging myself at a public outlet."

Cinco hung up the phone. He sighed. "Jeeves. You're fired. I can't afford you."

"You cannot fire me, George. We have a long-term contract." It played back Cinco's words agreeing the conditions of employment and a three-year contract.

* * * *

Cinco stopped writing his novel and sought employment. It was the only way he could afford Jeeves. It was ironic, since it was to be free from distractions that caused him to hire Jeeves in the first place.

Since Cinco was not around most of the day to order Jeeves around, the android downloaded fiction writing software and began work on a novel about an android detective with a human sidekick.

CHAPTER 4. LOST IN TIME

Winterbottom entered Doctor Aaron Gamostein's office, a room which could only be described as a shambles. His eyes wandered to a blackboard full of scribbled formulas, drawings of geometric shapes that were like optical illusions and mathematical equations. None of it made the slightest sense to Winterbottom. After he doffed his floppy hat, he made his way through piles of books and overflowing wastebaskets to sit on a straight-backed chair facing Gamostein's desk. The famous physicist had on a rumpled, stained suit; his long uncut hair flared out from his head wildly; and his spectacles were perched precariously on his forehead. He was deeply engrossed with something on his computer, which sat among a jumble of papers, reports, magazines and books. He was completely oblivious of Winterbottom's entrance.

Winterbottom cleared his throat.

"Be with you in a minute," Gamostein growled.

The archaeologist waited patiently for several additional minutes. Finally, Gamostein yelled, "I did it. I got that damn frog across the road." He pumped his arm a few times in triumph and gazed up at his visitor. Grinning sheepishly, he said, "Darn computer games. They're so addicting." He stood up and extended his hand. "You're Doctor Winterbottom, I presume."

As Winterbottom rose to shake Gamostein's hand, his well-starched field jacket and trousers crinkled noisily. "The honor is mine, sir, to meet the man who discovered the chronoton, the elementary particle of time. In the years to come, I'm sure it will prove to be a great boon to mankind."

Gamostein waved his hand as though to dismiss the compliment. "Perhaps. So far, however, no time travelers from the future have dropped in on me to get my autograph. Besides, someone would have made that discovery soon or later. It was inevitable once you posited the evolution of the universe since the big bang, quantum theory, relativity, the graviton, dark matter, dark energy and the multiverse. The thing is to come up with a single theory that explains everything. Now that would be a discovery. The God theory I call it. But, enough of my meandering. I understand that you've volunteered to be my guinea pig, so to speak."

Winterbottom curled up the corners of his thin lips. "Yes Doctor, I understand that the university engineering department has designed a time machine using your theory of elementary time particles."

"That's true. And it works. We have sent objects and animals forward and backwards in time using the device. But so far, no human beings. In fact you may be in luck. As a demonstration, I intend to send my cat to this very moment from two weeks in the future. It should arrive any second."

As though on cue, a shabby black cat appeared seemingly out of nowhere to land on the Winterbottom's lap, startling him so that he leaped up and tipped over his chair. After gaining his aplomb, he brushed cat hair off his lap, righted his chair, and said mildly, "Amazing. And you claim that the creature arrived here from two weeks in the future."

"I assume so. That's when I intend to send him back in time. Sorry about his landing in your lap though."

Winterbottom thought for a moment. "But suppose you forget to send him?"

Gamostein shrugged. "A paradox. In two weeks there might be two identical Jakes; that's assuming Jake is really my cat's name. You see, I haven't named him yet since he just arrived. Hmm." He got up and went to the blackboard, erased about a quarter of it, and began to write mathematical formulas furiously. Finally, he scratched his head, getting chalk dust in his hair, and said, "Schrödinger's uncertainty principle comes into play in this case. The actual outcome is unclear mathematically."

"I see. So the consequences of time travel are not always predictable?"

"Precisely. That's why I think you're a brave man to volunteer for this project. We really don't know what dangers a time traveler may face. We've made educated guesses, but we really don't know. Your position is similar to the first men to venture into space."

Winterbottom puffed out his chest. "Well, I'm no stranger to danger. There are many hazards that archaeologists face while on a dig: irate natives, poisonous snakes, scorpions, tomb robbers, bandits, uncooperative governments, exotic diseases, ancient curses, to name only a few. Besides I was almost eaten by the Azathoth on Mars and attacked by the Cthulhu in Woodstock, New York."

"Good. The world needs men like you: men who are not afraid to risk their lives in the name of science. But, before you commit yourself, I would like to give you our assessment of the dangers I believe you may face."

"I understand. Forewarned is forearmed."

Gamostein began to pace with his hands folded behind his back and slightly bent over. Winterbottom was reminded of the twentieth century comedian Groucho Marx. A position Gamostein often took when lecturing students. "I'm assuming that because of your occupation that we will be sending you to the past. The first danger you may face is the possibility of an object occupying the same space as yourself in the time period that you are sent. We will minimize this hazard by launching you from deepest space." He gazed over his glasses at Winterbottom. "Have you ever been outside of the solar system?"

"No. But, as I said before, I have traveled to Mars. A highly developed civilization exists there underground. But they're not friendly. They sacrifice strangers to their demon-god, Azathoth. Uh, I have a question. How will I return to earth? I'm not a space pilot."

"Oh, the space-time machine is automatic. It will fly you into deep space away from any stellar systems. By the push of a button it will send you into the past at the selected date and time. Once it arrives in the past, it will fly you directly to the designated spot on Earth, which will be in a remote area near the chosen location. On return, it will do everything again in the reverse order. All you have to do is close a few switches."

"I see. Press on."

"As I said, you will be launched from deep space where the hazard from other objects in minimal. Yet, it is not zero. There's the off-chance that a micrometeorite will exist in the exact same location as your craft in the period you wish to visit. But, the odds against it are astronomical. Nonetheless ... you never know.

"The second danger is more likely. Although we will take every precaution and give you weapons with which to defend yourself, there is always the threat of something in the past that may cause you harm. For example, if you go to the era when saber-toothed tigers existed, you could be mauled and eaten by one. Or, more likely, you might go to a period where a war is going on; you could become the target of an arrow, spear, bullet or bomb. Also, you must be careful about the local mores and prohibitions. For example, your knowledge of modern science and technology could get you burned at the stake as a witch in certain ages."

"I'm prepared to face such hazards. But, after what you said about the cat, what concerns me is the possibility of creating a paradox. Suppose I do something that prevents my own birth. For example, cause the death of an ancestor before my later ancestor is born? How do I avoid this?"

The physicist chuckled. "I see that you do not really understand the nature of time travel. Suppose you went to the past and did kill your ancestor. It wouldn't make a bit of difference. Do you know why? It is because when you return to the present, you will not be returning to the universe you left. Just the fact of your going to the past at all would create a 'paradox' if only a single future existed from any point of time. In that case time travel would be impossible.

"The thing is that from each instant of time, there are an infinite number of possible futures. Parallel universes exist for every possibility. Some are only slightly different. Others are vastly different. Sometimes the difference is so minuscule that you may not detect any change whatsoever. You might believe that you had returned to the universe you left. In other cases, the changes would be so great that the universe you return to would be insanely different from the one you knew. When you go to the past and return, you move sideways in time, as well as backward and forward. The more the present is changed by your actions in the past the more sideways slippage."

"It sounds complicated. I don't ... think I understand."

"Allow me to illustrate. I want you to be very clear on this point before you make your final decision to go through with the experiment."

Gamostein went to the blackboard, erased everything that had been written on it previously and drew a horizontal line from one edge to the other. On the right side of the line he placed a large dot. He pointed to the dot. "Now, let's say this is the present moment. If I send you back to the past ..." He moved his finger from right to left along the line. He stopped near the left edge and drew another dot. "Your arrival in the past changes the entire future from that moment on. So the next moment in your future would be here." He drew a short diagonal line from the dot and placed another dot on the end of it. He chalked in another horizontal line starting at the second dot. This line was parallel to the first line. "Now suppose you perform an action that changes history." He placed a second, large diagonal line emanating from the second dot and a dot at the end of it. "Okay. At this point you return to the present." He drew a third horizontal line parallel to the other two and made a large dot at the right end of it. This dot was vertically displaced from the very first dot he had drawn. "As you can see, the universe here is much different from the one you started from, although from your standpoint – as the time traveler – you would be at the same location in time." He glanced at his watch. "Let's say at exactly three forty six in the afternoon of the twenty-sixth of January of the year twenty fifty two A. D."

"This moment."

"Correct. The exact moment you left to go to the past." Gamostein grinned and brushed his hands as though his illustration had explained the whole concept.

Winterbottom was more bewildered than ever and stared wide-eyed at the diagram. "Uh ... I think I grasp the concept. You mean, I don't actually change the present in this universe. I just sort of create a new ... uh, present. But ... but what happens to the real present."

"There is no such thing as a 'real' present. The other parallel presents are as real as the one you are living in. Actually, since we are continuously moving from the past toward the future, in essence the present does not exist. But as I understand your question, the present as it seems to exist from my point of view remains unchanged."

The more Gamostein explained, the more confused Winterbottom became. "What do you mean when you say 'seems to exist from your point of view'?' The same moment also exists for me, doesn't it?. Time and the material universe are objective things. They exist other than in our minds, regardless of what some nihilistic philosophers may say."

"Oh, I am not saying that the universe at any particular moment is simply a subjective phenomenon of our minds. Although an objective material universe exists at the present moment, it is but one of an infinite universes that exist at the same moment. We are not aware of them because they are in dimensions other than our familiar three. As the great Albert Einstein has demonstrated, the universe is relative to the observer and depends upon where we are and our motion relative to the things we are observing." Gamostein had warmed up to his subject and waved his arms about as he spoke. "Time travel theory has its basis in the theory of relativity as well as quantum theory and indeterminism. You see, I was not the first to theorize that a time particle must exist. I simply performed the experiments that proved its existence. The first to hypothesize a time particle was the genius mathematician, Doctor Hoygold. His premise, in his brilliant paper on the topic, is that in order for the universe to exist as it does, there must be a time particle with wavelike properties. The theory of chronotons reconciles relativity with quantum theory and allows the possibility of time travel."

Winterbottom rolled his eyes. "I'm afraid the entire subject is a bit too technical for my understanding. After all, I'm only an archaeologist, more used to dealing with chips of clay than atomic particles. Tell me though, if I'm extremely careful to change the past as little as possible, will the universe I return to be identical to this one?"

"The odds are very good. I'd say almost astronomical in your favor. You see, according to Hoygold's theory, there's a damping effect in time that keeps things relatively stable – although this has yet to be proven. The thing is, to be on the safe side, you should simply observe. Try not to touch anything, move anything or disturb the past in any way. Well, now that I have made you aware of the hazards, are you still determined to go through with it?"

"Oh yes. It's been my dream for as long as I can recall to see ancient Greece in all its glory. To hear Socrates or Plato lecture in person."

"Well then, you seem to be ready to go ahead with your part of the project. Of course, there'll be a training period. You'll have to learn how to operate the space-time machine, and what to do in an emergency, although for the most part, it functions automatically once we've set its parameters. An artificial intelligence program does all the calculations and controls the operation of the equipment. Nonetheless, there are a small number of manual controls. Also, if for some reason, you cannot return to the shuttle during the rendezvous window, you might need to modify its program slightly. Naturally, you'll also have to brush up on your ancient Greek, language, customs and so forth. Would you like a tour of our facilities now?"

"Be delighted."

Gamostein strode down the space station's corridor at a pace that made the Winterbottom hurry to keep up, although his legs were longer than the physicist's. They halted before a wide metal door which Gamostein opened by placing his thumb on a reader. With a loud rumble, the massive door slowly opened. Beyond it was a large shuttle bay in the center of which was a one-man spaceship. Technicians, scientists, engineers and mechanics swarmed over it, making adjustments, taking measurements and servicing its mechanical and electronic parts.

Gamostein put an arm around Winterbottom's shoulders and made a sweeping gesture with his free hand. "There it is, the space-time machine, a marvel of engineering designed for atmospheric, space and time travel." He led the archaeologist to the ship's access door. The cockpit's interior was cramped, and Winterbottom's eyes bugged when he saw the enormous number of dials, meters, switches and other controls on the instrument panel. He wondered if he would need to learn what they were all for. He knew he could not even program a VCR properly. "Will I have to know ..." He gulped. "What all those dials and switches are for?"

"Hardly. Most of them are for the people who service the ship and the engineers. You'll be concerned with but a half dozen controls. Of course, there are manuals aboard that describe each instrument, if for some unknown reason you need to know the purpose of any dial or switch. The important ones, the ones you'll actually use, will be explained during your training." Gamostein showed Winterbottom one of the manuals, which was double the thickness of the Manhattan phone book.

"Right now, I want you to see this." He pointed to a small computer screen and the keyboard below it. He patted it. "This is where the software that controls and monitors the chronoship resides. Let me demonstrate." He pressed a button, and a brightly colored menu appeared on the screen with the words Program Selection above it. The third item in the menu was Chronotravel Parameters. He selected this option with the mouse. Another menu appeared. The items were *Current Date and Time, Destination Date and Time, Orbital Distance to Earth Zero, Map Coordinates* and so forth. Next to each item was a series of numbers. For example, across from the Current date and time was 01:26:2052/16:11:35: followed by a blur after the last colon. When the 35 changed to 36 as Winterbottom watched, he nodded. Of course, this was the current date and time. He glanced at his watch to confirm. Since his watch was two minutes ahead, he reset it to the time on the screen.

After they explored the ship, Gamostein took him on a tour of the space station.

Time Travel Training

Winterbottom started his training the next day. It lasted eight weeks and included, besides lessons on the operation of the time-space vehicle, a comprehensive study of the language and customs of ancient Greece, target practice with ancient weapons, intensive physical training and martial arts, and additional instruction in the theory, practice and hazards of time travel.

At the end of this period, he felt competent to run the space-time machine and ready to venture into the unknown. He had one last question for Gamostein. "When I return from the past, what benefit will there be to you since I'll be in another universe on a different time track?"

"Ah, I see you are still a bit confused about the ins and outs of time travel. As you say, you will not return to this universe. But, of course, another Charles Winterbottom from a different time track will arrive. It's like the business with Jacob, the cat that appeared the day you first walked into my office. I never actually sent it back in time. The one that arrived on your lap was from another time track."

"Uh ... I guess I understand. But if you didn't send the cat back in time, how could it appear when it did?"

"I could have; in fact, I was planning on sending some animal back in time as a test at the time."

Winterbottom mind whirled. He wondered whether that was one of those time paradoxes he had heard about. "So this other Charles Winterbottom will get all the glory in this universe. I suppose they'll have a ticker tape parade down Broadway for him."

Gamostein laughed and clapped Winterbottom on the back. "Don't you worry. You'll be a celebrated hero in whatever universe you wind up in. Perhaps they'll heap even more honors on you than we would. After all we're operating on a limited budget here."

Winterbottom smiled wanly. "Oh. Of course." He was beginning to have doubts about the project and wondered whether Gamostein and his crew really knew what they were doing. But, it was too late to quit. Too much time and money had been invested in him. Besides, the press would crucify him as a weakling and coward for backing out at the last minute, maybe infer that he never had any intentions of going back in time, that the whole project was a publicity stunt. So far the media had made him the celebrity of the hour. They had dubbed him "Our Brave Chrononaut." People who recognized him from the media net asked for his autograph.

Launch

The big day finally arrived. He squeezed into the tiny space-time ship to the sounds of a marching band, the glare of lights from the media and the roar of the crowd of VIPs lucky enough to have the pull to view his departure. He strapped himself into the acceleration couch. There was a countdown in which he checked over gauges and indicator lights as he had been taught. When it reached zero, he pressed the GO button and zoomed into the great emptiness of space. This moment was viewed by billions all over the solar system. Anchor men from the major news networks burst into tears as he flew off the space station.

This did not mean that he would be going back in time any time soon. First, the automatic pilot of the ship must take him far into the emptiest part of deep space, away from the solar system with all of its hunks of rocks and bits of space debris circling it. Actually, it was four boring months before he reached an area deemed safe to travel to the past. He whiled away the time talking to the media and to technicians at the space station, studying books on ancient Greece, exercising or playing chess with the shipboard artificial intelligence, who was named PAL and who had more doubts about the mission than he did.

About a half light-year into the deepest vacuum of space, it was time for him to initiate his journey into the past. He changed into the dress of the place and time that he had chosen, which was Macedonia of Alexander the Great. He was not particularly interested in the brilliant general and tyrannical king, but in his adviser and mentor, the greatest philosopher of all, Aristotle. Of course, actually getting to meet such esteemed personages would not be easy. He decided on presenting himself as an ambassador from a fictitious barbarian kingdom in northern Europe.

Before leaving his own time, Winterbottom had the onboard computer generate an authentic-appearing scroll that announced him as representing King Wenclicose of Moreoveria. He also brought along a cache of gold coins and jewels to present to Alexander as a gift. He chose the summer of 333 BCE, a few months before Alexander's defeat of the Persian King Darius. Although this was during the war between the empires, during the summer months the armies sometimes took a respite due to sultry weather.

When Winterbottom felt fully prepared for his great adventure, he made several checks as instructed, sent a final message to the Earth he had known, took a deep breath and pulled the lever that would take him back in time 2300 years. Nothing happened, except that a green light on the control panel came on and a red light went off. Thinking that there might be a malfunction in the time machine, he sent a message to Earth over the hyperspace communicator equipment. Even though it was sent through hyperspace, at the distance he was from the solar system, it would take four hours for the space station to receive his message and for him to receive a reply. While he waited impatiently, he gazed out at the stars. After a check of the constellations, he realized that the stars were not in the same positions as they had been when he had first arrived at his present location. He checked an astronomical program in the onboard computer. It told him that the positions of the stars were as they had existed 2300 years ago. He knew then that no reply would come over the hyperspace communicator. He had actually been sent to the past.

He strapped himself into the acceleration couch and flipped the switch that would return him to earth. There was another long period of boredom until he was in orbit around the Earth. Bracing himself for reentry, he pushed the Earth Landing button. There was the usual fiery trip through the upper atmosphere, and then a smooth landing in a desert region near the city of Phrygia, the place where legend said that Alexander cut the Gordian knot. This is where Winterbottom expected Alexander's army to spend their rest and recuperation period.

Landing in the Past

The space-time ship had a cloaking device that camouflaged it as a rock outcropping. Winterbottom turned this on and hiked toward Phrygia, five miles northeast. To his dismay, before he reached the city, he noticed a great cloud of dust ahead of him. It had been raised by Alexander's army. He had arrived on the same day as the conqueror. Before he could find a place to hide, advanced scouts on horseback were upon him. They quickly surrounded him. Their captain said in the Greek of the times, "Who are you wanderer? Greek or Persian?"

"Neither." He bowed. "I am an ambassador from the land of Moreoveria. I have traveled far to pay my respects to the God King Alexander from my own monarch, King Wenclicose, The Mighty."

The captain spat. "I never heard of Moreoveria, or King Wenclicose. To me, you look like a Persian spy." He dismounted and unsheathed his sword preparatory to parting Winterbottom's head from his shoulders. "Kneel and pray to whatever gods you worship."

Winterbottom's eyes bugged out and sweat dripped down his back. This was about as sticky a situation as an archaeologist could get into. "Please sir, I have proof; a message to Alexander from my king." He held out the scroll to the soldier.

The captain took the scroll. "It has a king's seal on it. I must bring it to headquarters and give it to a scholar to read." He gazed at Winterbottom, suspicion still in his eyes. "If you're an ambassador, how is it that you are wandering about in the desert alone? I would think that this king of yours would've provided you with an escort, slaves, baggage, camels and so forth."

"Ah, we started out with a great troop, but met with disaster. We were attacked by bandits. Only I survived. I was knocked unconscious. The bandits must've thought me dead."

"An unlikely story." Nevertheless, the captain gave orders for a horse to be brought to Winterbottom. As soon as he was mounted, the small troop rode to Alexander's camp, where Winterbottom was put under guard while the captain brought the scroll to the king. An hour later, he returned and bowed to Winterbottom. "Apparently, you are who you say you are. At least that's what the scholar Aristotle thinks after reading the scroll you brought. Pardon me if I have offended you by my suspicions."

Winterbottom grinned broadly. His highest hopes were about to achieved. Aristotle was here in Alexander's camp. In a few moments, he would be meeting two of the greatest men in history. "Oh, I forgive you completely, captain. I could hardly blame you for being cautious with strangers. You are at war, after all."

Winterbottom was escorted to Alexander's tent, where he knelt down and touched his head to the ground in obeisance. When told to rise, he presented the gold and jewels he had brought to the conqueror and expressed greetings from the fictitious king. Alexander, who was a bit tipsy, introduced him to Aristotle and his other advisers, and sent slaves to fetch food and more wine. "So tell me about this kingdom of Moreoveria. Where is it located? And what does your king want of me?"

Winterbottom made up a lot of stuff on the fly. Mostly he praised Alexander, saying that word had reached their kingdom of what a wise and excellent ruler he was and that he was a daring and ingenious general. That tales of his exploits had reached even to Moreoveria which was far to the north. His king simply wanted to express his friendship to such a great ruler.

"See Aristotle," Alexander said. "And you thought that only savages lived up north. After I chase Darius back to Persia and conquer the lands to the east, perhaps we should send an expedition up north."

Oh, oh, thought Winterbottom, *I hope I haven't changed history by putting such ideas in Alexander's head.* "It's an extremely long way to my land through rough and dangerous territory. Besides, Moreoveria is a poor country, hardly worth the effort of a great conqueror such as yourself. It has so little to offer."

"Ha. If it is so poor, why is your king sending such gifts as these?"

Winterbottom was saved from replying by the arrival of the food and drink. It was quite a sumptuous feast, and all present dug in furiously. While they ate, Winterbottom wondered how he could get to talk to Aristotle. He had a host of questions he wanted to ask the philosopher about his works. In addition, he was being bothered by a mosquito that kept buzzing around his head. Finally, he swatted at it so that it went directly toward Alexander and stung the conqueror on the arm. Aristotle laughed as Alexander slapped at the insect. "Ah," he commented, "you may be a god-king to our people, but to that mosquito, you're but a meal."

Alexander joined in the mirth, and the entire company enjoyed the joke.

What no one was aware of, not even Winterbottom, was that the mosquito carried an extremely deadly disease. If Alexander did not get the proper treatment, he would be dead in two months. As a result, the Persians would conquer Greece again, and Hellenic influence would wane. Thus, the Romans would never achieve the civilization and power they had gained in Winterbottom's original timeline, Christianity would remain an obscure Jewish sect, the Mongols and the Vikings would divide Europe between them, and all of world history would be changed completely. If Winterbottom had returned to his own time at that moment, he would've found a world he would not have recognized.

During the feast Winterbottom expressed an interest in philosophy and was later invited by Aristotle to his tent. As adviser to Alexander, the philosopher was able to bring along all the amenities. Thus, his tent was cluttered with jars of this and that, scrolls, and other items which Winterbottom couldn't help but admire. Such antiquities as were present would've kept him busy as an archaeologist for years. And everything was whole, not jumbled pieces and fragments that he would have to put together like a jigsaw puzzle. He had a portable recorder hidden in the folds of his clothing into which he muttered notes as he examined each item. He also recorded the anecdotes, words of wisdom, philosophizing and small talk directly from Aristotle's mouth. He was in heaven. When he returned home, he would write several books about his experiences. He even questioned Aristotle on the real meaning of certain obscure language in his writings. This almost caught him out though, when Aristotle asked him, "How did you know that was the direction of my thoughts? I hadn't even written about that as yet."

"From followers of yours who have visited our country," was Winterbottom's lame reply.

Alexander Falls Ill

Two days later Alexander fell ill. Winterbottom was arrested and thrown into a dungeon. He was accused of spying, treason and suspicion of attempted assassination. Although he was tortured, he kept to his story, threatening that his king would make war on the Greeks for his ill treatment. It did no good. His jailers laughed, saying that the great Alexander would welcome such an invasion.

On the verge of death, Alexander ate some moldy meat which had the effect of an antibiotic which killed the germs that caused his fever. Once fully recovered, he felt so good he gave a general order to release all political prisoners. The timeline that Winterbottom was on took another turn, and the world of his future returned to one that was much closer to the one he left. This phenomenon would have interested Doctor Gamostein very much had he known about it. He would've figured that it proved Hoygold's theory of a damping effect of changes to the timeline caused by a time traveler.

After being freed, Winterbottom figured that he had better return to the future before he got into more trouble. But, as he hiked through the desert towards where the time-space machine was hidden, he crossed the path of a caravan from which he purchased food and water. As he conversed with the merchant, his eyes lighted upon a beautiful young woman with dark eyes grooming the camels. He had never seen anyone as lovely, and his heart thumped in his chest at the sight of her. The merchant followed the direction of his gaze and smiled. He jerked his thumb in the woman's direction. "You like? Her name is Desdemona. She is for sale."

"You mean she's a slave?"

"Yes. I can let you have her cheap. She's too skinny for most men's taste. I am getting low on supplies, and she does not do enough work for the amount that she eats."

Winterbottom caught the girl's eye. She smiled shyly at him. His heart went thump, thump, thump. He was in love. "How much do you want for her?"

"Two hundred drachmas."

From what Winterbottom had learned in the short time he had been in ancient Greece, this was an exorbitant price for a female slave, even one as beautiful as Desdemona. Nonetheless, he was leaving the past. Why haggle? He counted out ten twenty drachma silver pieces into the merchant's palm. The merchant bowed and fetched Desdemona, who was pleased when she was told that she had been sold to the handsome stranger. Winterbottom also bought a camel and supplies.

As Winterbottom and Desdemona rode away from the merchant, the timeline took another large jump. The merchant used the money from the sale of Desdemona to buy more camels. The camel seller celebrated in a notorious brothel and bar. As he staggered away, thugs murdered and robbed him. As a result, one of his descendants in Winterbottom's original timeline was never born. That descendant would have invented a more accurate timepiece, giving mariners the ability to gauge longitude. Hence, all the voyages of discovery that took place in the fifteenth and sixteenth century did not occur until the eighteenth. As a result, the United States did not exist as such. Instead, the North American continent was divided into several smaller countries. Germany won World War One, thus dominating Europe, Northern Africa and The Middle East. Propped up by a strong German Monarchy, the Czar was able to put down the Russian revolution. Thus, monarchy prospered in the West during the twentieth and twenty-first centuries.

By the time Winterbottom and Desdemona reached the space-time machine, the archeologist was in a quandary. He loved the woman dearly, more so than when he met her four days before. But what was he to do now. If he took her with him, he didn't know what the consequences would be. Gamostein had warned him not to take anything from the past, much less a human being, although he did take one very beautiful ceramic pot. He visualized that diagonal line going off the board. His other option was to stay in the past himself. But it would be a betrayal of everything he stood for as an archaeologist not to return with all the new data that he had gathered regarding Greek pottery and Aristotle. So with a stiff upper lip, he made love to Desdemona one last time, gave her money and the camel and sent her on her way with a scroll announcing her freedom.

Little did he know, as he gazed longingly at the retreating backside of her camel, that he had impregnated her. A descendent of his and Desdemona's became an inventor in the fourteenth century and came up with the same idea for an accurate timepiece as the camel merchant's descendant would have had he been born. Again the timeline was dampened, again confirming the Hoygold's theory.

Return

Eight months after the space-time machine took off, Winterbottom's return was tumultuous. He received the cheers of everyone who worked on the project, the press and several VIPs. He even got congratulatory calls from the president of the United States and the secretary-general of the UN. After an extensive debriefing, a complete medical checkup, and a news conference, he was finally able to relax.

On his last day on the space station, he was visited by Gamostein who asked, "What was it like visiting the past?"

"More or less as I had imagined it. The whole time though, I had the awful dread that I would change the present drastically by some action of mine."

"I thought about that too. Mathematically, according to my calculations, the odds were heavily in favor of you changing the timeline drastically. If that had happened, you would never have returned to us, but would've wound up in another universe."

Winterbottom became quiet. When Gamostein had left the room, he thought to himself, *I believe I have. In my original universe, you had a mustache and a full beard. In this one, you're clean shaven. I suppose after a while I'll get used to little incongruities like that.*

Gamostein's Beard

As Gamostein walked back to his office, a coworker came up to him and remarked, "I don't know, Doctor. I think you looked better with a beard."

"Really? Well, maybe I'll let it grow back. I shaved it off yesterday on a whim."

CHAPTER 5: THE SEARCH FOR PARADISE

"I'm sorry I'm late," apologized Winterbottom. As he knocked water off of his floppy brim hat, a puddle formed at his feet. "It's darn hard to get a taxi in New York when it's raining. So I decided to walk."

The man he came to see, the famous expert on lost lands, Doctor Quentin Love, rose to greet him. He was in his early sixties, a dust-covered academic with a full white beard and unruly long hair. He grinned. "You're forgiven. I've often run into the same problem. We're glad that you decided to accept our invitation. Before we get started, allow me to introduce the other two people involved with the proposed enterprise. This lovely young lady is my daughter, Ardent."

Ardent, an attractive, well-endowed brunette in her early thirties, held out her hand.

Winterbottom, who always had an eye for a well-turned ankle and other attributes on women, took it and gallantly kissed it. "Charmed to make your acquaintance, Miss Love."

She smiled pleasantly and winked at him. "You may call me Ardent. The pleasure is all mine. Your exploits are well known throughout the archeological community."

Winterbottom wondered whether she meant his exploits in field work or with the ladies.

A man with bushy eyebrows, a well-trimmed dark beard and thinning hair stepped forward. He was older than Ardent, but younger than Love. He didn't offer his hand, but merely said, "I'm Professor Boris Ambitchov, Doctor Love's assistant. It wasn't my idea to invite you here. I believe you'll simply laugh and call us mad when Love tells you about our discovery. Or perhaps you'll think us dupes of a confidence man."

"Now, now, Boris," said Ardent. "Doctor Winterbottom may be more open-minded than you give him credit for."

Boris simply glowered for a reply.

"Yes, I'm definitely an open-minded person, especially after traveling to Mars and back in time."

"It's the notoriety of that time travel business that brought you to our attention," said Professor Love. "Please be seated, and I'll attempt to explain the reasons behind the expedition we've planned. You may make up your own mind as to whether we're onto something important or simply chasing a wild chicken."

"Goose, father," corrected Ardent.

This brought a smile to Winterbottom's lips as an obscene image came into his mind. He plumped into a chair and threw his hat at the hat rack. He missed, causing the hat to fall limply to the floor. He leaned back and put muddy boots on Love's desk. "I'm all ears." Actually, he was all eyes because Ardent had crossed her legs, flashing a goodly amount of thigh. Ambitchov noticed and glared at him.

Love folded his hands and began to speak in a professorial style that invariably put students to sleep. "Throughout the ages, every civilization has among its myths a mysterious land of milk and jam where everything is beautiful, peaceful and abundant, and everyone lives forever..."

He was interrupted by Ardent, who winked at Winterbottom again. "Honey, not jam."

As she leaned forward, Winterbottom stared into her cleavage and thought, *Did she just call me honey? I wonder what the jam part meant.*

Love continued, "This land has been variously called Paradise, Eden, Atlantis, Shanghai La, Erewhon, Middle Earth and other names. Since this myth is so prevalent, it's my contention that a land of milk and jam must exist somewhere. I've spent a lifetime researching these myths ..."

"My father is the foremost authority on the Paradise myth."

Love gazed down modestly. "Perhaps I am, but only because others have not shown much interest. However, to go on ... While on a trip to Alexandria, we visited the crypts below what was once the ancient great library. In an odd niche in a wall our guide came across a papyrus document overlooked for centuries. Our guide sold this valuable document to me for the measly sum of two thousand dollars American. It was in an obscure ancient language that took months to decipher. When I did, I realized that it contained specific information on the location of Eden."

"Interesting."

"More than interesting. It's what I've worked my whole life to find. Now, it's a simple matter of mounting an expedition to make the discovery of the millennium."

"And you need my field experience."

"Exactly. Are you game?"

"That depends. Whereabouts is this marvelous land?"

"In Bhutan."

"Of course. It's a land that's quite primitive, rugged and mysterious. I've been there and found it quite exotic, with breathtaking scenery. Some people call it paradise. But Doctor, I don't understand. It's a well-known country. What's new there to discover?"

Ambitchov blurted, "See, I told you he'd be skeptical."

Love ignored his assistant. "The document I've obtained talks about a hidden mountain valley in the Himalayas, so difficult to get to that no one has been there for centuries. This valley is the true Eden, Atlantis, Middle Earth, the mythic Paradise."

"I see. And you're sure that your papyrus is authentic?"

"Absolutely."

"Well, I'm game. But there's a problem though. The government of Bhutan has an extremely cautious approach regarding visitors to their country. Anyone entering Bhutan must be either guests of the government or tourists, who must travel on a preplanned, prepaid, guided package tour. Independent travel is not allowed."

"Not only that," remarked Ambitchov, "we made inquiries. The area in which we wish to travel is explicitly off limits to foreigners."

Ardent said, "We think they know what's hidden there and don't wish to share their prize with the world at large. That's precisely why we hired you. You have a reputation for getting into places that others cannot." She winked at him.

Winterbottom wondered whether that remark was meant to be flirtatious. Ambitchov turned beet red for some reason.

"I do. But I usually work alone." He winked back at Ardent. "What you have in mind will require a large and expensive expedition."

"Does that mean you're not up to the task?" asked Professor Love.

"Not at all. I love a challenge. I'm ready, willing and able." Winterbottom stared into Ardent's wide eyes as he said this.

She winked back at him and replied in sultry voice. "I'll bet you are. Let's hope that you've got the right stuff. We'd hate to be disappointed."

The Journey

After Winterbottom studied Love's papyrus and Ardent's body for a while, he thought it best if they mounted their expedition from India. In Calcutta, he contacted people on the fringe of the underworld to obtain guides and haulers who, if the pay was right, would go anywhere and not ask questions. He left it to the Loves and Ambitchov to obtain the necessary equipment. They rented a jeep and two trucks to haul the stuff to Assam, in the far northeast corner of India. From there they sneaked into the Manas Tiger Preserve, which borders the Royal Manas National Park in Bhutan in the foothills of the mighty Himalayas. The expedition entered it from the eastern region of wet alluvial grassland around the Benki and Hekua rivers. Even with four-wheel drive vehicles it was slow going through tall thickets of elephant grass and swamp.

In the middle of the night, they crossed the Manas River which demarcates the border between India and Bhutan. Once over the border, things started to go wrong. An elephant herd stampeded their tents. They were lucky that no one was in them at the time. A porter was seriously injured by a tiger, a charging rhino almost horned Ambitchov, and Ardent evaded Winterbottom's advances, although she winked at him from time to time. In another incident, a lammergeyer vulture dropped a bone on Doctor Love's head, rendering him unconscious for an hour. They also lost a guide who was bitten by a pit viper.

When they reached thick forest, they abandoned the vehicles. All their supplies had to be hauled on the backs of porters. Above them flew numerous buzzard, kites and eagles. After many days, they reached the sub-Himalayan deciduous forests of the highlands. However, the monsoon started, making them trudge through muddy ground and ford swollen rivers in forests filled with the cries of talking mynas, lorikeet, rufous-bellied niltava, rubycheek, crossbill, malkoha, pheasant, and magpies

As they approached the foothills of the Himalayas, they traveled by night, slogging through the rice paddies of Drukpa farmers in the area. After more day of trudging, they ventured into the higher altitudes where the chestnuts, oaks, and alder gave way to deciduous and evergreen hardwoods.

The most difficult part of their journey began in the Middle Himalayas, whose peaks varied from six thousand to fourteen thousand feet. They made their way through extensive forests of conifers, oaks, maples, laurels and magnolias. From there began a most arduous and dangerous climb through passes of the Inner Himalayas, the highest mountain chain in the world. Once they reached the permanent snow line, they donned parkas and got out their mountain climbing gear. The temperature dropped to below freezing, and snow squalls and blizzards halted their progress for days. For warmth, Winterbottom offered Ardent whiskey from his canteen, which she accepted, winking at him, but she refused to snuggle in his bedroll.

One day, as they trudged across a glacier, probing for hidden chasms, Ardent cried, "Look. What's *that*?"

In the distance a tiny manlike figure with extremely long arms, covered with white fur and carrying a spear shuffled along.

"It's a Yeti," cried Professor Love. "Quick, get out the camera with the telescopic lens."

"Uh, Professor," said Winterbottom, "I don't think we'll need the telephoto lens." He tapped Love on the back. In a semicircle surrounding them were the ape men brandishing spears and Stone Age axes.

The Big Feet, grunting and gesturing, herded them to an area between two steep cliffs and into a cave. In the back of the cave was a stone throne upon which sat a young woman Yeti. Although she was covered with fur and had long arms, her face was that of a beautiful Asian woman and the curves of her body were voluptuous. Their captors bowed to her and chattered in a strange grunting language. They made the adventurers kneel and touch their foreheads to the ground. When they were allowed to rise, the figure on the throne asked in Bhutanese, "Who are you people? I've never seen such pale skin."

Ambitchov acted as spokesperson. "We're explorers from a land far to the west. We've heard of a pleasant and beautiful hidden valley. We wish to see it for ourselves."

Winterbottom thought, *does he mean Ardent's cleavage?*

The queen replied, "I know of the valley of which you speak. But a great beast guards the entrance. You will not be able to enter. Go back to your homeland."

"Oh great queen of the Yeti, cannot you please at least lead us there? If there is a beast, let us deal with it."

Her smile had a bit of mischief in it. "Perhaps. But there's a price."

"If it is within our means, we will pay it." Ambitchov's expression became one of greedy anticipation.

"One of you must stay behind as my prisoner." She pointed at Winterbottom. "The one with the funny thing on his head will do."

Ambitchov grinned. "Certainly, that will be no problem. His usefulness to this expedition has come to an end anyway."

Ardent protested angrily. "That's hardly fair after all his hard work and sacrifice getting us here. Why he must've saved your ass a dozen times." She turned and winked at Winterbottom. "Why don't you volunteer, Boris? Talk about useless people. All you've done is grumble this whole trip."

To avoid further argument, they decided to draw straws to see who would remain with the Yetis. As luck would have it, Professor Love drew the short straw. "Aw nuts," he complained. "I was so hoping to see Paradise before I died."

Ardent rubbed his back. "Maybe, it's for the best, Papa. You are old, and your heart is weak. The next part of our journey will be most difficult." She winked at Winterbottom.

Love sighed. "I'm sure you're right, Ardent. Please take many video and still pictures though."

"I will, Papa."

The Yeti queen appeared disgruntled that the old man remained instead of the young, strong one. Nonetheless, she assigned two Yeti as guides.

The Way to Paradise

Several days later, with the Yeti in the lead, the tiny expedition moved slowly to conserve energy and avoid altitude sickness, as they were in the highest part of the mountains. At the end of two hours, they came to the end of the rocky moraine and ventured onto a glacier that consisted of pinnacles of ice. Since the ice was hard, they donned boots and crampons and followed the Yeti closely to ensure they stayed on the correct route. It was easy to get lost twisting through and over the pinnacles. Abruptly the spikes ended, and the glacier became smoother. Nearby were snow fields and steep faces that looked ready to avalanche, but ahead was a gently rising plateau. One of the Yeti and Winterbottom went ahead to anchor rope over hidden crevasses. Winterbottom used sign language to communicate with the Yeti.

By the time they reached the edge of the plateau, the weather had worsened. A gusty wind blew snow, and Winterbottom feared avalanches. Finally, they approached a snow hardened steeper section that they could climb without difficulty. After they rested in a sheltered spot to eat and drink, the party looked around for the easiest route up the mountain.

After a while the angle eased slightly but became more exposed. Cautiously they tested each footstep; one false move meant a thousand foot drop. Although the Yeti kicked steps in the knife-edged top of the ridge, to move the climbers had to lean over, drive axes into the opposite side and hold slippery snow with mittened hands. Time slowed to a crawl; for Winterbottom it seemed an eternity to reach a wider section of the crest. Billowing clouds engulfed them, and gusts threatened to throw them off the mountain. They clawed their way to the summit, hanging to the side by ice axes.

Winterbottom gazed around and realized that they were headed toward the smaller of a double summit. Their position was precarious so they traversed back along to a small spot that caught less wind, where they could sit astride the ridge to rest. In the distance tremendous peaks poked through the clouds.

The Yeti pointed to a small valley between the double peaks and motioned the way to get there. They returned the way the group had come, leaving the trio to their own devices. To reach the path indicated by the Yeti, they had to jump into steep snow. Luckily, their heels sunk in well. A few meters down they turned inwards and climbed down. Because they were roped together, if one tripped, they would all slide to their deaths. Gradually the angle eased and the snow became softer, so soft in fact that all it needed was the weight of unsuspecting climbers to start an avalanche.

By this time, twilight had turned into night. The climbers broke out flashlights. Winterbottom turned to Ardent, "Be extremely cautious here." Ardent winked back at him. They gently, tiptoed along towards the ridge.

The Red Dragon

Early the next morning they reached the first summit. From there, it was an easy climb down to the tiny canyon-like crevice. "Where do we go now, Charlie?" growled Ambitchov, who had slipped several times only to be rescued by either Winterbottom or Ardent. "I think those Yeti have put one over on us. Paradise couldn't be at this altitude. It's much too cold."

"If I read the Yeti signs correctly, it's up that way." Winterbottom pointed toward where the crevice curved so that whatever was beyond could not be seen. "Paradise should be just beyond that rock outcropping." He hummed *"Just a Stranger in Paradise"* while gazing ardently at Ardent. She winked at him and giggled.

"Stop that," cried Ambitchov. "This is a scientific expedition, not a songfest." He tramped heavily toward the curve. Ardent and Winterbottom followed at a more leisurely pace. Moments after Ambitchov disappeared around the outcrop, there was a horrendous animal roar and a bright light. Ambitchov flew back toward Ardent and Winterbottom as fast as his legs would carry him. "Dragon, dragon," he screamed. "That Yeti queen wasn't lying."

When the other two calmed him down, Winterbottom asked, "What happened?"

"After I rounded the curve, I saw a high wall with a golden gate. As I headed toward it, an enormous red dragon flew out and spouted a huge flame right in front of me. We'll have to kill it to get into paradise." Ambitchov reached back for his elephant gun, loaded it and strode forward again. This time Winterbottom and Ardent followed closely behind him.

When they came around the corner, the dragon lay in front of the gate glaring at them. As it rose up on its front legs, its head was as high as a church steeple. Again it roared and spouted flame, missing frying the trio by less than a meter. Ambitchov raised the gun and fired two shots at the monster's chest. When the bullets struck, they bounced off the serpent's scales and ricocheted around on the rocks.

The dragon looked startled and laughed. It said in Bhutanese, "Did you think you could harm me with that peashooter? What are you people doing here? What lies behind this gate is forbidden to human beings. Go away."

Winterbottom asked it if it spoke any other language. It replied, "I speak every language known to man or beast. *Parlé vous français? Sprechen se Deutsche?*"

"We speak English. Is there no way that we can persuade you to allow us in? We promise to obey any rules you set down. We just want to see what paradise is like."

The dragon rubbed its chin with its talons. Ardent winked at it. The dragon winked back. It said, "You're an attractive young lady. You remind me of a former resident of this place. Only she usually ran around in the nude. Perhaps, I'll allow you in if you undress."

"How dare you? What do you take me for?" Nonetheless, she winked at him.

"You're a feisty one. Okay, here's the deal. All of you must remove your clothes and leave all your guns and supplies here. Once inside, you must not drink from the fountain, and you must not eat any fruit from the large tree in the center of the garden. I'll allow you the rest of the day to look around. Be back here by sunset."

Because Winterbottom was anticipating the sight of an Ardent nude, he did not pay attention to these instructions. Ambitchov grumbled about having to leave his guns and cameras behind. Ardent said, "I'll turn my back while you two gentlemen undress and go into paradise. After you're out of sight, I'll remove my clothes and enter. This will save us a lot of embarrassment." She turned her back.

After a time, the dragon said, "Your two companions have gone into Eden and can longer be seen. You humans are really funny about this clothing bit. We dragons never wear anything."

Ardent winked at him. "That may be. But you also must turn your head while I undress."

"Then how will I know that you've actually done so."

"I'll allow you one quick peek."

The dragon turned away, and Ardent quickly undressed. "You may peek now." When the serpent turned back, she ran through the gate. The dragon smiled as it watched her jiggling fanny. As soon as she was out of the dragon's sight, she found a fig tree and made a bikini out of the leaves.

Entering Paradise

Winterbottom and Ambitchov strolled along the path admiring the beautiful flowers and friendly animals. They were amazed by the sight of a sheep lying with its head resting on the hide of a lion. The weather was superb, seventy-two degrees Fahrenheit and bright sunshine. Winterbottom said, "It certainly is a wonderful place. It really is a paradise."

"Do you really think so? Personally, I don't see anything so great about it. It reminds me of the rain forests in South America."

"Um. You're probably right. I saw something back aways that I'd like to investigate further."

"Go right ahead. I'll meander on."

After Winterbottom turned around and headed back the way they had come, Ambitchov continued on. He thought, *that fool doesn't realize what treasure lies ahead. If this really is Eden, the tree of knowledge is here somewhere. If I can find it, I'll be the smartest person on earth and become rich and famous.*

The path circled and meandered around like a corkscrew. Finally Ambitchov came to a clearing in which a great tree grew. Its branches were laden with a golden fruit of a type he had never seen before. He drew closer to examine it. A sign was posted. It read in Bhutanese: *The Tree of Knowledge. It is forbidden to eat the fruit. Dire consequences will result for anyone who disobeys this commandment. By order of The Creator.*

Ambitchov gazed all around. There was no one in sight, neither man nor beast. He gazed upward and laughed. *Creator, my butt. That dragon or some official from Bhutan wrote this. I don't believe in any creator.* He took another look around and quickly snatched a low-hanging fruit. He waited a few moments. Since he wasn't struck by lightning and no voice came from the sky, he took a large bite of the fruit. It was delicious, better even than the food in his favorite French restaurant. As he swallowed, he felt all sorts of odd facts enter mind.

Looking for Love

As Winterbottom strolled back towards the entrance, he thought, *Yes, this place is really nice. There's one thing missing. The lovely curves of a pretty woman.* In his mind's eye, he brought up an image of Ardent Love in the nude. He hurried, anxious to catch a glimpse of her flesh. Nonetheless, he arrived at the gate without seeing her. The dragon was still lying there, with one eye open. Winterbottom addressed the dragon, "Sorry to disturb your rest, old chap, but did you happen to see which way the young lady went."

The dragon pointed with a talon and drawled, "She went that-away, pardner."

Winterbottom saluted the dragon. "Thank you, you're a real gentledragon." He followed the indicated path. After walking a long way through a winding path, he spotted her sitting on the edge of a lovely fountain whose center contained marble statues of a group of mermaids and fishes. To his disappointment, the portions of Ardent's anatomy that he most wanted to see were covered with fig leaves.

As he approached, she winked at him, but turned away. "Mister Winterbottom! Please have the decency to cover your private parts with something."

"Uh ... oh ... sorry." He hurriedly ripped some large leaves off a bush and used some vines to make a loincloth. "Uh, Ardent. You may look now."

She turned toward him and winked. "So. Did you or Boris find anything interesting in this so-called Eden?"

Winterbottom grinned. "Not yet. But, my dear, you and I could make this place a real Paradise." He wiggled his eyebrows suggestively.

"Are you trying to come on to me, Mister Winterbottom? I don't really appreciate advances of that nature from a colleague during a scientific endeavor. It smacks of sexual harassment."

"But it's you who have been coming on to me this whole trip. Every chance you get, you wink at me."

"Oh you fool. Don't you realize ..." But before she could finish that sentence, Winterbottom grabbed her and kissed her full on the mouth, his tongue darting between her open lips.

She pushed him away and gave him such a hard slap that he stumbled into the fountain head first. "Oh my," she cried. "Are you all right?" She reached in to help him, only to find that he had shrunk to half his original size. She pulled him out and realized that he had turned into a ten-year-old boy. She laughed. "It serves you right, you womanizer. This must be the Fountain of Youth. Now you'll have to wait until you grow up to start messing around." She dipped her hand in the water and took a sip. Using the water as a mirror, she was gratified to see that her laugh lines were gone. She went to search for something to carry some of the magical water home. "Stay right here, little boy. I'll be right back."

Since Winterbottom had always been a naughty boy, he ignored her orders and wandered away. After a long time, he came upon Ambitchov, who was sitting under a fruit tree muttering to himself. "There are infinite universes ... time travel is possible ... there are particles smaller than mesons ... our galaxy is being sucked into a black hole ... angels and demons exist ..." and on and on. He looked as though his head would explode.

"Boris, what's the matter with you?"

Ambitchov gazed at him in a dazed manner. "Huh? Who are you, little boy?"

"Charlie Winterbottom. I fell into the Fountain of Youth."

"Oh yes. I now know where that is. I know everything."

"It's getting late. We must leave, or the dragon will come after us."

"Yes. Where is Miss Love?"

"She went to look for something to carry water in."

They strolled back toward the gate. Ardent was waiting there. She had half of a coconut shell in one hand. "Charlie, you naughty boy, you disobeyed me," she scolded. "What should I do with you?" She winked at him.

Now, although Winterbottom had the body of a ten-year-old, he had the mind of an adult. "How about a good spanking?"

She ignored him and headed for the gate. The dragon was waiting for the trio as they exited. "You people have sinned. You disobeyed orders." He gazed skyward suggestively. "As punishment, one of you will have to stay and keep me company." It pointed a talon at Ardent. "I choose you."

"Me," she cried and burst into tears. "Why me? I only took a little bit of water from the Fountain of Youth. I'll put it back."

"That won't be necessary. Besides, you may like it here. You can live in Eden and partake of the fountain anytime you like. Besides, over the centuries I've accumulated a vast treasury of jeweled necklaces, diamond rings, gold bracelets, garment of the finest silk, furs, and so forth. You may wear any of it while you stay with me."

Ardent winked at the dragon. "Really? And what would I have to do for you to gain those riches?"

"Simply converse with me once in a while. I'm very lonely. Since I've been assigned here thousands of years ago, I seldom get to talk to anyone."

"Oh, you poor thing. Of course, I'll stay." She shook hands with her two former comrades and winked at each one. "Good-bye. When you see my father, tell him where I am. I'm sure he'll want to visit me."

After the two men departed, the dragon asked Ardent, "I noticed that you always wink at people. Why is that?"

"Oh that. It's a tic. I've had it since childhood. I hate it. It's always getting me into trouble."

"Well, my dear, perhaps I can cure you of it by magic."

"Oh would you? I'd be ever so grateful."

Return to the Yeti Queen

After several weeks of hair-raising mountain climbing, the man and the boy made it back to the Yeti camp. When they were brought before the queen, Doctor Love was sitting in a throne that was only slightly lower than the queen's. After the usual bowing and scraping, Ambitchov told Love and the queen all about their adventures in Eden. "And how have you been, Quentin?"

"Very well. The Queen of the Yeti's and I are married according to their custom. I am her consort. I'm sure she'll allow me to visit my daughter in Eden fairly often. In fact we may go there soon, so that Ardent can meet her new stepmother. When you fellows are ready to leave, Queen Grgstymkl and I will send Yeti guides to escort you back to civilization."

* * * *

After Winterbottom and Ambitchov returned to New York, Winterbottom was sent to a foundling home, and Ambitchov made the rounds of TV quiz shows, winning millions of dollars, most of which he spent on doctors in an attempt to find a cure for his awful headaches.

CHAPTER 6. LEMURIA

Fifteen years later, a warm tropical sun beat down on Winterbottom as he took a sip from *A Gilligan's Island*, a fruity cocktail made with vodka. He now had the appearance of a twenty-five-year-old man and had returned to his former occupation of archeology. He turned to his latest mistress, the gorgeous Honey Bunn, whose swimsuit consisted of tiny bits of strategically placed cloth tied together with strings. They were sitting in lounge chairs poolside at a luxury hotel in Maui. "Isn't this great? I'm glad you suggested Hawaii. I needed the rest. The archeology business can be quite stressful at times. On one expedition, I actually lost height as well as weight."

Honey Bunn adjusted her sunglasses and stretched, a sight that brought a broad smile to Winterbottom's lips. "Oh Charlie, it was so sweet of you to bring me here. I've got a surprise for you for later."

"Really? What is it?"

"If I told you, it wouldn't be a surprise, now would it?" A tiny giggle burst from her lush pouty lips.

Winterbottom felt inner warmth to match the heat of the sun. He loved the little surprises that Honey Bunn gave him. They always pleased.

Suddenly, a hulking dark shadow fell upon him. He gazed upward to see what had blocked the sun. To his utter disgust, it was his overweight unwholesome fellow archeologist, Heinrich Schmidt. Schmidt wore a Speedo, which was mostly covered by overhanging belly so that he appeared to be grossly nude.

"Charlie Winterbottom. I heard that you were vacationing in the islands. How are you?"

Winterbottom snorted. "Doing well, as you can see, Heinie." He nodded toward Honey Bunn. He sat up to shake Schmidt's limp hand. "What are you doing here in Maui? Taking time off from archeology too?"

"Nope. Chasing leads about a find that will make me famous."

"Really?" Winterbottom knew that Schmidt was always after some Chimera or other. *Well, this time I'm not going on one of his crazy wild goose chases no matter how much he tempts me.* "Allow me to introduce you to my roommate. Honey Bunn, this is a fellow archeologist, Doctor Heinrich Schmidt. We've been on several digs together."

"Digs! I love your archeo-ology talk. It sounds so scientific." She put out her delicate hand with its blood red pointed nails. "Pleased to meet you, Mister Schmidt."

"Actually, it's Doctor Schmidt, but you may call me, Heinie. Everyone does."

Honey Bunn burst out in an uncontrollable giggle.

Schmidt turned red. He tore his eyes from Honey Bunn's breasts and directed his attention to Winterbottom. "You might be interested in what I've found, Charlie."

"I doubt it." He sighed. "But I suppose you're going to tell me about it anyway."

Schmidt lowered his voice conspiratorially. "I've discovered the location of the lost continent of Lemuria or Mu, its true name."

"Suppose you have. What good does it do? Lemuria is at the bottom of the Pacific Ocean."

"That's why I wanted to talk to you. You were sent back in time by the physicist, Aaron Gamostein. Perhaps you could talk him into sending you and me to ten thousand B.C."

Winterbottom laughed. "Oh Heinie, you're such a fool. Believe me, time travel is not that simple. Besides, Gamostein's operation has been shut down for lack of funds. It was quite expensive sending even one man into the past. It cost over a billion dollars for me to visit the time of Alexander."

Schmidt's face fell. "Oh well. I guess that's that. Nonetheless, I'd like to show you what I've found. Can we get together sometime?"

Honey Bunn said, "Oh Heinie, why don't you come to our room tonight and show us your arti-facts. I belong to a Theosophy Organization. We discuss things like Lemuria and UFOs and other paranormal stuff all the time. I'd be fascinated to hear more about Mu. We're in room three-ten, on the third floor."

She had a sparkle in her eye that Winterbottom had not seen before, even when they made love. He figured that it was because she was from California and an enthusiastic aficionado of astrology and other paranormal nonsense.

Schmidt gave her a little bow. "Thank you, Ms Bunn. I'm happy to accept your kind invitation. I'll come by about ten this evening. By the way, have you noticed a certain similarity of meaning between your last name and my nickname?"

She gazed at him over her sunglasses without comprehension. After a few moments, it hit her, and she giggled uncontrollably for a while. "Oh, you naughty man." Suddenly her expression became serious again. "Y'know, I've learned from Theosophy that there are no coincidences. There must be a mystical bond between us."

"Or behind us."

Winterbottom glared at Schmidt and Honey Bunn. He did not like the direction the conversation was taking. It seemed like flirting. He also did not want Schmidt to come to their room that evening, but saw no way of preventing it since it was Honey Bunn who extended the invitation.

Schmidt said, "See you two tonight then." He walked away.

When he was out of earshot, Winterbottom said, "Why did you invite him to our room? The man will simply go on and on about his insane theories."

"Why Charlie, I believe you're jealous. Besides, Lemuria really existed many eons ago, before the flood even. I want to hear what he has to say about the lost continent."

"I see. My blood is beginning to boil. I'm going for a swim to cool off."

"Go ahead. I'm still working on my tan."

Winterbottom got up and dove into the pool.

Lemurian Artifacts

Nine that evening, Winterbottom and Honey Bunn returned to their room from dinner. When they arrived, Winterbottom said, "Okay. What's the surprise you said you have for me? I want to experience it before Heinie arrives."

"Okay, Char-lee. Hide your eyes."

Winterbottom covered his orbs with his hands. He heard her unsnap her purse. A moment later, she said, "You can look now."

He removed his hands from his face. She pointed to the coffee table. It held a small pipe and a plastic bag with a dark flaky substance inside it.

"What's this? It looks like marihuana and a bong."

"Oh Charlie, it's not grass. It's a mind expanding drug made from a special mushroom. I bought it from a Hawaiian shaman. After smoking it, a person has mystical visions. The shaman used it to perform magick. He turned me into a bird."

"A bird?" Winterbottom turned away to hide the smile on his face. Obviously, she had hallucinated being a bird after inhaling the drug and believed that she had actually turned into a bird. "I'm afraid that I'm not quite ready for such mind-bending experiences."

"But that's not all it does, Char-lee. It enhances the act of love tremendously. It turns it into a mystical experience."

No wonder that shaman gave her a hallucinatory mushroom, thought Winterbottom. Nonetheless, the thought that their love making would reach new heights of pleasure was tempting. "Okay. After Heinie leaves, we'll smoke some of that stuff. Put it away now."

Honey Bunn returned the bong and the ground up mushroom to her purse.

A little later, Schmidt knocked on their door. He hauled in a large briefcase. After Winterbottom and Honey Bunn greeted him and showed him to a chair, Honey Bunn asked, "Would you like a drink?"

"Thought you'd never ask. I brought liquor too." He pulled a bottle of tequila from his briefcase.

Honey Bunn cried, "Oh, tequila! I know how to make a splendid cocktail with it and other ingredients. Should I whip it up."

"Absolutely." He handed her the tequila.

She went to the bar and poured half the bottle into a shaker. She added a good amount of vodka and bourbon. To this she poured in small amounts of various fruit juices. Finally she added ice and shook the container vigorously. She poured three water glasses full of the mixture and handed one to each man.

They sipped their drinks for a while and made small talk. Winterbottom asked Schmidt what he had been doing since they left Woodstock. This gave Schmidt the opening he needed. "I went to Peru. Very interesting place. Legend has it that the Incas are descended from Lemurians who fled there when their continent sank into the Pacific."

Honey Bunn clapped her hands together. "Oh Heinie, how fascinating. I'm thinking about going back to school and taking archeoology. I'd love to go to somewhere like Peru on a dig. You know UFOs visited there thousands of years ago. I read a book all about it."

Schmidt took three crystals molded into the shape of skulls from his suitcase. "I found these in Peru. Note the way the skulls are shaped. No human skull is shaped like that." He handed one to Honey Bunn and one to Winterbottom.

Winterbottom pretended to examine the crystal skull and nodded. "I see." He handed it back.

Honey Bunn went over the skull minutely. "This *is* fascinating. And you believe these crystal skulls were made in Lemuria? That Lemurians had such odd shaped heads."

"Absolutely."

Winterbottom said, "How can you be so sure? Maybe the ancient Incas made them and simply shaped them that way for some reason. Artists don't always craft objects exactly as they appear in nature."

"Ah hah. Along with the crystal skulls, I found this." He pulled out a terracotta tablet. On it was inscribed a crude diagram.

Winterbottom looked it over. He twisted it this way and that. "What's it supposed to be?"

Schmidt said, "You're holding it upside down. Turn it this way. It's a map." He pointed out features of the diagram. "These are the Himalayas. Below them is the Indian subcontinent. On the right is Australia."

"But it shows a big land mass covering the area between India and Australia."

"Of course. Lemuria."

"Oh, let me see," cried Honey Bunn. She ran her fingers over the etched lines with a spellbound lascivious expression on her face. "Oh Heinie, what a wonderful discovery."

By this time they had finished their drinks. She refilled their glasses.

Schmidt related more of his adventures in Peru. "And after I left Peru,

I went to California where I examined caves in Mount Shasta that I had heard about from a medicine man. And that's where I found this." His voice rose in triumph. Apparently what he was going to show next was the *piece de resistance* of his collection. He took out an unusually shaped box, intricately carved with alien figures and odd designs. He allowed Winterbottom and Honey Bunn to look it over.

Honey Bunn said, "There's something inside. I hear it rattling around, but I don't see anyway to open the box."

Schmidt replied, "It took me a long time to discover its secret. Here, let me show you." He took the container from her hands and laid it on the coffee table. He placed two fingers of his left hand on a certain carving, and three fingers of his right hand on another carving at a different spot on the object. The lid popped open. Within was an off center hexagonal trapazehedron crystal that glowed from an inner light of a strange hue.

Winterbottom and Honey Bunn stared at it in wonder. Winterbottom said, "What a strange crystal. It seems somehow alien. The non-symmetrical shape and the odd light, I mean."

Schmidt snapped the lid closed. "You do not want to stare at it for too long. It's dangerous."

"What do you mean? Is it radioactive?"

"No. But there's a warning on the box that I was able to decipher because of its similarities to ancient Inca glyphs. The warning reads, roughly translated, *He who gazes at the crystal will invoke the Haunter of the Dark*."

Winterbottom chuckled. "Rank superstition. It reminds me of the curses that the ancient Egyptians placed on anyone who opens their tomb."

Honey Bunn said, "I wouldn't laugh, Charlie. The Haunter of the Dark could be a powerful demon. It may be that the Lemurians used this crystal to call it up from the underworld. They probably worshiped it as a god."

Schmidt added, "I agree. It's not wise to ignore such warnings."

Winterbottom said, "Pah. You two are so superstitious. Do you have any more artifacts to show us, Heinie?" He hoped not and that Schmidt would soon leave.

"No. I'm afraid not. It's too bad we can't go back in time to get the proof I need for my hypothesis."

Honey Bunn said, "You've got a lot of proof right here. I don't know why people don't believe your theories. I do." She took a sip of her drink. "Let's toast Lemuria."

They clinked glasses and said in unison, "Here's to the ancient continent of Lemuria."

They also drank to Schmidt's theory, to the artifacts, to the Incas, to archeology and to friendship. Winterbottom's glass was empty. "Is there any more of this left, Honey Bunn."

"No, and I can't make any more. We're out of vodka. Say, I've got an idea. Why don't I break out the sacred mushroom? We could probe the mystical unknown."

Schmidt's eyes went wide, although they were somewhat glazed from so much toasting. "Sacred mushroom. It's been a long time since I smoked any of that stuff."

Winterbottom snorted. It was not the mystical unknown that he wanted to probe. He had hoped that he and Honey Bunn would be alone when they smoked the drug.

Honey Bunn took out the bong and pouch of sacred mushroom. She packed the flakes into the bong, lit it, sucked in a long draw of the smoke and held it. She passed it the Schmidt, who did the same. Schmidt gave it to Winterbottom. They passed it around until the drug had burned to ash. Soon they were rolling around on the floor with the giggles.

Between bouts of silly laughter and trying to teach the archeologists how to meditate and do yogi, Honey Bunn said, "Say. Wouldn't it be a hoot to stare at that crystal in your box?"

"Absh-aloutly not," Schmidt said, slurring his words. "Too danger-ouch."

"Oh come on. Letsh stare at it to …," said Winterbottom, "… prove that there'sh noshing to ancient curses and warnings."

"Okay, but don't shay you weren't warned." He pressed the carvings on the box to cause the lid to pop open, removed the crystal and laid it on the table. After Honey Bunn turned off the lights, they held hands and stared at the glowing crystal.

The darkness around them grew darker. Winterbottom saw images inside the crystal. Strange alien sentients dressed in long dark robes wandered in a place of murky gloom. One stared directly at him with menacing eyes. The being drew closer and closer until it was in the room. It let out a raucous evil laugh as stood looking down on Winterbottom.

"Fools," it cried. "Do you not who you have summoned? I am the Haunter of the Dark. You were warned and now you shall pay for your folly." The eldritch creature turned to Schmidt. "You shall get your wish. We'll see how much you enjoy it."

It raised its arms in gesture of invoking magick and chanted in a language Winterbottom had never heard before.

Elsewhere

Suddenly he, Honey Bunn and Schmidt were elsewhere. All the fuzziness caused by the alcohol and sacred mushroom had cleared out of his head. He peered around. They were on a vast plain. Although a noonday sun beat down, there was a definite chill in the air.

Honey Bunn cried, "Where are we? How did we get here?"

"Damned if I know," said Winterbottom.

Schmidt said, "It was the Haunter of the Dark. He sent us here. And I think I know where here must be."

"Where?" cried Honey Bunn and Winterbottom together.

"Lemuria. The Haunter of the Dark said he was granting my wish."

Winterbottom snorted. "Careful what you wish for. It may come true."

"Do you think we're really in Lemuria?" asked Honey Bunn. She seemed pleased by the prospect.

"Whether this is Lemuria or some other place, the important thing is what do we do now. How do we get back to Maui?"

Schmidt said, "If this really is Lemuria, the magi of the Lemurians may be able to help us. We need to find the ancient race."

Winterbottom made a sour face. "And exactly where do we look? According to the map you showed us, Lemuria is a continent of thousands of square miles."

While they were debating, Honey Bunn peered around. "There's something over there." She pointed in a northwesterly direction.

Winterbottom shaded his eyes and looked where she pointed. In the distance a great number of creatures were moving around. "Looks like a herd of animals to me."

"Maybe they're cows."

"And where there are cows, there are cowboys," Schmidt remarked.

Winterbottom rolled his eyes. "You've got to be kidding. Well, let's head that way. I guess it's a good a direction as any."

They hiked for hours through the long grass of the endless plain. After a while, mountains appeared on the horizon, and the animals they had observed could be seen clearly.

"They look more like elephants than cows," said Winterbottom.

Nonetheless, they trudged on. Soon it became apparent that they were neither elephants nor cows, but mammoths.

"Holy cow," cried Schmidt. "Real mammoths. I wish I had my camera."

"What now?" Winterbottom asked. "I don't think we should get too close. We might get trampled."

"There's a hill over to the left. Let's head for it. We can observe the mammoths from there."

The hill in question was lightly wooded. Winterbottom thought it might be a good place to spend the night as the sun was low in the sky. "Okay. Let's step up the pace. I don't think it's a good idea to be out on this plain at night. Who knows what lurks in this long grass."

Honey Bunn's expression turned to one of horror. "Do you think there are snakes? I hate snakes."

"Could be. Or worse creatures."

She began to be more careful where she trod

As they neared the top of a hill, an enormous catlike creature with large fangs appeared from between the trees. It crawled on its belly toward the edge of the hill on the side that faced the mammoth herd.

Obviously it was stalking them.

Honey Bunn let out a squeal of fright. The sabertooth turned its head and glared at the trio. It licked its lips, raised itself to a standing position and started toward them, slowly at first, but increasing its speed to a fast jog as it came closer.

"Run," cried Schmidt. "It's after us." He turned around and sped down the hill. Winterbottom and Honey Bunn followed. With their longer legs and more athletic bodies, they soon passed him. He chanced a quick glance back. The sabertooth gained easily. Puffing and huffing, Schmidt raced forward. His legs moved so fast that his heels hit him on the backside. He tripped over a large pile of mammoth droppings and fell on his face.

When the mammoth herd heard the commotion and spotted the sabertooth, they stampeded. The trio was trapped between the stampeding mammoths and the sabertooth. Honey Bunn and Winterbottom stopped in their tracks to keep from being trampled by the enormous beasts, which were twice as tall as a modern elephant with huge curved tusks.

Schmidt simply ran out of steam. He collapsed. The sabertooth leaped at him for the kill. It sprang high in the air from ten feet away. Schmidt curled up into a ball and closed his eyes in anticipation of being torn to shreds by the powerful beast.

Lemurians

At the midpoint in its leap, the sabertooth went limp and fell to the ground dead. Several persons came out of the woods. They shouted in a strange language and raised their weapons, long blow guns fashioned from bamboo cane, to point at the trio. They were a strange people, seven feet tall with green snakelike skin. Because their only clothing was a loincloth, it was obvious that they were a mixed group of males and females.

Winterbottom and Honey Bunn gaped in amazement, for the alien creatures were handsome and well endowed. Except for their color and height, they would be mistaken for exceptionally good looking athletic men and women. Schmidt remained curled up in the fetal position, shivering uncontrollably.

Honey Bunn knelt down by him. "The big tiger is dead, Heinie. You can get up now."

Winterbottom raised both hands over his head palms out in what he figured was a universal gesture of peace. He smiled. "Hi guys. Thanks for saving our companion's life."

The giants approached slowly. From their expressions, it was difficult to determine whether they were friendly or hostile.

Schmidt stopped trembling and rose to his feet. He too gazed with wonder at the strange looking people. One of the women, either their leader or spokesperson, spoke in language that sounded familiar to him. After a moment's thought, he realized that it was a dialect of Incan. The giantess seemed to be saying, "Who are you little people? What are you doing on our hunting ground?"

Schmidt replied in Incan. "We wandered away from our home and are lost. I am called, Heinrich Schmidt. The taller man is Charles Winterbottom. The woman is Honey Bunn."

"You are lost children then? Although you are small, in many ways you seem adult. I am Anahuarque, a high priestess of the Tiahuanaco people. You will come with me." She turned to the other tribespeople and gave some orders. They lowered their blowguns, which had been pointed at Winterbottom and his companions. Anahuarque held out her hand. "Do not be afraid, little ones."

"What's going on?" Winterbottom asked Schmidt.

"She thinks we're lost children. I think she's going to adopt us."

"Do you think it's a good idea to go with them?" asked Honey Bunn.

"What other choice do we have? Otherwise we could wander around until we were eaten by a sabertooth or trampled by mammoths or starved to death. Perhaps they have shamans who may help us return to our own time."

Schmidt stepped forward and took the hand of Anahuarque. From the rear, they looked like a mother and young son out for a stroll. Winterbottom and Honey Bunn followed. The sabertooth was gutted and tied to poles. Anahuarque led a group of five hunters, two of which bore the dead sabertooth, and our intrepid comrades down a path through the woods. The other tribespeople stayed, apparently to continue their interrupted hunting expedition.

As they made there way through the forest, they saw many strange animals that were extinct in modern times. Schmidt pointed some out. He was an expert on the creatures that existed in the Pleistocene era. Above them in the trees they heard the raucous cries of lemurs, small large-eyed primates. The column halted to allow ground sloth to pass. It was as large as an ox when on all fours. Another time they encountered peccaries, large boar of the pig family. A stag-moose gazed at them from a distance for a few moments. After sniffing the air, it turned tail and scampered away.

"That was an odd looking elk," said Honey Bunn.

Schmidt explained, "It's an ancestor of both moose and elk. It has traits of both. It has the stilt legs and face of an elk, but is like a moose in other respects."

"Heinie, you're sure a smart guy. Where did you learn all that stuff?'

Schmidt puffed out his chest. "Books, my dear. And science journals." He turned to Anahuarque. "Where is your village exactly?"

"In the mountains."

"The mountains? How far must we walk?"

"For many sunrises and sunsets."

Heinie groaned. He had never been one for hiking.

Winterbottom asked him what had passed between him and the Lemurian.

"We've got a long road ahead. Their village is in the mountains."

"My feet hurt already," complained Honey Bunn. "I'll never make it."

Winterbottom said, "Don't worry, we'll get you there. After we stop for the day, I'll make a travois. I'll haul you along, babe."

"What's a tra-voy?"

"It's like a cart without wheels."

That evening Winterbottom found some broken tree branches and vines to build the travois. Anahuarque looked curiously at the vehicle. She laughed and said something in Lemurian. Schmidt translated. "Anahuarque says that the little girl will grow up to be a weakling if she does not carry her own body. Also, she wondered why Honey Bunn wore those leather things that raise her heels on her feet."

"Weakling? Tell that bitch I'll take her on any day and twice on Sunday. As for my shoes, these cost a couple of hundred bucks."

"Now, now. We're guests of these people. We don't want to antagonize them."

Winterbottom said, "You paid two hundred dollars for those? That's not what you told me when you charged them to my card."

Anahuarque cuffed each of them on the head and shouted something. Schmidt said, "She says, 'Stop quarreling children, or I will have to punish you.'"

In the end Honey Bunn refused the travois. She removed her high heels and walked barefoot. "I won't give that bitch the satisfaction."

It took them several days to hike through the tropical forest. Besides the danger from carnivores and large beasts, they suffered from tropical heat, insects, snakes, lizards and exhaustion. Once the sun had set, the darkness was absolute, the insects became ferocious, and the forest came alive with strange bird calls, animal cries and other unidentifiable sounds. Anahuarque rubbed a noxious smelling ointment on the trio to stave off the insects. She and the other Lemurians lit torches to light the way.

Sometime after sunset they camped for the night. They built a bonfire and constructed tents that they carried in backpacks. They broiled meat from animals they killed and served it with fruit and vegetables picked and dug up from the forest as they passed through it. They also passed around pouches of a slightly intoxicating fruity wine drink, sang alien songs to the accompaniment of alien instruments and told stories, which Schmidt translated.

Once the meal was finished, everyone went to their tents. Winterbottom, Honey Bunn and Schmidt shared a tent with Anahuarque, who treated them as though she was their mother. This made

Winterbottom uncomfortable as the Lemurian woman was extremely handsome and slept in the nude. When he stood next to her, his eyes were level with her ample breasts. Every night he tossed and turned as lascivious thoughts ran through his brain.

Travel Travail

After several days traveling in this manner, they came to a river. The Lemurians had cached canoes. Once the adventurers and Anahuarque boarded one, the other Lemurians pushed it into the river and climbed aboard. Winterbottom, Honey Bun and Schmidt were grateful for the chance to get off their feet. The Lemurians paddled upstream on the swiftly flowing, crocodile-infested river. Along the way they encountered hippopotami and mastodons bathing in the river and saw other large animals on the bank that had come down to the shore to drink or bathe

Several days went by as they paddled up the river. As they had done in the forest, each night they pulled onto shore and made camp. After a while they came upon a rocky gorge where the tumultuous water threatened to overturn the canoe. However, the Lemurians were skilled oarsmen and kept their craft steady and away from dangerous rocks. Finally they came upon the origin of the river, a waterfall that plunged hundreds feet over a cliff. They beached the canoe, and began an arduous climb to the cliff top. This was especially difficult for Schmidt, who was afraid of heights. He needed much help from Anahuarque, who practically carried him much of the way.

When they reached the top, Winterbottom peered into the distance at the mountains and groaned. They did not seem much closer than they had at the beginning of the trek. Above the chasm, the stream was much smaller and finally petered out. They continued hiking on dry grassland again. After a while their surroundings became more arid until they were in a desert of shifting, blowing sands. The Lemurians donned loose fitting robes with hoods as protection from the sun. Anahuarque created similar outfits for the humans by resizing robes originally made for the larger Lemurians.

The trek through the desert was even more painful than their previous hike. A hot sun beat down on the troop as the slogged through loose sand up and down the slopes of dunes. A constant wind blew sand into their faces and made its way into their garb, causing itching where it stuck to their perspiring skin. Water had to be rationed. Soon their tongues were thick from lack of moisture, and their lips became chapped and cracked.

Just when Winterbottom thought that he was going to perish from heat exhaustion and thirst, they arrived at a muddy oasis. All the travelers immediately fell to a prone position and stuck their heads into the refreshing water. When everyone had drunk their fill, the Lemurians filled water vessels. They camped at the oasis for a single night, during which Winterbottom heard the howling of dire wolves.

It took two more weeks to traverse the desert. A few kilometers after the last oasis, they arrived at the foothills of the mountains. Plant life became more plentiful. Soon they were among trees again as they roamed up one side of a hill and down the other. Game was also present. As a result the trip became more pleasant. The entire company became more cheerful and began to converse again.

One morning Honey Bunn pointed at something in the sky. "Wow. Look at the size of that red bird."

Winterbottom and Schmidt peered at the creature she pointed out. Schmidt said, "That's no bird. Look how sinuously it slithers through the sky."

Winterbottom cried, "It's a dragon. I thought they were only in legends and fairytales."

"Apparently they existed in Lemuria."

The Lemurians had also spotted the creature. They chattered excitedly among themselves, pointing with their blowguns and spears. Their chatter was too rapid for Schmidt to follow. As the little troop gazed upward, several more dragons joined the red one. Most were green, but some were other colors. However, the red one was the largest and obviously their leader.

Anahuarque gave orders to hide in a nearby copse before the flock spotted them. Everyone hid within the trees and peered out at the dragons. A herd of mammoths were grazing in the field. The dragons attacked the mammoths like hawks after rabbits, swooping down and carrying the monstrous creatures away.

After a few more days they were into the mountains. Traveling again became extremely difficult. Winterbottom, who had previous mountaineering experience, was able to follow the mountain trails without too many problems. However, for Honey Bunn and Schmidt, whose fear of heights overcame him several times, it was a trip out of a nightmare.

Titicaca

After several days of climbing, they overlooked a pleasant mountain valley from a ridge. A great city was spread out in the midst of acres of farmland, meadows and woodland. Within it were thousands of one and two story houses of stucco and stone, taller buildings and elaborate palaces. A pyramidal structure with a shiny object on top that reflected the sun dominated the central plaza. The bright light prevented Winterbottom from seeing exactly what capped the pyramid.

Anahuarque pointed to the city and announced to Schmidt, "Titicaca, our home."

Schmidt stood with his back against the side of the mountain as far away from the cliff edge as he could get. "It-it's a large city. I was expecting a village of crude huts."

Anahuarque laughed. "Did you think that because we were out hunting in the manner of our ancestors that we are savages? We are civilized beings with a long history. Our forbearers came from up there." She pointed at the sky.

"They were colonists from another planet?"

"Yes."

"Which one? Were they from another star?"

She shrugged. "That part of our history is lost in the mist of legend. All I know is that our wise men say that they arrived on earth over a million years ago."

"The pyramid in the center of the city is quite striking. Is it the seat of power of your nation?"

"In a sense. It's the first building built by the original colonists and is sacred. I am a priestess and seeress of the old ones. The sacred pyramid is where I prophesize and do other priestess duties."

"That's great. We are in need of someone with power in order to return to our own time and place."

"What do you mean your own time and place?"

Winterbottom had picked up bits and pieces of the language by comparing Schmidt's translations to the original Lemurian. It was the one thing he was good at, learning new languages. As a result he understood some of what passed between the Lemurian woman and Schmidt. "We have traveled through time. We are from a time ahead." He wondered whether she would understand the concept of time travel.

She frowned at the two human men. "You must be powerful magi to go from one time to another. I thought you were children, but now I realize that you are really small adults." She tousled Winterbottom's hair in a friendly manner. Honey Bunn glared daggers at her. "When we get to my home, you must tell me all about how you managed to travel to our time from a time yet to be. But for now, we must be on our way. I wish to be off the mountain before dark." She started down the winding path.

Since Winterbottom did not understand all of her reply, Schmidt translated for him. As they followed the Lemurians down the mountainside, Winterbottom remarked, "They must be a sophisticated people. She understood immediately what I meant by traveling through time."

"A little too sophisticated," said Honey Bunn. "I need to keep my eye on that bitch."

Schmidt said, "The exciting part of her knowing about time travel is that there may be people here who know how to accomplish it. Maybe even Anahuarque herself. Perhaps we have hope of returning to the twenty-first century after all."

After another arduous descent and a short hike through the farmland that surrounded the city, they entered Titicaca. As they strolled through the metropolis, Winterbottom peered around curiously. The natives they passed stared back at them with the same curiosity. The inhabitants were similar in appearance to Anahuarque and her companions in that they were extremely tall with green skins. In most other respects they resembled humans. None of the men, however, had beards or moustaches. The only hair was on their heads. Although their garments were varied in both color and style, there was no attempt to conceal any part of their bodies. Because the weather was pleasantly warm, many walked about nude.

It was a crowded busy place, much like the cities in Winterbottom's world. Besides pedestrian traffic, various types of vehicles were driven through the wide boulevards, which were paved with carefully laid stone blocks so that they were as smooth as an asphalt highway. Winterbottom was surprised to see that in addition to animal and human hauled carts and litters, there were motorized three-wheeled vehicles, which did not spew fumes of any sort and were elaborately ornamented.

Through Schmidt, he asked Anahuarque how they were powered.

She replied, "From the rays of the sun and through magic."

Winterbottom wondered what sort of magic could run wheeled vehicles. He figured it was really solar energy, or perhaps atomics, which powered them.

Anahuarque explained that there was additional transport that ran underground throughout the city and that for long distance travel they used something called a *pachacamac*.

Winterbottom wondered what a *pachacamac* was. Could it be some kind of flying machine? So far he had not seen anything except birds and dragons in the sky. Hence, he assumed that it was a high-speed ground vehicle.

One by one and two by two the Lemurians who had been on the hunting expedition said their good-byes and left the group for their homes. The two who carried the sabertooth headed for the center of town.

"I wonder where they're taking it," Honey Bunn said.

"Should I ask Anahuarque?" asked Schmidt.

"No. I'm happy to see the last of that awful thing. It was starting to smell."

They passed through a street market which had many things for sale including foodstuffs, shiny colorful cloth, trinkets, jewelry, bottles of wine, and prepared food. Anahuarque stopped and purchased steaming tortilla wrapped meat from a vendor and bottles filled with greenish liquor. She told Schmidt that these items were for dinner.

Anahuarque's Home

Anahuarque's home was constructed in the Roman manner. Except for the door and windows, the front was flat stucco with no decoration. It was two stories high. Only the upper story had windows.

Since it was near the center of town, the central pyramid was clearly visible. It had thirteen great steps. The object at the top was a crystal eyeball. As they approached, it turned in their direction. Winterbottom had the eerie feeling that it was watching them. He whispered to Schmidt, "Doesn't the pyramid look exactly like the one on a dollar bill?"

"By golly, you're right. Perhaps this pyramid is the origin of the symbol."

Anahuarque led them through a foyer into an atrium. Servants came forward, bowed and greeted her. She ordered food and drink. She treated the three humans as honored guests. They all sat at a long table. She had Winterbottom sit on her right, Schmidt on her left and Honey Bunn next to Schmidt.

After the food and drink were served, she said – Schmidt translated her words for the other two – "There is an ancient legend that one day small creatures would arrive from another world. I am curious about where you three actually came from. You mentioned a time that not has happened yet. Tell me how you achieved such a feat of magick?"

"It was not really our own doing. " Schmidt went on to explain how he had collected various artifacts having to do with Lemuria. "I wanted to show them to Charlie. Although there was warning on the container, we opened a box that contained an odd-shaped crystal. When we stared at it, the Haunter of the Dark appeared and sent us to your time and place."

Winterbottom yawned. Schmidt's rambling stories always made him sleepy, even when they were in Lemurian. Honey Bunn was also restless and began to tap on her wine glass with her spoon.

"It seems your companions are tired from the long journey. We will finish this conversation tomorrow. My servants will show you to your rooms."

Schmidt looked disappointed. He was hoping to ask Anahuarque about the Lemurian civilization and whether their men of magick also had the ability to send them back to their own time.

Anahuarque ordered a servant to find rooms for her guests and wished them a restful sleep. The servant showed them to bedrooms located on the second floor. Strangely, Schmidt's and Honey Bunn's rooms were on one side of the building and Winterbottom's was on the other. Winterbottom tried to speak to the servant to tell him that he wanted to stay in the same room as Honey Bunn, but the man refused to listen. He gave Honey Bunn a quick kiss and wished her a good night.

Honey Bunn said, "That bitch deliberately put us in separate rooms. She's got something up her sleeve."

"I'll complain to her tomorrow. Tonight, I really am tired. I don't want to do anything except sleep. Okay, sweetheart?"

"Well ... I'm sort of tired myself. See you in the morning, darling." She had an odd expression on her face.

They kissed again, and Honey Bunn went into her room. Winterbottom followed the servant to the other side of the building. He was ushered into a luxurious apartment in the center of which was an enormous bed covered by a canopy of pink lace. He turned to the servant to try to communicate that there was some mistake, but the fellow had already left the room. Not sure what else to do, he headed for the bed. He parted the curtains. To his absolute amazement, Anahuarque was lying there in the nude. She smiled up at him. "Do you understand any of my language?"

He nodded as he took in her amazing body, all seven feet of it. Although her skin was green and serpent like, she was one of the sexiest women he had ever seen – and that was quite a few. "A little. Speak slowly."

"I have admired you from the time I first laid eyes on you little people. I wish to have you as one of my consort slaves. You will not be required to do any physical work. Simply keep me amused."

"B-but I am committed to another." Winterbottom did not wish to be a consort slave to this woman, although she was very beautiful. In fact, he would have preferred to remain with Honey Bunn.

She scowled. "You mean that little person you were found with. I will dispose of her."

"Please don't do that. I will do whatever you ask."

She smiled and patted the bed. "Remove your garments and lie here."

He undressed. "What are to become of my two companions?"

"Suitable employment will be found for them. The funny looking one seems to be a scholar. Perhaps he can work in the temple library. The female has attractive features. I will give her to one of my male friends to play with."

"We will become slaves then?"

"Of course. Since you are not of our race, what else could we do with you?"

"I see." Winterbottom realized he must go along with her dictates for the present until he could tell the others their fate and devise an escape plan.

As he crawled into Anahuarque's bed, the door was flung open. Honey Bunn charged into the room wielding a dagger she must have found somewhere. She shrieked, "I knew something was up. That snake woman had her eyes on you right from the beginning."

Winterbottom said, "Wait sweetie. Don't do anything rash."

Anahuarque sat up. "So. The little female has spirit after all." She shouted out, "Guards. Come quickly. I am being attacked."

Two male Lemurians ran into the room. With their long strides, they were able to grab the maddened Honey Bunn before she could reach the bed. She kicked, punched and tried to stab them, but they were too strong for her. One twisted her wrist so that she dropped the dagger. She screamed out curses against Anahuarque, the guards and Winterbottom.

Anahuarque said, "Remove her from my sight. Take her to the dungeon."

The guards dragged the screaming fighting wildcat from the room.

Winterbottom said, "They won't hurt her will they?"

"No more than necessary to get her into a cell."

"What will happen to her eventually?"

"She is guilty of attempted violence against a priestess of the temple. She will be executed."

"Please have mercy and let her go. Honey Bunn has a temper I realize, but I don't believe she would actually hurt anyone. She's simply jealous."

"I see that you wish no harm to befall the female little person. Well, if you want me to show mercy to her, you will have to please me very much." She stroked Winterbottom's cheek with her large hand.

He crawled into the bed and used all his expertise to make smoking hot love to her. It was not unpleasant for him, even though she was so large and her skin had the texture of a serpent.

Breakfast Conversation

The next morning Winterbottom and Anahuarque bathed in a pool in another section of her apartment. Slave women scrubbed and washed Winterbottom's bottom and top, and slave men performed the same actions for Anahuarque. After their bath, Anahuarque gave Winterbottom native garb to wear, and they strolled down to the atrium arm in arm. A sumptuous breakfast was laid out. Schmidt had already arrived at the table and was indulging in one of his favorite pastimes, eating. He rose and bowed when the duo entered the room. He said in Lemurian, "Good morning, Anahuarque," and in English, "Up to your old tricks, eh Charlie, bonking every female in sight."

"I had no choice. I've been chosen to be Anahuarque's slave consort."

"Well, I suppose there are worse things. Is your other girl friend sleeping in this morning?"

Winterbottom sighed. "She's been thrown into the dungeon. It's a long story, which I'll tell you about later."

Anahuarque interrupted their conversation. "Please do not speak in your barbaric mother tongue. You both have learned my language. It is rude not to use it."

Winterbottom said, "I'm sorry, my dear. I was simply telling Heinie my new status. Shall I also tell him about your plans for him?"

"I will tell him myself. We need a new librarian in the temple. Since you have knowledge of many things, I have chosen you to be our new slave assistant librarian."

"I am honored. When will I begin my duties?"

"I will take you to the temple right after the morning meal. The head librarian will instruct you in the work."

Winterbottom did not like the idea. It meant they would be separated. He needed to consult his fellow archeologist to devise an escape plan and a way of rescuing Honey Bunn. Nonetheless, he could not think of any valid excuse to prevent him from going to the temple. "May I tag along too? I have been curious about the temple ever since I first viewed it."

"Of course, my little lover man. I will take you on a tour."

Schmidt said, "Are any of the priests and priestesses that I will meet magi?"

"Some are adepts, yes. Why do you ask?"

"I wish to learn magick."

"I thought you already knew magick. Did you not summon the Haunter of the Dark using a crystal and force the demon to bring you here?"

"Well, uh, sort of. But the crystal was an artifact from your land, and I no longer possess it. As long as we're on the subject of artifacts, what is the significance of crystal skulls?"

"You also were in possession of crystal skulls? They are used in our rituals of worship."

"Fascinating. Tell me more about your religion."

"You will learn that soon enough. Everyone is required to worship the sleeping god at least once every ten sunrises. I will tell you this much. Its eye at the top of the temple observes everything we do, causing it to dream about us."

Winterbottom said, "I noticed that it turned our way as we neared the temple yesterday."

Anahuarque lowered her voice to a whisper. "Recall that prophetic legend I told you about. There is more. It is said that when a child of our people is born as a result of a mating between one of our people and a *guara* the sleeper will awaken and call down death from the sky."

"What's a *guara*?" asked Schmidt.

"It is a mythical creature with pale skin and hair on parts of its body other than its head. They are said to be small like you."

"In our language such creatures are known as *elves* or *gnomes*. This sleeping god, does it have a name?"

Her voice dropped even lower. "It is forbidden to pronounce its real name in case it should hear and awaken. But, for your enlightenment, I will say the name with my lips without making the sounds." She moved her lips.

The men stared. She seemed to be mouthing Yog-Sothoth. They looked at each other. The Yog-Sothoth was a monster from outer space according to a fictional horror story.

Winterbottom said, "I know the name. It is ..."

Anahuarque reached over and cover his mouth. "Do not say it. Do you wish to bring death upon us all? Besides, it is a capital offense to say the name aloud. Since you two are finished with breakfast, we will go to the temple."

The Pyramidal Temple

It was only a short walk to the pyramid. Nonetheless, the eye at its tip stared at them the entire way, seeming to follow their every movement. On the way, Winterbottom related in English what had transpired the evening before. Schmidt shook his head. "That girl. She's got quite a temper. It's lucky that she did not do any real damage. We'd all be in trouble. How are we going to get her out of the dungeon?"

"I've appealed to Anahuarque for mercy."

Anahuarque said, "I heard my name mentioned as you were conversing in your barbaric native tongue."

"I just told Heinie what a lovely person you are and what a tremendous lover. I am extremely happy to be your slave consort."

She smiled broadly. "Thank you. Before we go into the temple, I must warn you to follow what I do to show respect for the sleeping god. The penalties for impiety are severe."

The men nodded. "We will show every reverence," said Winterbottom.

The pyramid before them was larger than Winterbottom had first estimated. It was a veritable mountain. Each of the thirteen steps was the height of a three story building. The entrance consisted of massive bronze double doors, which were decorated with various horrible monsters doing awful things to naked Lemurians. Winterbottom wondered whether the scenes were of the Lemurian's concept of hell.

Anahuarque stood before them and raised her arms. "Oh great sleeping god, allow us entrance to the sacred temple."

The huge doors opened slowly with a loud grating that hurt Winterbottom's eardrums. Anahuarque stepped forward into an enormous chamber. Hundreds of thick columns held up a ceiling several meters above their heads. The room was ill lighted with torches on some columns. Winterbottom and Schmidt followed her. After three paces, Anahuarque halted, went to her knees and knocked her head three times on the stone floor. The men did the same. They rose again and ventured forward into the gloom. After stepping forward several paces, they came upon a statue of a monster so horrible that it was difficult to look at. Its eyes were closed as though in slumber. Anahuarque again knelt down and prostrated herself. Again the two men did the same. She cried out, "Awesome one. I beseech thee to have mercy on us and remain asleep for many more seasons. I revere and fear thee." The men repeated this prayer. They rose. Anahuarque placed the thumb of one hand on her nose and waved her fingers. Winterbottom had to stifle a giggle as he imitated the motion.

Afterward Anahuarque took them through a small door which led to a stairway. They climbed up several levels, exiting at what Winterbottom estimated was about the height of the top of the first step of the pyramid. They entered a dim hallway, at the end of which was a doorway with hieroglyphic symbols on it. Schmidt whispered to Winterbottom, "If I read those symbols correctly, they say *The place of knowledge of the ancients.*"

They entered. The room contained many shelves of books and scrolls. Schmidt's eyes went wide with pleasure, like a kid in a candy store. A Lemurian in the robes of a priest approached. He bowed. "May I be of service?"

Anahuarque said, "I have brought someone to help you, Acahuana." She pointed at Schmidt. "This one is to be your new slave assistant. He is a scholar."

"Ah, good. Many thanks, Priestess Anahuarque. I have great need of such a one. Come with me, little man." He led Schmidt away.

Anahuarque said, "Now Charlie Winterbottom, I will show you the many wonders of our temple."

She took him to an elevator which they rode up several levels. When they disembarked, they were in a place that contained many machines, some familiar and some strange. Winterbottom was awed to learn that they had computers and television and many other devices that he considered inventions of the twentieth and twenty-first centuries. He asked, "Do you also have machines that fly?"

"No need. We travel to distance places by teleportation. We have traveled as far as the moon and the red planet, but those places are dead worlds and special clothing and equipment is necessary."

"The red planet is not quite dead. It has an underground civilization. I have been there."

"How interesting. You will have to tell me about it sometime." Her expression was one of disbelief. Apparently she considered Winterbottom and Schmidt storytellers and prevaricators.

They went up higher in the pyramid. She took them through a museum. Among the artifacts Winterbottom viewed there was crystal that seemed identical to the one that summoned the Haunter of the Dark.

"Do not look too closely at that," Anahuarque warned. "It has been known to drive men mad."

"I believe it." Winterbottom looked away.

Finally they went to the topmost level and through a dark tunnel. Anahuarque lighted the way with a glowing globe. At the end of it was a solid looking iron door. Several heavy flat bars were also affixed across it. Someone thought a lot of strength was needed to hold back whatever lay beyond it.

Anahuarque pointed at it. "The abode of the sleeping god."

"You keep your god a prisoner?"

"We must. Should it wake and get loose, it would rampage through the city killing everyone. Nothing could stop it."

They returned to the bottom of the pyramid and left for Anahuarque's home.

The Dungeon

After Anahuarque and Winterbottom shared another meal, Winterbottom asked, "What of Honey Bunn? When will you release her?"

"As soon as I find a suitable master for her. I will ask around for a male who is wishes to obtain a concubine. Do you wish to visit her?"

"I would. I feel responsible for the trouble she is in."

"Since she does not speak our language, perhaps you can calm her down and warn her of dire consequences if she acts violently again. Tell her of the fate that awaits her so that she will be prepared."

"I will explain everything. I hope she will listen to reason."

"If she wishes to live, she had better."

She called one of the guards and said, "Lead this little man down to the dungeon cell where the little pale female is kept. He is allowed to speak to her for a twentieth of a day."

The entrance to the dungeon was in the atrium. The guard opened a trapdoor concealed by a carpet. Carrying a glowing globe to light the way, he led Winterbottom down stone steps to a damp underground hallway that had the stench of death and decay about it. On each side were barred cells. The odor of urine and feces added to the foul odor. Emaciated Lemurians, both male and female, gazed listlessly at them as they passed. The guard halted by the last cell in the row. Inside Honey Bunn sat on a stone bench weeping, her clothing disheveled and torn. Her arms and face was covered with bruises. She glanced up as Winterbottom approached, and her expression turned to one of absolute fury. She lunged at the bars.

"It's your fault that I'm stuck in this stinking dungeon, you cheating bastard."

"Please calm down, Honey. In the first place, I did not want to have anything to do with Anahuarque. She forced me to make love to her. She's made me into a love slave."

The fury in her face faded to mild anger. "And you hated it," she said sarcastically. "I had always heard that you were womanizer, Charlie. All those stories were true, weren't they?"

"Yes. But it was different between you and me. I have real feelings for you. However, what you think of me is not important now. Anahuarque promised to release you from this dungeon on the condition that you hold your temper."

She wrinkled her nose as though smelling a bad odor. "Well, if your love mistress orders it, I suppose I can do that. When do I get out?"

Winterbottom cleared his throat. "There's ... uh ... one other thing. Once you're released, you'll become a love slave to a Lemurian male."

"What!" she screeched. "I'd rather rot in this stinking cell."

The guard made a threatening move toward her. Winterbottom restrained him and moved closer to the bars. "You must do this if we are ever to escape these creatures. There's no way Heinie and I can rescue you from this dungeon."

She stared at him for several moments. "Hmm. I see what you mean. Well, I'm no virgin. I suppose I could play the whore for a while. But you two better come up with a plan to get away from here soon. And as far as you and I are concerned, Charlie, it's all over."

Winterbottom looked down sadly. "I understand. I'll see you soon once you're released to a male Lemurian."

Escape Plan?

A few days later, Honey Bunn was released in the custody of Acahuana, Schmidt's boss in the temple library. He was excited to have such a lovely well-shaped woman, even though she was small. He liked small females. Honey Bunn did not fight his advances and flirted openly with him whenever Winterbottom was nearby.

Schmidt's duties were cataloging new arrivals and distributing them and returned items to the proper shelves. When Schmidt was given a couple of hours off, Winterbottom conferred with him. "Okay, Heinie, you're the brainy one. Have you any ideas for an escape plan?"

Heinie raised his eyebrows. "Escape to where? Back to the wilderness to be eaten by sabertooths or trampled by mammoths? We're better off here. We don't have it so bad. We're well fed, get almost anything we want and the work is not difficult. For you especially." He raised one eyebrow and smirked.

"So you think we should stay here as slaves for the rest of our lives." Winterbottom was disgusted with Schmidt's cowardice and lack of adventurous spirit.

"Certainly not. What we want to do is return to our own time. The only way we can do that is for me to discover a magick formula that will allow us to do that. As a librarian, I'm in the perfect position to learn what magick is available. There's an entire section devoted to magick and the paranormal. All I need to do is find the correct book or scroll. You must be patient, Charles."

Winterbottom realized that he was right, but patience was not his long suit, especially when he thought of Honey Bunn being in the arms of Acahuana every night. He wanted to do something, but did not know what.

Days went by swiftly turning into weeks. One day Honey Bunn asked, "When are we going to leave this Godforsaken city?"

He told her what Schmidt had said.

"Oh Charlie, I don't know how much longer I can hold out. It isn't that Acahuana is cruel or anything. In fact he's kind of nice. But I'm afraid that I'm getting used to a lazy sort of life. It's like being on vacation all the time. I'm growing fat and lazy."

"I'll talk to Heinie again. By the way, what sort of lover is Acahuana?"

She winked at him. "He has no problems in that area. Being a big man, everything about him is large, if you know what I mean, Charlie." She let out a giggle.

The blood rushed to Winterbottom's head. Was she being cruel as revenge for his making love to Anahuarque? If so, she had achieved her goal. The hurt was almost too much to bear. He walked away without another word.

Anahuarque's Illness

More weeks went by. Schmidt still had not found the formula to travel back to their own time. After that hurtful conversation, Winterbottom saw little of Honey Bunn. When he did, she was with Acahuana who had affixed a jeweled collar around her lovely throat with a golden chain attached to it. He held the chain like a man with a dog on a leash. This sight brought a sour taste into Winterbottom's mouth and a cold chill to his heart.

At this time, Anahuarque came down with a strange illness. Some mornings she had bouts of nausea. Other times her appetite increased. Often she had cravings for strange combinations of food. She needed to urinate a lot, and her breasts were swollen and pained her.

One day Winterbottom said, "Something is wrong. You should see the medical priest."

"You're right, Charlie. Besides the symptoms you have seen, I've missed two bleeding times."

A chill went down Winterbottom's spine. Could it be possible? They were different species. How did it happen? It was against nature. What would the child be like? Green but not as tall as its mother? Pale and hairy like Winterbottom with serpent like skin like its mother?

The next day they visited a priestess with medical training. She confirmed Winterbottom's suspicions. Anahuarque was pregnant. "You're entering your second trimester," she told the Lemurian woman. "Congratulations."

"How soon before the baby is born?" asked Winterbottom.

"The egg should be laid in about three months. With the proper warmth, the child should appear a month later."

"I don't understand. Egg? Laid? What do you mean?"

The medical priestess chuckled. "Typical male. He knows nothing about what we women go through."

They left. When they returned to Anahuarque's home, Winterbottom said, "Where I come from a female is pregnant for nine months."

"Really? How do they stand it? I'm ready to lay today."

"Also, when they give birth, a tiny child comes through the birth canal and is born alive."

"Are you teasing me? What happens to the egg? Does the child break it inside the mother? How awful."

"It's not like that at all."

"You're being silly. Such a thing is not possible."

Lemurian Gynecology

After that conversation, Winterbottom went to the temple library. "Hi, Heinie. Do you have any books on gynecology?"

"Possibly. Why do you ask? Planning on delivering a baby?"

Winterbottom told him what the medical priestess had said. "I want to check how the birth process works in Lemurians. I think Anahuarque is going to lay an egg."

"Who's the egg's father?"

"Me, I'm afraid."

Schmidt laughed so hard he could barely stand. When he got himself under control, he said, "Charlie my boy, you sure have a way of getting yourself into messes." He led him to section on medical information. They found a book on advice for young mothers. Schmidt had to translate for Winterbottom. He read aloud, "The normal gestation period of a healthy female is four months …"

"That much time may have already gone by since conception."

He read on. "When labor starts, the mother should go to the nest prepared for her and sit until the egg is laid. It would be helpful to have the father nearby to comfort her. Once the egg is laid, she must sit on it to keep it warm until it is hatched. This may seem boring. However, it is wonderful feeling to know that soon, a wee one will breaking through the shell. The father can be helpful in this regard by sitting on the egg while the mother takes a break. If the egg does not hatch after one moon, a medical priest should be called." Schmidt looked up from the book. "Do you want me to go on?"

"I've heard enough. I had better get back to Anahuarque. For all I know she's laying now. Have you found a book on traveling forward to our own time yet?"

"Not yet. Too bad we don't have that magic crystal to summon the Haunter of the Dark."

"Y'know, I just remembered something. Remember the first day that Anahuarque brought us to the temple. She gave me a tour of the pyramid. On the tenth level there is a museum. I saw a crystal like the one that summoned the Haunter of the Dark."

"Why didn't you tell me this sooner?"

Winterbottom blushed. "I forgot about it. Do you think the Haunter of the Dark will really send us back to our own time? Or will it simply send us somewhere worse?"

Schmidt shrugged. "Hopefully I've learned enough magick since I've been here to control such a demon."

To Winterbottom, he did not sound confident.

Anahuarque Lays an Egg

When Winterbottom arrived back at Anahuarque's house, the servants were all aflutter. They told him that Anahuarque had been having pains all morning and was calling for him.

"Where is she now?"

"In the birthing nest," said the head maid. "I'll take you to her."

Winterbottom followed the slave woman to a room he had never seen before. Anahuarque was resting inside a kind of round tub lined with stuffed silks surrounded by pillows. She was perspiring profusely and groaning. Winterbottom went up to her and took her hand. "I'm right here, darling."

"Thank the sleeping god you've come. I'm about to lay."

"The servants told me. Is the pain terrible?"

"Not as bad as I anticipated. This is my first egg. I did not know what to expect. Ohhh. Here comes another contraction." She groaned loudly. "Oh, I think the egg is almost here." She squeezed Winterbottom's hand and screwed up her face.

Suddenly she raised her arms and waved them up and down. She began to cluck like a chicken. "Cluck, cluck, cluck."

She rose up and pulled the skirt of her gown to reveal that something was protruding from her female parts. She clucked some more and bore down. More of the object appeared. With a popping sound, a green egg fell out onto the soft cushion below her. Winterbottom stared at the melon-sized object. Anahuarque let out a deep sigh and settled herself slowly on the egg.

She smiled tiredly at Winterbottom. "I wonder whether it will be a male or female."

He returned her smile. "As long as it's healthy." The thought that he had fathered whatever was in that egg boggled his mind.

Schmidt Hears Rumbling

After Winterbottom left the library, Schmidt went to Acahuana and asked for the afternoon off. The head librarian rubbed his chin and thought about it for a few moments. "I suppose so. This day there are not many new items to be cataloged and put on shelves. You have been a good worker and very thorough. However, report back here immediately after the dinner twentieth. I am expecting a group of mystics. They will want to check out occult scrolls. You know that section well and can easily find what they are looking for."

Schmidt bowed. "I will return as quickly as I can." He thought, *that may be never if I can summon the Haunter of the Dark.*

He took the elevator to the tenth floor and was amazed at how many arcane artifacts were displayed. He stopped to examine many items as he strolled through the museum, which was an archeologist's and occultist's paradise. Time flew by. Finally he realized that he should not be spending so much time browsing. Acahuana would be expecting him back to help with the visiting occultists. He searched around until he found the crystal that Winterbottom had told him about and dropped it into a sack which he tied to his belt.

Now to find Charlie and Honey Bunn, he thought. As he started for the elevator, however, he heard thumping from somewhere above. There was a rumbling, and the building trembled so that he had to hold on to a display table to keep from falling. *An earthquake,* he thought. *It's lucky this building is pyramidal. It's the most stable shape.*

He decided that he dare not use the elevator. He found a stairway. The trembling halted but the thumping continued from somewhere above. Curious, he started up the stairs. The higher he climbed the louder the thumping. Finally it changed to a loud clanging as though someone was beating on a metal barrel. He came to the top level of the pyramid and walked through the dark tunnel. He stared at the barred door. The thumping and clanging was definitely coming from it. Something huge, fierce and strong was trying to escape.

"The sleeping god has awakened," he cried. *Yog-Sothoth wants out.* He dared not say the awful name aloud. He was frozen with fright and kept staring as the monster hammered so hard that dents appeared in the thick steel door. There was a loud crash, and one of the metal bars that had been bolted to the wall fell to the floor.

The sound brought Schmidt out of his terror-stricken paralysis. He turned and ran back through the tunnel and down the stairs as though a thousand fiends were after him. He did not stop until he reached the ground floor and was out the door into the street. *We must leave quickly,* he thought. *Lemuria is doomed.*

Acahuana's house was closer than Anahuarque's, so he went there first. He knocked on the door and asked to speak to Honey Bunn. When he was ushered into a parlor, Honey Bunn was relaxing on sofa. She had adopted the Lemurian habit of wearing garments that revealed rather than concealed. In addition, her neck and arms was adorned with gold and jewels. She sipped Lemurian wine as she munched on a box of chocolates.

Schmidt blushed to see her nipples and privates exposed through the transparent silky cloth. He gulped before speaking. "Honey Bunn, I've found the means to return to our own time. Put something decent on. We must find Charlie and go."

Honey Bunn shook her head and smiled sadly. "I'm not going back." She held up her arm with the golden bracelets encrusted with jewels.

"This is the life I've always dreamed about. I'm the favorite concubine of a rich and powerful man. I don't have anything to do except lay around all day eating chocolate and sipping wine. I allow Acahuana to make love to me whenever he's not too tired, which is not all that often. Besides, he's a kind and caring male. I'm sure that after a while I shall be in love with him."

"That's all very good, but Lemuria is doomed."

She laughed. "I know. It's going to sink into the sea someday. But who knows when that will be."

"That's not it. The sleeping god has awakened. The Yog-Sothoth is breaking out of its prison and will destroy everyone."

"And how do you know that?"

"I was up there where the demon is kept. It was hammering on the walls and door to get out."

"I'm sure that its prison was built strong enough to hold it. It will tire itself out and go back to sleep."

"I wouldn't count on it."

"Pah. Away with you. I'm happy and comfy here. What do I have waiting for me in the twenty-first century? Charlie has cheated on me with that snake bitch and will probably cheat with someone else after we return. Then I'll be back where I started, manless, jobless and homeless. No thanks. My days of looking for someone to take care of me are over. I've found him. Good-bye, Heinie. Tell Charlie, I wish him all the luck with his Lemurian priestess."

She turned away and signaled the servant to show Schmidt to the door.

As Schmidt walked toward Anahuarque's dwelling, he looked toward the great pyramid. The eye on top was no longer gazing at the city. It was pointed upward as though searching the sky for something. He shuddered, wondering whether the Yog-Sothoth will break loose from its prison or whether Honey Bunn was right and it would simply go back to sleep once it wore itself out.

After a servant answered his knock at Anahuarque's home, he said, "I would like to speak to Charles Winterbottom please."

"He is in the birthing room. He has become a father this day."

"Really? I'd like to congratulate him."

The servant led Schmidt to the birthing room. Winterbottom was sitting naked in the birthing nest. "I see you've gone as native as Honey Bunn, Charlie."

"I'm keeping my son or daughter warm until Anahuarque gets back. She went shopping for baby clothes."

"I'm surprised that you cannot tell whether it's a boy or girl."

"That's because it hasn't hatched yet. Do you want to see?"

"Sure." Schmidt leaned over the nest wall. Winterbottom rose up to allow him to see what was underneath him. "It's a green egg!"

"Of course. You're the one who showed me those motherhood books. The Lemurians are not mammals."

"But they have breasts and resemble us."

Winterbottom shrugged. "I don't believe they originated on earth. What amazes me is that my sperm would be compatible with Anahuarque's reproductive organs."

"Well, it's a mystery we'll probably never resolve. I've got the crystal. We must summon the Haunter of the Dark and leave for our own time as quickly as possible."

"Can't we wait another month until my child hatches?"

"No. The Yog-Sothoth has awakened. This city is doomed."

"What? How do you know this?"

"I just came from the top level of the pyramid where it's held prisoner. It's beating the door down."

"Maybe it can't get out. That door looked pretty strong. Besides, we need to get Honey Bunn."

"She refuses to leave. She says that she's the happiest she has ever been in her life."

"Did you tell her about the Yog-Sothoth?"

"Like you, she believes that the prison it's in will hold it. I'm not so confident."

Just then, there was a commotion outside. It sounded as though many people were running and screaming.

Yog-Sothoth on a Rampage

The outside door crashed open. Anahuarque rushed into the room out of breath. "Quick, hand me our darling egg." Winterbottom gingerly placed the orb in her arms. "Now you two, bring the nest."

"What's happened?" Winterbottom asked.

"The sleeping god has awakened. We must hide. It is rampaging through the city, eating every citizen in sight."

She led them to the cellar door. After they opened it, Winterbottom and Schmidt struggled to get the birthing nest down the stairs and into the dungeon area. They moved it to the empty cell at the end of the row. Anahuarque placed the egg in it, climbed in herself and carefully sat on it. The servants and guards also came down into the dungeon area. They clung to each other in fright.

"We must go now," Schmidt whispered to Winterbottom.

Winterbottom turned to Anahuarque. "I need to leave." He kissed her. "Take good care of our son or daughter."

"Where are you going?" she screamed. "You'll be killed by the sleeping god if you venture out."

"We'll avoid it somehow. There's something that Schmidt and I must do now."

Her brows knitted into a frown. "You've found a way to return to your own time, haven't you?"

"Yes. I really love you, Anahuarque darling, but we do not belong here."

"Coward. It's because of the sleeping god. You're deserting me when I need you the most."

This was the first time anyone had ever called Winterbottom a coward. People had called him many other bad names, but never before coward. He was torn. Should he stay in Lemuria to look after his lover and child, or should he return. Then he recalled that Honey Bunn was in deadly danger also. "Yes. I suppose I am. I'm leaving."

Anahuarque called to her guardsmen who had entered the dungeon to escape the Yog-Sothoth. "Grab them. Don't let them leave."

Four guards rushed toward Schmidt and Winterbottom. Winterbottom used a karate kick in the privates of one to disable him. Schmidt grabbed a whip off the rack on the wall where the torture instruments were stored. He snapped it at the other three guards, keeping them at bay. He and Winterbottom rushed up the stairs, slammed the cellar door on the heads of the guards coming up behind and moved a heavy piece of furniture over it.

"That'll hold them a while," Schmidt said. "Now we must summon the Haunter of the Dark."

"Not yet. First we need to get Honey Bunn, even if we have to force her to come with us."

Schmidt sighed. "I suppose you're right. But we must be careful to avoid the Yog-Sothoth."

They went out into the street. Lemurians were running in all different directions. The monstrous, twenty meter tall Yog-Sothoth could be seen plainly above the houses. The ground shook under its thread. Every so often it reached down and grabbed one or more Lemurians to stuff into its mouth. Its stench, when it wafted in their directions, was so awful it made Winterbottom want to vomit.

As he and Schmidt were running towards Acahuana's house, a huge fireball streaked across the sky. Seconds later there was a huge explosion whose shockwave knocked the two men and several Lemurians to the ground. The central pyramid disappeared in a great mushroom cloud, and the earth began to shiver and shake.

Winterbottom and Schmidt struggled to their feet. Schmidt cried, "Look." He pointed in the direction of the bay. A monstrous tsunami, hundreds of feet high, was building. In moments it would inundate the city and crush everything in its path.

"We need to leave this instant." Schmidt took the crystal from its sack. "Stare at it Charlie. It's our only hope."

Winterbottom gazed into the crystal as the enormous wall of water descended upon them. Everything went black. He heard the evil laugh of the Haunter of the Dark, and Schmidt reciting the words of power that he had learned from the magical books in the Lemurian library. "Return us to whence you took us," he cried.

Aftermath

A blinding light struck Winterbottom in the eye. His head felt as though someone had hit him with a hammer. He gazed around. The light was from a window. He was back in his hotel room. It was a mess. Bottles and glasses were all over. The bong lay on the floor. A couple of lamps had been knocked over. Schmidt was struggling to a sitting position.

"Boy, that was close," he said.

"What do you mean? Oh my head hurts from all the booze and mushroom. I had the weirdest dream or drug trip."

"When was that? The night before we left Lemuria?"

"That was the dream. All about Lemuria."

"Charlie, my boy. That was no dream. We really were sent to Lemuria by the Haunter of the Dark."

"Ohmigosh! What happened to Honey Bunn?"

"I'm afraid she perished with Lemurians, either from the tidal wave, the\ affects of the meteor crash or was eaten by the Yog-Sothoth."

"Oh no. We weren't able to save her." Winterbottom wept, not only for the loss of Honey Bunn, but also for the loss of Anahuarque and the egg he fathered. Schmidt tried to comfort him. After a while he stopped sobbing.

Schmidt said, "Why don't you go for a walk on the beach? It'll make you feel better. I'll clean this mess up."

"Good idea." Winterbottom left the room.

After he was gone about five minutes, Schmidt was sure he would not return. He called out, "Honey Bunn."

The woman came out of her hiding place in the closet. She smiled at Schmidt. "He fell for it hook, line and sinker."

"I feel sorry for the poor chump. He believes that he was really in Lemuria."

She put her arms around him. "You sure are good at mesmerizing someone."

"Nothing to it. It has to do with animal magnetism."

"You'll have to explain it to me sometime. I love all that paranormal stuff. But I'd better pack my clothes before he returns."

"And I'll clean up the mess as I promised him. Do you think it was the right thing to do, playing a trick like that?"

"Absolutely. If he knew that I cheated on him with you, he'd probably knock your block off. Charlie does not take things like that well. He'd probably keep pestering me to come back to him. This way it's a clean break. He thinks I'm dead and that he had quite an adventure."

CHAPTER 7. DINNER WITH DRACULA

A Knock on the Door

Winterbottom placed an icepack on his head, which throbbed from the wild party, he, Honey Bunn and Heinrich Schmidt had the night before. If his head had not hurt so much, he would have tried to puzzle out whether they had really traveled to Lemuria or whether it had been simply a nightmare brought on by the strange powdered mushroom they had smoked. On the one hand, it seemed impossible to travel ten thousand years into the past and five thousand miles around the globe by simply staring at the crystal that Schmidt had obtained in Chili. On the other hand, Honey Bunn did disappear mysteriously, and Schmidt had also experienced traveling to Lemuria.

He poured a small amount of tequila into a glass and downed it quickly. There was nothing like a little hair of the dog for ridding oneself of a hangover. He leaned back against the headboard to allow the liquor to take affect. Someone rapped sharply at his door.

"Come back later to clean my room," he cried. "I'm resting."

"I'm not the maid," a man's voice replied. "Doctor Winterbottom, I have business I wish to transact with you."

"Just a minute." He slipped on his bathrobe, combed his hair with his fingers and went to the door. He peered through the peephole. A young man stood outside the door. He was pale-skinned, had thick dark brown hair slightly on the longish side, and wore a dark suit with a white shirt and striped tie.

"You're not going to preach some religion to me, are you?" asked Winterbottom.

The young man grinned. "Nothing like that. Actually I want to hire you. Please let me in so I can explain."

Winterbottom's funds *were* on the low side. Honey Bunn had been a high maintenance mistress, and the trip to Maui had cost him an arm and a leg. He had always been a spendthrift, and his credit cards were just about maxed out. A job at this point in his career could be what the doctor ordered.

He opened the door and let the young man into his hotel room. "Sorry about my appearance, but I and a couple friends had a little party last night. I slept in this morning."

"No problem." The young man put his hand out. "My name is Robert

Tepes."

Winterbottom shook his hand vigorously. "Pleased to meet you, Mr. Tepes. Obviously you already know who I am. Please have a seat." He pointed to the desk chair. He, himself, sat on the edge of the bed. "Would you like a spot of tequila?"

"No thank you. I never drink during the day. What I want your help with, sir, is to locate my family. You see, I am an orphan. My parents died when I was very young and left a considerable inheritance, for which I am grateful. However, I know nothing about my ancestors except that they came from an Eastern European country. I don't even know which one. What I want to hire you to do is help me find any living relatives."

"Who administers your estate? Wouldn't he or she know something?"

"That's a problem. The firm that was hired by my parents has been sworn to never give me that information."

"That's odd. But why come to me? You probably want to hire a private detective or a genealogist."

Tepes leaned forward. "It's because of the secrecy thing. My parents were probably trying to protect me from something. You see, I'm a great fan of yours. I've followed your career closely. Your exploits have been written about extensively in the press. Why you've discovered an underground civilization on Mars, exposed a pagan cult, traveled back in time and found the Garden of Eden. I'm surprised you haven't written a book."

Winterbottom grinned. He loved to be praised. "I intend to some day."

"Because of your spirit of adventure and great deductive abilities, I believe you're just the man to help me. I have a feeling that there may be something sinister or unsavory about my relatives in Europe. Someone like you could help me deal with them ... if we can locate them."

"I'm beginning to understand. It sounds like an interesting project. Without seeming to be crass, what sort of salary are you offering?"

Tepes looked thoughtful for a few moments. "Would two thousand dollars a week plus expenses be sufficient?"

Winterbottom did a quick calculation in his head. Tepes was offering more than one hundred thousand dollars a year if the job lasted that long. He could live in the style he wanted to become accustomed to and maybe even get out of debt. "I'll take it."

"Good. And there will be a bonus if you actually discover who my relatives are. I'll have my lawyers draw up a contract. When can you start?"

"As soon as I get dressed. I have a laptop."

"Great. Here's your first week's wages." Tepes handed him an envelope stuffed with twenty hundred dollar bills. "You understand, of course, that there may be danger."

"Danger? From what source?"

"After you find out who my relatives are, I want you to accompany me to meet them. If it turns out that there's something nefarious about them, we may be in for some trouble."

"It sounds like you're anticipating that will be the case."

"There were hints in letters left by my parents. For some reason they did not want me to know who my relatives are."

"Well, I'm no stranger to danger. I would be happy to accompany you to meet your nefarious relatives."

They shook hands again.

Winterbottom showered and dressed. He said, "Before we start, I'd like to get some breakfast. Shall we go down to the buffet?" He glanced at his watch. "They should still be serving."

An outdoor breakfast buffet for guests was provided by the hotel. Winterbottom was hungry and loaded his plate with hotcakes, bacon, and an omelet. He also took orange juice and coffee. Tepes had only black coffee and a Danish. "I'm not a breakfast person," he said.

They found a table with a good view of the beach. Winterbottom liked to stare at the young women in bikinis as they strolled by. After putting away his breakfast, he sipped his coffee and said, "Tell me about yourself, Robert ... or would you prefer Bob or Rob? You may call me Charlie. Your history may help my search. For example, what happened to your parents?"

Tepes shrugged. "Robert is fine. I don't know what happened to mom and dad. It's another mystery. When I asked my guardians the same question, I was simply told that they died. And that I should not concern myself with how. They said, 'They're dead. What difference does it make how they died?'"

"Where are they buried? Perhaps we can derive clues from their tombstones."

"In Chicago's Graceland Cemetery. I've visited the gravesite. Only their names appear on the tombstone. No dates."

"I know Graceland. It's an interesting place. It's strange that are no dates on your parents' tombstones though. Oh well. Who raised you?"

"I had a nanny until I was old enough to go to a private boarding school. That was my life from the age of seven until I graduated from a four-year college, living in dormitories."

"What about those letters you told me about? Maybe something in them could give us a clue."

Tepes looked embarrassed. "I destroyed those years ago in a fit of anger and frustration."

Winterbottom patted him on the back. "That's all right. There are still plenty of resources available to us. Let's return to my room now. I'll see what I can Google."

When Winterbottom did a search on Tepes, he came up with many websites devoted to the fictional character Dracula and the famous nobleman Vlad Tepes who impaled many people. He turned to Tepes. "Do you think the famous medieval prince of Walachia who warred against the Turks could've been an ancestor?"

Tepes shrugged. "Anything's possible. How could I tell? Besides, we're looking for relatives currently alive."

"It might be a clue, however. It's a good likelihood that your parents came from an area of Romania, possibly Walachia or Transylvania. Let me try a genealogy site." He did searches on several genealogy web sites, but still could not find any persons with the name of Tepes. He posted a query asking for anyone who thought they might be related to a Robert Tepes whose parents migrated to the United States. "Well, that's about all I can do for now. Give me a number where you can be reached. I'll call you if anyone answers my post."

Tepes wrote down his cell phone number. "Call any time, day or night. Thank you for your work so far."

"I assume this is the easy part of what you want me to do, depending upon who answers my post."

They shook hands, and Tepes left.

Three days later Winterbottom received E-mail from a Vladislav Tepes. It read, "It is very possible that we are related, Robert. I would be pleased to have you visit me. I will compensate you for all your expenses. My home is located near the village of Bran which is near Bra ov. When you arrive in Bran, call me. I will send someone to take you the rest of the way." This was followed by a telephone number. It was signed, "Cordially, Prince Vladislav Tepes."

He called Robert Tepes immediately. "I received a reply from a possible relative. If he is, you're related to royalty. He signed it Prince Vladislav Tepes."

"I wonder if that was what they were keeping from me, that my relative was a noble. Back when they emigrated, Romania was under communist rule. Perhaps they feared that the Reds would come after me."

"It's one plausible explanation. Perhaps we'll find out more when we visit him. He's invited you all expenses paid."

"Wonderful. I wonder what a prince of a Balkan country is like."

"We'll find out. Do you want me to make the arrangements for travel?"

"That would be great."

"I feel I should do something to earn my salary. I'll reply to Vladislav's email in your name. May I tell him that you're bringing a friend?"

"Fine. I'll start packing now. Will you be able to leave soon?"

"As quick as I can make airline reservations. This hotel in Maui is costing me an arm and a leg. I'll be happy if we can leave tomorrow."

Travel to Brasov, Romania

Actually it took Winterbottom's travel agent a few days to make the arrangements. The first leg of their journey was a Delta flight from Maui to LA. They left Maui at noon local time and arrived in LA at eight in the evening Pacific time. Their connecting flight to JFK did not leave until ten P.M. so they ate a snack at the airport. Five hours later they disembarked at JFK at six in the morning.

With Robert Tepes' concurrence, they booked a hotel in Manhattan. By the time they retrieved their luggage and took a taxi into the city, it was ten before they checked into their midtown hotel. They did a little sightseeing and returned to their room for a nap. Since Winterbottom was familiar with the New York nightlife, he took his employer to several nightclubs and bars. They had a wild time and fell into bed inebriated around midnight. Winterbottom found Tepes a pleasant companion who was a lot like himself, ready for a good time with plenty of wine, wild women and song. Exhausted, they slept the next day away.

Their flight to Bucharest left at three the following afternoon. When they boarded the Romanian Airline flight, they still had hangovers. The leg of the journey from New York to Bucharest took ten hours, which meant that they did not arrive until eight A.M. local time. Again, they took a taxi to their hotel and slept most of that day.

The following day they did more sightseeing. They visited the Romanian Peasant Museum, the National Art Museum, Patriarchal Cathedral and the Russian architectural wonder, Saint Nicholas Students' Church. Tepes was an aficionado of the arts and architecture. He was pleased that they spent the time at these places. Winterbottom, on the other hand, was bored, but felt obligated to tag along.

They ate dinner in a Hungarian restaurant. The food was heavily spiced with paprika. For the main course they had their choice of beef goulash, chicken goulash, pork goulash and the special goulash. The desert choices, however, were fancy cream-covered cakes filled with custards or fruit filling. The coffee was dark and strong and served in small cups.

Afterward they went to the Casino Palace to gamble for a while. Winterbottom lost a hundred dollars, and Tepes broke even at the blackjack table. Afterward they went to Club Prometheus where they drank and danced the night away.

The next day they took the train to Brasov. They shared a compartment with a beautiful, but mysterious woman dressed in black and wearing sunglasses although the day was cloudy. She was very pale; her skin was almost the color of the white handkerchief which with she dabbed her lips. Her name was Ilona Szilagy. The other person was a rather hairy man by the name of Lycan Thrope. They both spoke excellent English.

Winterbottom, always interested in good-looking women, asked, "Where are you headed, Ilona?"

"A place you probably never heard of. It's a tiny village, called Bran."

"Now, isn't that a coincidence," said Tepes. "That's where we're going."

Lycan Thrope, who had not said a word until this point, simply sat looking melancholy, said, "My destination is also Bran."

Winterbottom noticed that Tepes kept staring at Szilagy as though mesmerized. He smiled. It seemed that his young boss had developed romantic feeling for the woman. He could not blame him. Although she was not really Winterbottom's type – he preferred robust healthy cheerleader type women – he had to admit that she was quite attractive in a wane sickly manner.

He said, "Since we are all headed for the same place, perhaps when we get to Brasov we can share whatever transportation is available."

"An excellent idea," Szilagy said. "You perhaps have never been in the area, but getting from Brasovto Bran can be difficult."

Thrope said, "I have my own means of travel." When he glanced at his watch, a panicky expression came over him. "This train is very slow. I hope we arrive before moonrise." He turned away and fixed his eyes on the scenery.

Winterbottom thought it was an odd turn of expression. Why moonrise?

Tepes said to Szilagy, "So you're familiar with Bran. Are you from there?"

"I have lived there on and off."

"Do you know a Vladislav Tepes?"

"Very well. Ah, I should've put two and two together. You are related?"

"Perhaps. That is what we are here to find out." He launched into the story of his parents' death and the mystery of his origin.

"I suppose your parents were trying protect you. You see, many people in the area do not like Prince Tepes, because of events long past and certain rumors about him."

"What rumors?" asked Winterbottom.

"I'd rather not say. I do not wish to spread gossip. You may judge for yourself what sort of man Prince Tepes is when you meet him."

The conversation turned to other subjects, finally becoming a flirtation between Tepes and Szilagy. Winterbottom became bored with it. Like Thrope he became engrossed in the scenery. In the beginning of the train trip, they had passed through lush farmland where everything was grown from corn and wheat to cabbage and turnips. In addition they passed several turbine wind farms. The tall wind turbines, which stood in even rows like soldiers at attention with their spinning propellers, seemed to Winterbottom to have their own sort of beauty.

After a while, however, as they entered the Carpathians, they passed through great forests of pine, ash and oak. The train chugged along through the heavily forested area and by many rivers and streams. Little towns and castles were placed precariously on the top of steep hills. Finally he was presented with a beautiful rosy sunset as the red globe rested for a few minutes on a mountain top.

As the sun slowly disappeared, Thrope became extremely agitated and nervous. He muttered in Romanian, "Will this damn train never reach Brasov?"

Winterbottom thought, *that fellow must have an important engagement.* "Pretty sunset," he said.

The others ignored his remark. Szilagy and Tepes were too busy chatting and giving each other admiring looks. Thrope was deep into whatever sorrow he had been contemplating.

Winterbottom returned to his scenery viewing. Although it grew darker, there was enough twilight to show that they were climbing steep cliffs and going through wild country. For a fleeting moment, he thought he spotted a great gray wolf. He was startled when Thrope let out a dog like growl.

Off in the distance he saw lightning flashes. A roll of thunder echoed in the hills. A light rain tapped against the window. The lights went on in the cabin making it impossible to see anything outside. A few minutes later, the conductor shouted in Romanian and English that the train was about to pull into the depot at Brasov.

On to Bran

The moment that the train halted, Thrope leaped up, grabbed his luggage and darted for the exit. "Nervous fellow," Winterbottom remarked.

Szilagy said, "It is because he has the mark of the pentagram on him."

"Pentagram? I didn't see any tattoos."

"It's invisible except for those of us with second sight. Don't worry about it. I'm probably being superstitious. Nonetheless, we're probably well off that we are rid of that fellow."

Tepes said, "He did seem to be an odd sort, like something was weighing on his mind. You never know with someone like that. They could snap at any moment."

Szilagy chuckled. "Here in Transylvania, you're likely to meet people like him fairly often."

They gathered their bags and left the train. Tepes politely carried Szilagy's suitcases, leaving Winterbottom to haul both his own and Tepes' luggage. As they stepped off the train, Winterbottom noticed Thrope running into the woods. He shook his head. "What an odd fellow."

They asked the station about transportation to Bran. He gave them a strange look and pointed towards the taxi stand. When the cab driver saw them approach, he flew out of the driver's seat, quickly stowed their luggage in the trunk, bowed and opened the rear door. Once they squeezed in the tiny backseat, he asked in Romanian where they wished to go. Szilagy, who was squished between Tepes and Winterbottom, replied, "The village of Bran. Do you know where it is?"

The cabby crossed himself. "I have been there once or twice. Are you tourists?"

"Sort of," Tepes replied. "My ancestors may have come from this area. I'm visiting someone with my family name."

The driver started the ancient Dacia with a grinding noise. It wheezed onto a road that led into the mountains. "What is your family name, young man?"

"Tepes."

The cab driver took one hand off the wheel to make the sign of the cross again. "You are to visit the prince then?"

"If you mean Prince Vladislav Tepes."

The man shuddered. "I cannot bring you all the way to the castle."

Winterbottom thought, *so the prince lives in a castle. This should be interesting.*

"That's all right. Just drop us off in the village somewhere. He said he would send someone for us."

"May God protect you," the cabby muttered.

As they headed up a narrow badly paved road, the storm that had been threatening all day broke. The rain came down so hard that the windshield wipers struggled to keep the vision clear. As a result the driver came near to steering off the edge of the narrow road several times in an area of steep cliffs. Winterbottom gulped and felt the blood drain from his face as one wheel went over the edge. Szilagy and Tepes were too interested in each other to notice.

Winterbottom was amazed and grateful that they had made it safely to Bran when the taxi pulled up in front of an inn. Tepes paid the driver, leaving a substantial tip, and the trio splashed through the mud to the entrance. The cabby swiftly unloaded their luggage, brought it into the inn and quickly drove away.

The Bran Inn was homey place with a low wood beam ceiling, crude stucco walls, an enormous fireplace crackling with flames and tables covered with checkered tablecloths and a small bar. The odor of alcohol and cigarette smoke permeated the room. Two men in crude baggy trousers, colorful peasant jackets and caps sat at the bar nursing large steins of beer and conversing in low tones. They paid no attention to the trio who had entered.

The bartender, however, a portly man with a large gray moustache and wearing an apron, came from behind the bar and greeted the strangers. "*Bun zi doamna si domn. Pot ajutor tu?*"

Winterbottom asked, "Do you speak English?"

"A little bit. You are English?"

"Americans actually, except Miss Szilagy."

"You are tourists then?"

"In a way. Actually we are here to visit Prince Vladislav Tepes."

When they heard that name, the two men at the bar stared at the newcomers with fear in their expressions.

The bartender's eyes went wide, and he took a step back. "You are friends of der prince?"

"Not exactly. We haven't met him yet but have been invited to his home."

The man waved his hands in a negative manner. "You not want go there."

Tepes asked, "Why not, my good man?"

"Things could happen. Better you return to America." Like the cab driver, he made the sign of the cross.

Szilagy whispered to Tepes and Winterbottom, "These village people are superstitious. Ignore him." To the bartender, she said in Romanian, "Please stop trying to frighten these people and show us to a table. Then bring three cups of coffee." She gave him an evil look. He hurried to obey.

After they were served their coffee, Winterbottom took out his cell phone and punched in the number that Vladislav had sent in his e-mail. The phone rang for a long time. Finally, the voice mail answered in Romanian, "Prince Vladislav Tepes is unavailable. After the beep, please leave your name and number. He will get back to you after sunset."

Winterbottom gave Robert Tepes' name and his own cell phone number. "Nobody home right now. Perhaps we should have some dinner. I'm starved."

Szilagy snapped her fingers. The bartender came at run. She asked for menus, which he quickly supplied. With Szilagy's aid, the two men chose the type of goulash they wanted. Winterbottom said, "How is the local wine hereabouts?"

"Excellent. Red or white, gentlemen?"

Winterbottom chose red and Tepes chose white. Two bottles and glasses were brought to the table. As they ate and chatted, the storm outside grew worse. Intermittent lightning and thunder crashed and echoed. The rain rattled on the inn's tin roof like machine gun fire. Cold drafts made them grateful for the flaming logs in the fireplace.

As they enjoyed their meal, the inn became darker and gloomier. After a while the innkeeper came around and lit candles at each table. The flickering of the candles cast weird dancing shadows on the walls. Every few minutes a flash of lightning made everything in the room become visible for a second or two. Afterward the room and its inhabitants faded into gloom, leaving only an afterglow on the retinas.

Winterbottom shivered as a damp chill penetrated the walls. They conducted their conversation in low tones, which started and halted as though they were anticipating a strange eldritch event.

Winterbottom's cell phone played The Jefferson Airplane's *Somebody to Love* loudly He fished it from his jacket. "Charlie Winterbottom here."

A voice with a thick accent tonelessly enunciated each English syllable slowly. "Do I have the cor-rect party? I wish to speak to Rob-ert Tepes."

"Just a moment." Winterbottom covered the mouthpiece with his hand. "I think it's Vladislav." He handed the phone to Robert.

"Robert Tepes here." A pause. "Yes, we're at the Bran Inn." Another pause. "You'll send someone at midnight." Pause. "Who is with me? My friend, Charles Winterbottom and a woman named Ilona Szilagy."

He turned to Szilagy. "Vladislav sends his greetings. He's looking forward to seeing you again."

Szilagy chuckled. "Perhaps he won't be so happy when he sees what I have for him. Don't tell him that. Just say that I'm looking forward to our reunion too."

Tepes repeated into the phone what Szilagy had said. After another pause, he said, "See you then." He folded up the phone and handed it back to Winterbottom. "Someone will pick us up at midnight." He looked at his watch. "We have a couple of hours to kill."

The bartender, who had been eavesdropping, said, "You cannot stay here. I do not want the one who comes for you in here."

Winterbottom protested. "But it's raining cats and dogs outside, and he won't be here for two more hours."

Szilagy said, "The rain has slowed. Let us leave where we are not wanted."

Tepes paid the tab, and they left. As they walked out the door, Winterbottom heard the bartender remark to the barflies, "Poor souls. They do not know what they are in for. The prince is cunning, sending *her* to lure them to Bran Castle."

The Gypsy Fortune Teller

Szilagy put her hand out. "See. The rain has slowed to a drizzle. Look. The clouds are breaking up. You can see a few stars and a full moon."

At that moment wolves in the forest began to bay.

Tepes said, "A full moon. How romantic." He placed an arm around Szilagy to protect her from the chill wind.

Winterbottom said, "But what are we going to do for the next two hours. We'll be chilled to the bone."

Szilagy pointed to a large wooden house-like wagon parked about thirty meters down the road. "Roma. Why don't we get our fortunes told?"

Tepes said, "Splendid idea. Perhaps I can find out whether Prince

Vladislav is really related to me."

"You would believe a gypsy fortuneteller?" asked Winterbottom.

"Well, let's go anyway. It's better than standing in the cold."

They strolled up to the wagon and knocked. A swarthy man with an enormous moustache, long black hair and a colorful vest opened the door. He asked in Romanian, "What do you want?"

Szilagy said, "According to the sign on the wagon, you tell fortunes."

"That is my wife's business. Come in, please."

He ushered them through what was their kitchen and sleeping area to another room created by a bead curtain stretched across the wagon. It contained a small round table covered by a colorful fringed cloth and several wooden chairs. Flickering candles on every flat surface in the chamber gave off a thick cloud of over-sweet fumes. A beautiful young woman in an off-the-shoulder blouse and brightly colored skirt sat darning stockings. "Esmeralda, customers." He returned to the other room where from the odors Winterbottom assumed that he had been cooking a cabbage dish that required much garlic.

Esmeralda came to her feet. "You each wish to have knowledge of future events. Who wants to go first?"

Szilagy said, "Robert, why don't you go first. I know you are anxious to know what the results of your meeting with the prince will be."

"Very well. I will do the young man. Please. All of you, please sit by my table."

They each pulled a chair near the table. Esmeralda took out a crystal and set in front of her seat. "Now, young man, tell me what question you would like answered."

"I want to know whether the person I am to meet tonight is really who he says he may be."

"I understand. Give me your hand." Tepes held it out for her. She turned his palm up and examined it. "Ah. I see that you are from the upper classes. According to your lifeline, there is a mystery about your origin. Also, you have experienced tragedy at an early age. I see that women are attracted to you." She fluttered her eyelashes at him

Szilagy gave her a dirty look. "Those things are obvious," she muttered.

Esmeralda ignored her. She let go of Tepes' hand and peered into her crystal. "I see that the man you are about to meet has a dark past. There is an air of mystery about him. Many things are hidden in the shadows. Nonetheless, many of his secrets will be revealed. However, there is danger in the path you have chosen." She raised her eyes to Tepes again. "That is all I can tell you. Much is hidden. Be wary of the man. He will try to conceal his real nature."

There was a pounding noise in the other room for a while. Esmeralda said, "Ignore that. My husband is doing repair work on the wagon. Who wishes to be next?"

Szilagy poked Winterbottom. "You go."

Winterbottom put out his hand. Esmeralda took it. "I see that you have traveled much and have had many adventures. Nonetheless, many revelations are still to come. You will learn to believe in things you assumed were impossible, and your faith in science will be shaken. Ah, I also see that you consider yourself to be a lady's man." She gazed into Winterbottom's eyes, which had a strange affect on him. Maybe not so strange, since she was an attractive, well-rounded woman. He had this sudden desire to kiss her. She turned away before he could act on his impulse.

She continued, "This belief that all women are attracted to you has gotten you in trouble in the past. Be very wary of who you go after. For example, should you try to seduce a married woman, you could be in deadly danger if she had a jealous husband who easily loses his temper … like mine."

Winterbottom blushed.

Esmeralda let go of his hand. "And what question would you like me to answer?"

"I am on mission for my employer. Will it be successful?"

She gazed into the crystal again. "Your future is cloudy. I see two possible outcomes. One will be disastrous and cause you to lose your most precious life and even your soul. In the second, you will be called a hero and have many more adventures in your life. Your biggest danger is your love of women as I've told you before. Beware those who tempt you."

"And now you, young lady."

Szilagy chuckled. "I'm neither young nor a lady." She held out her hand.

Esmeralda examined it. "Your lifeline is extremely long. In fact I see no end to it. However, it is broken at one point, as if you finished one life and started an altogether different one. You have parted ways with someone you loved in the past." She looked up at Szilagy. "I see that you are nervous about a reunion. What is your question?"

"I am wondering how the person whom I have come to see will receive me."

The psychic consulted her crystal again. "Not well, I'm afraid. Darkness will try to overwhelm you. I see a new love coming into your life. Danger is ever present. Whether you will overcome it is in doubt. Perhaps the new love will be your guardian." She glanced sideways at Tepes. "That is all I can say at this time."

Winterbottom glanced at his watch. "Good. I'm afraid it is time for us to leave. It's quarter to twelve."

Tepes asked, "How much do we owe you?"

"Whatever you think my revelations and advice is worth?"

He handed her several large bills. Her eyes went wide, and she grinned widely. "Thank you very much." She grabbed his hand and kissed it. "Come again, any time."

They wished her a good night. She held the beads to allow them to pass. Her husband sat on a rocker smoking a thin cigar. Winterbottom saw what the hammering had been. Great ropes of garlic, silver crucifixes and pentagrams hung from many places in the room. "You people are leaving now?"

"We are expecting someone to meet us."

"Be careful of wolves."

Esmeralda repeated the warning. "They are most dangerous when the moon is full."

They exited the wagon. Winterbottom peered around. He thought he saw red eyes at the edge of the woods reflecting the moonlight. He recalled the howling he had heard earlier and shuddered. With caution, they strolled back to the inn. Their luggage was piled outside. They could see no light from its windows. Apparently, it was closed for the night. The silence at midnight in that lonely place made him nervous.

Bran Castle

The quiet did not last long. From a long way off, Winterbottom heard hoof beats. They grew steadily louder. Suddenly, four black horses pulling a carriage thundered around a curve in the road at a reckless speed and screeched to a halt in front of them. The coachman was all in black with a hood that hid his face. He did not get down to help with the luggage. As a result, Winterbottom had to climb up to the top of the carriage and had Tepes hand him the bags which he secured to the luggage rack.

By the time Winterbottom leaped down and entered the coach, Tepes and Szilagy were already seated. The moment he closed the door, the coachman cracked his whip, and the horses started off as though being chased by wild animals. He was thrown into his seat by the lurch. "My, this fellow likes to drive fast."

The coach swayed and rocked like a ship on a stormy sea. The passengers clung to straps to escape being thrown about the interior. Despite the noisy clopping of the horse's hooves and squeaking of the wagon, Winterbottom swore he heard growling and barking. He put his head out of the window. Trailing them was a pack of the largest wolves that he had ever seen. He thought, no wonder the gypsies warned us about wolves, and the coachman drove the steeds so hard. He turned to Szilagy and Tepes to tell them about the wolves, but they had their arms around each other, kissing.

Winterbottom thought about Esmeralda's warning to not allow himself be carried away by temptation. *She should've warned Robert, as well.*

The trail up the mountain was steep and had hair raising serpentine curves and switchbacks. Nonetheless, the coachman kept whipping the team, and they sped ever faster with the coach swaying back and forth inches away from falling into the chasm below. It halted in front of Bran Castle, a bleak medieval fortress with many tower and turrets. To reach it, a moat needed to be crossed. As soon as a drawbridge was lowered and a gate of iron bars was raised, the coachman's whip snapped and the coach sped into a courtyard.

As the trio exited the coach, the iron bar gate clanged shut and the drawbridge was raised again. There would be no turning back. The coachman tossed down their luggage and drove around to the back of the castle. Winterbottom stared at the bleak edifice before him. Its bleak Gothic design of dark stone blocks was daunting. As he and his companions hauled their luggage toward the great oaken doors with iron straps, a flock of large bats flying off the roof were silhouetted by the silver glow of the moon.

Winterbottom banged the huge knockers on the double doors. After several minutes, they squealed open on rusty hinges. A servant with a twisted body ushered them into the main hall. "The master will be with you shortly. He has been expecting you." The man spoke English with a heavy Romanian accent. He took their luggage and climbed the stone staircase.

Winterbottom looked around. The anteroom was large with stone walls covered with tapestries depicting medieval scenes, knights in battle against a Saracen army, a prince being crowned by a bishop in church, rows of persons being impaled and a pastoral scene with the castle in the background. Light came from an iron candle chandelier hung from the high ceiling by a chain. Two high back wooden chairs faced each other on opposite walls. The cold dampness of the chamber made it feel tomb-like. It had not been cleaned for a long time, for enormous cobwebs hung from the ceiling.

"Spooky place," remarked Tepes, shivering slightly.

Szilagy said, "You get that feeling at first. After you're here for a while, you'll get used to it."

A tall man entered from a door in the rear and approached with his hand extended in greeting. He had a thin face as pale as death with bulging eyes His thick waxed moustache ran from cheek to cheek, and his long black curls brushed his shoulders. His jeweled cap had an eight-pointed star at the peak. Like the person Winterbottom had spoken to on the phone earlier, he had a thick accent and pronounced every syllable with the same intonation. "My guests from Am-er-i-ca, I greet you warm-ly. I am Prince Vlad Tepes. Which of you gen-tle-men is Rob-ert?"

Robert stepped forward and shook Vlad's hand, "I'm Robert Tepes and am pleased to meet you. However, I was under the impression that your given name was Vladislav."

Vlad smiled grimly. "I use that name with west-er-ners be-cause of the bad rep-u-ta-tion of my an-ces-tor ... known as the Imp-al-er, as you well know. Al-though he has been much mal-igned, man-y in this part of the world re-gard him as the great her-o who saved Wes-tern Eur-ope from the Turks."

"Ah yes, I know the history well. He was brutal in his methods, but as you say, kept the Turks at bay. You have traced your ancestry directly to him?"

"I have an an-cient bi-ble where all is re-cord-ed."

"That's great. Perhaps it will show whether we are really related. But, I am being impolite. I want to introduce my companions. This is Ilona Szilagy."

Vlad chuckled. "Il-ona and I know each other well. I am sur-prised to see you here, my dear."

"We will speak of the reason for my visit later, my prince, since it is a private matter."

Robert said, "And this is my friend, Doctor Charles Winterbottom."

Vlad's eyebrows raised. "Not the fa-mous arche-olo-gist?"

Winterbottom took Vlad's hand. It was as cold and clammy as a corpse's. "That's me. My friends call me Charlie."

"Then I hope we will be good friends in time, Char-lie. Wel-come to Bran Cas-tle. All of you. Please foll-ow me to the din-ing room. I have had the ser-vants pre-pare din-ner. My other guests are wait-ing."

Dinner at Bran Castle

When they entered the dining room, the other guests came forward to greet them. A short middle aged man in an ordinary brown suit was first in line. He wore thick spectacles which made his eyes seem enormous. He had an extremely high forehead and thick bushy eyebrows.

Vlad said, "May I pre-sent Doc-tor Bor-is Siv-an-a. He is a med-i-cal doc-tor in case any of you be-come ill." For some reason he thought this funny and chuckled. Winterbottom, Robert and Ilona each shook his hand and introduced themselves.

Next to grasp their hands was a younger man with long brown hair, a van dyke and wearing a sport coat, a T-shirt and jeans. Vlad introduced him as Laslo Varga, a distant cousin from Hungary. Varga clicked his heels and bowed.

Winterbottom asked, "And what's your occupation?"

"I am in the Hungarian parliament. Are you interested in politics, Doctor Winterbottom?"

"I am, but am away from the States too much to get involved."

"Perhaps later, we could discuss current events."

Vlad said, "Ah Char-lie, I would not take him up on his off-er if I were you. Las-lo is Hung-ar-ian, and you know how they like to ar-gue."

The three women were young in appearance and beautiful but thin and pale. Bianka was a brunette, Gizella had dark red hair, and Julianna was blonde. Vlad did not say what their family names were.

Winterbottom said, "What a pleasant surprise to meet such beautiful young ladies here."

All three giggled and gazed at him hungrily in a manner that made him uncomfortable. Gizella said, "And we are happy to meet such a handsome and famous man. We have heard much about your red-blooded exploits." She licked her lips.

Bianka said, "And look how he blushes. I can only imagine how the blood rushes to his head when he makes love."

Julianna smiled broadly and winked at him. Winterbottom noticed that her canines were extremely long and pointed.

Vlad said, "Now, now, girls. Don't be greedy. Leave the poor fellow alone."

The servant with the twisted neck entered the room from another door. "Dinner is served, master."

"Let us take our seats, please," said Vlad. He held the chair for Szilagy. Robert, Winterbottom and Varga did the same for the three younger women. The seating arrangement was thus: Vlad sat at the end with Szilagy on his right and Robert on his left. Varga sat next to Szilagy and Bianka sat on Robert's left. Winterbottom sat on her left, Julianna was to his left, and Gizella was across the table from him. Sivana sat at her right.

As a result Winterbottom was surrounded by the three young ladies. Although in most situations, this would delight him, something about these women gave him the creeps. Perhaps it was the greedy way they stared at the veins in his throat or perhaps the cold clammy feel of their hands when he touched them. He recalled the gypsy psychic Esmeralda's warning about his impetuousness with women getting him into trouble. Nonetheless, when they kept flirting with him, by habit he flirted back.

They were interrupted when the first course of dinner was served. To Winterbottom's amazement, the servant who served it was Jeeves (AKA Larke). As the android set the soup in front of him and poured his wine, he whispered, "Larke. What are you doing here?"

Larke (AKA Jeeves) replied in a low voice, "It's Jeeves now. I had a falling out with my last employer. It's difficult getting work in the US when you're an AI. I answered an ad to work for Prince Tepes. So here I am."

He backed away and continued to serve the other guests and Vlad.

Winterbottom slurped a spoonful of soup. "Um. This is very good. I don't think I've ever tasted soup with this particular flavor before. What is it?"

"Blood soup," Vlad replied. "I am glad you like it."

Winterbottom thought, *blood soup and the young ladies talking about my blood. I wonder why the subject of blood keeps coming up.* Mention of blood actually made him uncomfortable. He hated the sight of it, especially if it came from a puncture of his own skin. There was also the particular pastiness of Vlad's and the ladies' skins, as though they were never in sunlight. Certain suspicions came to him that he dismissed as superstitious nonsense. There were no such things as ... Even in his own mind, he did not name where his thoughts had led him.

Vlad remarked to Robert, "Tell me about your-self. Who were your par-ents? Per-haps we can de-ter-mine wheth-er we are act-ual-ly re-lated."

"Their names were Irma and Wolfgang. However, I don't know what my mother's maiden name was. In fact, I know almost nothing about them. I'm not even sure that they came from Romania."

"Act-ual-ly this part of Ro-ma-ni-a was part of the Hung-ar-ian-Aust-ri-an Em-pire be-fore World War One. It was a-ward-ed to Ro-ma-ni-a at the end of the war. Ear-li-er in its his-to-ry it was the in-de-pend-ent state of Tran-syl-va-nia. But, of course, you knew that."

Robert nodded.

"Jeeves," Vlad called. When the android appeared, he said, "Fetch the fam-i-ly Bi-ble, the one with all the names on the fly-leaf."

The fact that Vlad was going to pour through a Bible relieved Winterbottom of his suspicions. If he were really one of those mythical creatures, he could not touch anything holy, such as a Bible. At least that was what the authors who wrote about such legends wrote.

The bible came with the salad. No salad bowls were placed before the three young women or Vlad. Robert also did not eat much of his salad either, because he and Vlad were studying the Bible. Several pages were devoted to lists of members of the Tepes family, which included their birth, marriage and death dates. The Bible was hand written and beautifully illustrated by monks. The names in the front started with Vlad II Dracula, who was The Impaler's father and was born in the fifteenth century. The names were numerous and added all through the centuries including people born in the early twenty-first century. Many were rulers of Walachia. The last entry was the marriage of Wolfgang Tepes to Irma Karloff. A footnote gave the date of their emigration to America.

"Ah, there they are," said Vlad. "It seems that you are a dir-ect des-cen-dant of the fam-ily who ruled Wall-ach-ia for cent-ur-ies. We are def-in-ite-ly cous-ins."

"Apparently. But I don't see your name listed here. There is no Vlad or Vladislav listed in the twenty-first century."

"An over-sight by my par-ents. They are these Tepes." He pointed at an entry. "Which makes me your sec-ond cous-in, I be-lieve."

Jeeves entered with the main course, which was a sausage goulash and noodles. When Winterbottom tasted the sausage, he was pleasantly surprised at its flavor. The spices were quite mild, yet it tasted exquisite. "What do you call this sausage?"

"*Singe cirnati,*" replied Vlad.

Winterbottom tried to recall what that would be in English. Finally it came to him. It was blood sausage. He lost his appetite.

The desert was sweet bread with raisins and nuts. Coffee and brandy were also served. When everyone had finished desert, Vlad said, "I imag-ine you are wear-y after your trav-els. Would you like Jeeves to show you to your rooms?"

A Night of Strange Happenings

The entire company agreed. Vlad called Jeeves. As the travelers followed him upstairs, Winterbottom said, "So Jeeves, what have you been doing since we left Woodstock?"

"For a while I was employed as a combination butler, housekeeper and accountant for a writer. However, we had personal differences. When my contract was up, he let me go. I tried freelance writing myself for a while, but could not make a go of it. That is when I answered Prince Tepes' ad on the Internet."

"How is he to work for?"

"I have no trouble. He is a lenient master. But I would not trust him too much if I were you. His bite is worse than his bark."

"What do you mean?"

"Lock your windows and doors tonight."

Winterbottom could not get the android to say more, but decided to follow its advice. Since his room was at the end of the hall, he wished Robert and Szilagy goodnight as they went into adjoining rooms.

His own chamber was dark and depressing, and a musty odor permeated it. Since the castle did not have electricity, the only lighting was by flickering candles and a dying fire in the fireplace. The outer wall was cold damp stone with a shuttered window hung with heavy drapes. The other three walls were of dark paneling and hung with portraits of people in ancient costumes, whose eyes followed him wherever in the room he went. The furnishings were a four-poster bed with dark heavy bedclothes, an antique wardrobe, a desk and a dresser.

Exhausted, he undressed, turned back the comforter and crawled into bed. As soon as he closed his eyes, he heard the howling of wolves outside, and the high pitched squeal of bats. Although bright moonlight shined through the window, he fell asleep quickly.

He had a dream. In his dream, he was in the trailer of the gypsies, sitting across from Esmeralda. Her crystal was in front of her, and she stared at him with large dark luminous eyes. He smiled at her. "What big eyes you have, my dear. Where's your husband?"

"Djordji is away on business."

"That's interesting. Perhaps his absence will allow us to get to know each other better."

She wagged her finger at him. "If you continue your womanizing, you will be in deep trouble. Look into the crystal to see your fate."

Winterbottom peered into the crystal. He saw himself and Esmeralda in her bed in the nude. As he reached for her, the trailer door opened, and Djordji burst in with a dagger in his hand. He and Winterbottom grappled and fought for a while. Finally, he got in a lucky punch and knocked his opponent out. He grabbed his clothes and rushed out into a moonlit forest. He took ten steps out of the trailer and was attacked by a wolf. He fought off the wolf using Djordji's silver dagger. It ran away with a deep wound. He dressed quickly and looked around for a path back to the castle. Suddenly a whole flock of large bats attacked him. He ran and ran, sweating and puffing. His legs felt leaden, but dared not stop. He tripped and fell.

He awoke from the nightmare, drenched with perspiration and twisted up in the comforter. "It was the paprika in the blood sausage goulash," he muttered. He belched a couple of times and felt better. As he snuggled back under the feather-stuffed comforter, he heard the knob on the bedroom door rattle. The door opened slowly. He had forgotten to lock it. Stealthy footsteps padded across the room toward the bed. The hair on the back of his neck stood on end. Was it Djordji coming to kill him for flirting with his wife? No. That was in the dream. He reached over and lit the candle on the nightstand.

A pale face surrounded by dark hair approached him. It was Bianka. She wore a thin transparent nighty through which her nipples and pubic hair were visible. She smiled broadly. Like Julianna, her incisors were long and pointed.

"Bianka. What are you doing here?"

"What do you think, you vital robust man? I want to sleep with you." She placed a hand on his cheek. It was cold and clammy with long pointed fingernails.

"Uh, don't you think we should first get to know each other better?"

Before she could reply, the bedroom door opened again. More bare feet padded across the floor. Bianka and Winterbottom turned to see who had entered. It was Gizella. She too wore a see-through nightgown.

"Stay away, Gizella. I was here first."

"What does that have to do with anything? I saw how he admired me at dinner." She addressed Winterbottom. "Who do you want in your bed, Doctor Winterbottom, me or Bianka?"

"Well, really ladies, I'm very tired tonight. Besides ..."

Julianna strolled into the room, also mostly undressed. "You two get away from him. Everyone knows that gentlemen prefer blondes."

"According to you," Gizella said sarcastically.

"Please ladies, I've got a headache."

The three women looked at him hungrily. Their eyes were big and bore into him. He felt immobilized and unable to fight against what was going to happen next.

"You take the left, and I'll take the right," Gizella said to Bianka.

"Hey, what about me?" cried Julianna.

"You can have the leavings."

"The hell with that." She grabbed Gizella by the hair and yanked her back away from Winterbottom.

Gizella took a swing at her but missed and hit Bianka in the nose. This started a free-for-all. The women punched, bit and scratched each other, tearing their gowns and rolling around on the floor. They screamed and cursed each other.

Meanwhile, Winterbottom was too stunned to do anything. When the ladies of the night had gazed into his eyes, it had mesmerized him. He felt that he had no choice but to obey whichever one won the fight.

While the cat-fight raged on, Vlad stomped into the room. "What the hell is all the rack-et? My guests are try-ing to sleep. Bi-an-ka. Giz-ell-a. Jul-ian-na. Stop im-med-iate-ly."

The women ceased fighting and rose to their feet. They curtsied and said in unison, "Yes, master."

"Get out of here and leave this man a-lone."

The women left, which lifted the spell they had on Winterbottom.

Vlad said, "I'm sor-ry if they both-er-ed you. I will pun-ish them. Are you all right?"

"I'm fine. They are certainly three wild ladies though. I never expected them to come into my room like that."

"I'll see that you are not dis-turb-ed any-more this night. Good-night, Doc-tor Wint-er-bot-tom. Sleep tight and do not let the un-dead bite." He chuckled.

"What?"

"Oh, just an old Tran-syl-va-ni-an joke."

He strolled out of the room, pulling the door shut behind him.

Winterbottom tried to go back to sleep, but images of the three women floated before his mind's eye. Also, the wolves started baying at the moon again.

The Morning After

Bright sunlight and someone knocking at his door awakened Winterbottom, who had finally fallen back asleep after hours of restlessness. He heard Jeeves mechanical voice. "Breakfast will be served in the main dining room at ten thirty."

Winterbottom glanced at his watch. It was a bit after ten. Since he was hungry, he decided to rise although he was still sleepy or mesmerized. He showered, retrieved fresh clothes from his suitcase and left his room. On the way to the stairway he met Robert. The man looked terrible. He had dark rings under his eyes, his hair was not combed, and he had not shaved.

"Are you all right, Robert?"

"Didn't get much sleep last night." He lowered his voice. "Ilona came to my room last night. We made love for hours. She's quite a woman. I actually feel weak, as though I had lost blood."

Winterbottom noticed what looked like two punctures wounds on his throat. "What are those marks on your neck?"

Robert grinned. "As I said Ilona is some wild lover. She's a biter."

Winterbottom had his suspicions. Yet, he had seen Ilona in daylight. She could not possibly be one of those mythical creatures.

When they entered the dining room, Varga and Sivana were already seated and indulging in a heated discussion. They ceased when Winterbottom and Robert entered. "Good morning, gentlemen," they said almost together. They both rose and bowed.

"Good morning, Laslo and Boris."

They all took seats, and Jeeves brought in a breakfast of crepes filled with strawberries and cream and strong black coffee in small cups. In addition, a bowl of fruit was set out.

Winterbottom asked, "Where is our host and the three young ladies that we dined with yesterday evening?"

Varga said, "Oh them. They are night people. I doubt whether you will see them before sunset. Boris and I were discussing whether it was possible to bring a person back from the dead other than by a miracle such as our savior has performed. My opinion is that even if it were possible, since the soul has fled, the resurrected body would a soulless monster. What do you think Doctor Winterbottom?"

"Charlie, please. I think it depends on how much the brain had deteriorated." He thought, *these people certainly have morbid thoughts, always talking about blood and dead people.*

Sivana said, "I understand that. But suppose a fresh brain were inserted in the body first. In other words, a brain transplant, much like a heart or kidney transplant."

Robert said, "I don't understand why such an operation would occur."

"Well," Sivana explained, "suppose a relatively young man died of a brain injury and an elderly man with decaying organs were in the same hospital. If one obtained the consent of the senior and the young man's relatives, you could transplant the brain of the older man into the young one's body." He licked his lips. "It's a win-win situation. The older man would get a younger healthy body, and the young man's relatives would get to see their loved one alive."

Winterbottom said, "But his personality would not be the same. In fact it may not be the same as it was in the older man either, since other organs than the brain have an affect on emotions."

"Very acute observation. You have studied the biology of human beings?"

"Somewhat. I wouldn't say studied exactly although I've read books on the subject."

Varga crossed himself. "What a horrible thought, one man's brain in another man's body. And what of his soul?"

Robert said, "I agree with Laslo. The whole idea sounds macabre to me. The older man's brain would be quite confused, and as Laslo said, probably without a soul."

Sivana said, "I don't believe in the soul. What we conceive as ego is simply electronic and chemical signals firing in our brain and other organs."

This discussion was interrupted by a loud pounding at the front door of the castle. Jeeves went to answer it. A few minutes, he ushered in a disheveled young man. His hair was wild, his clothes were torn and dirt encrusted, and he was barefoot. To Winterbottom's amazement, it was Lycan Thrope, the man they had met on the train.

Thrope rushed up to Sivana. "Doctor Sivana, I'm so glad you're here. Remember that operation you said you would perform? I decided to go ahead with it."

"Good my boy. We will go over the details after breakfast. You look terrible. What happened to you?"

"The usual. I told you how I'm affected by the full moon. We discussed all that over the phone. This time I not only lost my shoes, but my luggage as well."

Sivana patted him on the arm. "I understand. Please have breakfast with us." He turned to Jeeves. "Set another place, and bring more crepes."

"Yes, master." There seemed to be a bit of irony in Jeeves tone.

Thrope sat down and had breakfast with them. The conversation turned to other subjects. Winterbottom noticed that whatever opinion Sivana expressed, or anyone else for that matter, Varga disagreed with them. The man simply liked to argue and loudly at that.

The Cemetery

After breakfast, Sivana and Thrope went to another part of the castle. Robert said, "I wonder whether Ilona is awake yet."

As if she had heard him, she walked into the dining room at the moment wearing sunglasses and a modest dress. "Good morning, Robert, Charlie and Laslo." She went over and kissed Robert on the lips.

Robert said, "Are you hungry my dear?"

"I am. What's for breakfast?"

"Crepes." Robert pointed to the empty crepe platter. "Jeeves, bring more crepes, please."

"Yes, master." The android took the empty platter and went through the kitchen door.

After Szilagy finished her breakfast, she said, "It's a beautiful day, Robert. Would you like to take a walk with me?"

"Of course, darling." Robert rose from his chair.

"Why don't you two come along?" Szilagy said to Winterbottom and Varga.

This invitation surprised Winterbottom. He would've thought that she would want to be alone with Robert. Nonetheless, he accepted.

Varga, on the other hand, said, "You call this a beautiful day? It's chilly and overcast. Leave me out of your plans. I am going to the library to read."

Szilagy whispered to Robert and Winterbottom, "I knew he would not go with us after I said it was a beautiful day. I know his type. He must disagree, always."

They went out a side door that led to the garden. Vargas was right; the day was overcast.. A chill wind blew. The garden was unkempt. Flowers and shrubs grew wildly, and it needed weeding desperately. Also, the choice of plants was odd. There were such items as deadly nightshade, skunk cabbage, and opium poppies. Altogether there was an air of rotten evil about the grounds.

Szilagy said, "Now that I have you two away from the house where no one can hear us, I want to tell you the truth about Vlad and myself. First I need to show you something."

Robert said, "What do you mean by Vlad and yourself? Are you more than friends?"

She laid a hand on his cheek. "It's nothing like what you're thinking. Have patience, dear Robert."

Winterbottom was also curious. He wondered whether there was anything to his suspicions, as incredible as they seemed. "Do you know anything about the three young women we met yesterday evening?"

"Not directly. But I can guess. Come with me. What I have to show you may answer both your questions."

She led them through the garden to the rear of the castle. An iron fence set off a family plot. They went through the gate into the cemetery, a jumble of grave markers, carved angels and crosses, and a couple of large mausoleums. Szilagy led them to the largest of these which was in the style of an ancient Greek temple. As she opened the carved brass door, it screeched like a banshee. Once inside Winterbottom was struck by the musty odor of the long dead. With the door closed, the thick stone walls muffled all sound except their footsteps and the pounding of his heart. They were in utter darkness until Szilagy turned on a flashlight. .

There were six stone sarcophagi. Szilagy said, "Look at the name on the largest tomb." She pointed with the light beam.

Winterbottom and Robert peered at the carved name and dates at the end of the sarcophagus. It read, "Prince Vlad Tepes Dracula III. 1431-1476 He who pierced many and drove away the Turks is buried here."

"Why, it's the tomb of the Vlad the Impaler. I thought he was supposed to be interred at a monastery in Snagov."

"In the nineteen thirties, archeologists opened his supposed resting place. They found the tomb empty. Apparently his corpse had been moved, perhaps to here. Shall we have a look at his bones?"

Robert said, "I don't think we should desecrate his grave."

"What do you say, Doctor Winterbottom? As an archeologist, I assume you've opened the tombs of historical characters before."

"I have, in the interests of obtaining artifacts of historical importance." Her gaze held his, and he began to hear little whispers in his mind, "You want to open it. You must see what's inside." He suddenly had an overwhelming desire to see what was hidden in the sarcophagus. "Yes. Let's have a peek ... for science."

It took all three of them to shove the heavy stone to the side enough to peer into the sarcophagus. To Winterbottom's utter amazement and dread, instead of bones or dust, what seemed to be a fresh corpse lay there. And it resembled their host, the present day Vlad Tepes.

"What is going on here?" cried Robert. "That's my cousin. But he's dead."

"Not really dead," said Szilagy. "Undead. He is not your cousin. He is your ancestor, Vlad the Impaler as written on his tomb. Come now, let's look at the other tombs."

They examined three other sarcophagi. The names on them were Bianka Baboescu, Gizella Zeklos and Juliana Georgescu. There were no dates. Winterbottom cried, "Those are the names of the three women we met yesterday."

She pointed the flashlight at another tomb. The carving on it read Ilona Szilagy 1497-. There was no date of death. "That's my tomb. If you were to open it, you would find it empty."

Robert said, "I'm confused. You're obviously not six hundred years old."

"I'm sorry, but I am. You see, I'm Vlad Tepes' daughter."

"But that doesn't make sense," said Winterbottom. "According to his tomb, Vlad Tepes died in 1476. How could you be born twenty-one years after he died?"

"The year 1476 was the year he became a vampire. He seduced my mother soon after. She became pregnant so he did not turn her into one of the undead. I am the result of that seduction. I am neither human nor vampire, but a half-breed. I do not crave blood, but am immortal. Direct sunlight hurts my eyes, and my reflection in a mirror is fuzzy."

Robert said, "All this is mind boggling." And then in any angry voice, "I can't believe I made love to my ancestor. You tempted me into incest."

"No Robert. I am not your ancestor. I never had children. If Vlad Tepes is really your ancestor, it would have to be through some other woman before he became a vampire, not my mother."

Winterbottom said, "So we've been the guests of the famous vampire known as Dracula. And Bianka, Gizella and Juliana are vampires too. I had my suspicions."

"You're correct."

"What does he want from us? To drain our blood and make us into vampires too?" *Somehow that doesn't make sense,* he thought. *He saved me from his vampire mistresses and did not try to suck my blood himself.* He felt faint when he thought of how close he came to losing blood.

Szilagy shrugged. "I couldn't say. The Prince has a Machiavellian mind. He might've invited Robert here for another purpose."

"And why are you in Bran?" asked Robert. "It was a strange coincidence that you and Thrope were in the same train compartment as us. Are you part of a conspiracy to make sure we arrived?"

"Absolutely not. Although Dracula is my father, he is my enemy. Nonetheless, I am glad you are here. I like you a lot. And you can help me with my plan."

"What plan?"

"To destroy him." She opened her purse and removed a wooden stake and a hammer. "He is evil incarnate. As his daughter, I could not ... do it myself. One of you must."

Winterbottom took the tools from her. "Although Vlad has behaved as a perfect gentleman toward us, he did impale all those people in the fifteenth century and deserves a similar fate himself. I'll do it." He went toward Vlad's sarcophagus.

Robert said, "Somehow this seems too easy. You would think that he would have either hidden his daytime resting place or had a non-vampire guard."

While Szilagy held the flashlight, Winterbottom bent over the vampire's body, set the stake where he figured the heart should be and raised the hammer.

The Trap Is Sprung

As quick as a blink, Dracula's hand came up and grabbed Winterbottom by the throat. Gasping for breath, Winterbottom dropped the hammer and stake. The vampire's fingers were as strong as iron, and he could not pull them away. He began to lose consciousness.

At the same time, the lids of three other tombs were thrown to the floor with a crash. The three women vampires crawled out of their coffins. Two grabbed Robert, and one attacked Szilagy.

Vlad tossed Winterbottom to the side, reached into his sarcophagus and pulled out three coils of rope. He tossed a length to each vampire lady. "Tie them up."

After his three guests were hogtied, he said to Szilagy, "Do you think I am such a fool as to leave the place where I spend my days dead to the world un-guard-ed?"

"But it's daylight. How can you be animate?"

"There is no day-light in here, although I ad-mit that it is diff-i-cult to stay a-wake. But I and my lad-ies will sleep in a lit-tle while." He took a cell phone from his pocket. When someone answered, he said, "Bor-is. I have them." A pause. "At the crypt."

After he hung up, he said, "We can go back to sleep, lad-ies." He turned to the three trussed up people. "Good-night. I will see you af-ter sun-set."

He and the three women vampires returned to their sarcophagi and closed the lids. A short time later, the crypt door opened. Sivana and Jeeves entered. "Put them in the cart, Jeeves."

"Yes, master."

The android picked up each of the wrapped up people, one at a time, and dumped them unceremoniously into a cart pulled by a donkey. Winterbottom cried, "How could you do this to your old friend Charlie?"

"I am simply following orders. I need this job."

The cart trundled back to the castle where Jeeves loosened the ties on their ankles enough to allow them to shuffle along. They entered a back door of the castle and were led down a narrow spiral stairwell. At the bottom, the stench of old urine and sweat greeted Winterbottom's sensitive nostrils. From there they went through a narrow, low-ceilinged corridor to a group of small cramped cells. It was obvious that the dungeon dated from the time of the inquisition. Faded bloodstains decorated the stone walls. The floors were covered with straw. The only toilet facilities were gutters with drains. There was no cot or washing facilities. The only light was from torches on sconces along the corridor.

Jeeves undid their bonds and shoved Winterbottom and Robert in one cell and Szilagy in the adjacent cell.

Boris Sivana stood rubbing his hands together. "Two fine male specimens. I'm sorry about the accommodations, lady and gentlemen, but don't worry, you will not be here long."

Robert said, "What's going to happen to us?"

"The prince promised the two of you to me for my experiments. He has his own plans for Miss Szilagy. I don't know what they are."

"And what are these experiments?"

"One of you will be used to cure Mister Thrope of his monthly illness. The other will help bring a new being into the world. That is all I can tell you now. I will see you later, when Vlad returns to the castle. Jeeves, keep an eye them."

"Yes, master."

Sivana walked away.

Winterbottom said, "Jeeves, what exactly is he going to do with us?"

"How would I know? I'm not a scientist. He has a combination laboratory and operating room in another part of the castle."

"Have you been there?"

"Once or twice. I helped set up some of the equipment. My chemical sensors tell me that you would find the odor repulsive."

"What is the stench from?"

"Dead things starting to decay, mostly human body parts."

Winterbottom shivered in dread. "Wh-where do the body parts come from? Does Doctor Sivana torture people by cutting them up?"

"I don't think so. The parts are from cadavers."

"That's a relief. What does he do with these body parts?"

"The one's that are not decayed he has sewn together to make a larger cadaver."

"That doesn't make sense. Why does he do that?"

Jeeves shrugged. "I don't have a clue. Actually, I believe Doctor Sivana is insane, even crazier than most of you humans."

Laslo Varga

Several hours later Sivana returned with Vlad Tepes. Tepes said, "I'm sor-ry that you had to en-dure these aw-ful dun-geon cells, but I did not have an-y other place to keep you."

Robert said, "You had better release us at once. Doctor Winterbottom is a famous archeologist. People will be looking for him."

Sivana said, "We will show them his corpse, died mysteriously of natural causes."

"How will explain the fact that both your guests died of the same mysterious illness?"

"Winterbottom will be the only one to die. You will stay a-live, but changed."

"What about Ilona?"

Vlad Tepes said, "My daught-er must be pun-ished for try-ing to des-troy me. That is the rea-son I have come down here. Jeeves, open Il-ona's cell."

As soon as the cell door was opened, Szilagy rushed out and tried to run down the corridor to the exit. Vlad flew after her and caught her. He made her look into his eyes, which put her into a trance. As he and she strolled away, she was like someone sleepwalking.

Sivana took an automatic pistol from his jacket. "Jeeves, open the other cell door. Don't either of you try anything. I'm an excellent shot. Mr. Tepes, you step out of the cell. Doctor Winterbottom, I'm afraid you'll have to stay where you are for now."

Sivana led Robert away. Jeeves followed along. Winterbottom was left alone in the gloomy filthy cell. He paced up and down for a long while contemplating his fate. He had to get out of his prison. That madman Sivana was going to kill him in some horrendous experiment. He examined the cell door. Perhaps he could pick the lock. He took out his Swiss army knife, selected a small blade, reached around the bars and inserted it into the keyhole. He wiggled and jiggled it, but to no avail.

He heard approaching footsteps and pulled his arm back into the cell. He thought, *Oh no. He's coming for me. Maybe I can get the gun away from him after he opens the cell door.*

But it was not Sivana who appeared. It was the Hungarian, Laslo Varga, who pointed a flashlight in Winterbottom's direction. The two men stared at each other for a few moments. "So, did Boris Sivana send you down here to get me?"

"No. But I was following him and Vlad and saw them come down here. They must've gone to another part of the castle."

"Then you're not in cahoots with them. Let me out of this cage, please."

"I can't. I don't have a key."

"Jeeves, the android, has one I think, unless he gave it to Boris."

"I saw him too. They brought you, Mister Robert Tepes and Miss Szilagy down here. Where are they?"

"Boris took Robert to his laboratory, wherever that is. Vlad hypnotized Ilona and brought her somewhere else. Jeeves may be with Boris, but I'm not sure of that. If you can get me out of here, we should rescue them. Boris is going to perform some horrible experiment involving Lycan Thrope, and I don't know what Vlad intends to do to poor Ilona. He's a vampire, you know. But, why were you following Boris and Vlad?"

"I'm not what I pretended to be. But we don't have much time if we're going to rescue your friend. Sivana may be experimenting on him already. I'll find Jeeves and get the key."

"Be careful. Boris is armed and a madman."

After Laslo's footsteps faded away, Winterbottom continued his pacing. He wondered whether he should trust the man. He admitted to not being who he was masquerading as. What was his game?

More time went by. He heard footsteps in the corridor again. He waited impatiently, expecting that it was Varga returning with the key. To his dismay, it was Sivana and Jeeves. They wore lab coats covered with bloodstains and carried a stretcher. On it laid Lycan Thrope. He was either unconscious or dead. Sivana had Jeeves unlock the cell where Szilagy had been. They put the stretcher in it and locked it. They came to Winterbottom's cell.

"What have you done to Lycan Thrope?"

"He's fine, simply recovering from the procedure I performed on him. He needs to be safely behind bars as long as the moon is full. He's a werewolf."

"Y'know, I suspected as much. What about Robert?"

"He's also fine and recovering from a similar procedure. You will find him fit as a fiddle. Now, Doctor Winterbottom, are you ready to assume your new life?"

"I don't know what you have in mind, but I'll have none of it."

Sivana laughed in a insane, evil manner. He pulled out his gun. "Jeeves, unlock that cell."

"Jeeves, don't do it. He's going to do something terrible to me. Remember the first law of robotics."

"I'm sorry, Doctor Winterbottom, but the programming that made me obey the three laws of robotics has been modified by Doctor Sivana. Vlad Tepes is my master, and I must obey him. He told me to do whatever Doctor Sivana asked. So you see, I cannot help you."

"Stop the blathering and open the cell," cried Sivana.

When Winterbottom was let out of his prison, he turned suddenly and with a karate kick, knocked the weapon from Sivana's hand. He smacked the scientist on the side of the neck with the side of his hand, sending him reeling. As he reached for the gun, Sivana cried, "Jeeves, grab him."

Before Winterbottom could pick up the weapon, arms like metal bands held him immobile.

Sivana said, "I didn't want to do this, but you've brought it upon yourself. I must sedate you." He took out a hypodermic needle and a small vial from his lab coat. He filled the hypodermic with the contents of the vial and jabbed it into Winterbottom's buttock. Seconds later Winterbottom felt dizzy, and everything went black.

Sivana's Laboratory

A bright light glared down on Winterbottom. He tried to move to keep it out of his eyes, but found that he could not move anything except his head. He turned to one side. As the fog in his brain cleared, he realized that he was in a laboratory strapped to an operating table. The stench of antiseptic, blood and decayed meat assailed his nostrils.

He heard a familiar voice. It was Robert. "Doctor Sivana, he's awake."

"Good. He must be conscious for the procedure to succeed. Attach the electrodes."

Electrodes? Winterbottom thought. *This is going to be bad.*

Someone approached him and began to attach electrical wires to various parts of his anatomy. It was Robert. "Robert, why are you helping this madman torture me."

Robert peered into his face with an evil glare. "In the first place, I am not Robert Tepes. I wear his body, but I am someone else. And Doctor Sivana is not insane. He cured me. Also, we are not going to torture you." He paused. "Well, there may be some pain, but it will not last long. Then you'll be a new man." He chuckled as though he had made a joke.

"I don't get it. What do you mean when you say you're not Robert, that you only wear his body? Who are you then?"

"You knew me as Lycan Thrope. However, when I leave here, I *will* be Robert Tepes."

"You're not making sense. Has Sivana driven you out of your mind?"

Sivana came over. "Thrope, go over to the power switches and get ready to throw them. Doctor Winterbottom, I will explain everything.

What I've invented is a method for transferring a person's life force, ego, soul or aura, whichever term you prefer, from one body to another. For example, to cure Mr. Thrope of his lycanthropy, I used my method to transfer his life force from his former body to that of Mr. Tepes. Hence, with a new genetic structure, Mr. Thrope no longer becomes a werewolf on full moon nights."

"What about Robert's soul?"

"Unfortunately it went into Thrope's body, which will be inflicted with the same illness."

"So, what have you accomplished? You've simply transferred one man's disease to another man and switched their identities. Not very practical if you ask me."

"You're correct. It can be of no intrinsic value, but it has a certain commercial value that can be exploited by unscrupulous people such as myself. Suppose an octogenarian billionaire should come to me and give me five million dollars to make him young again. I could transfer his essence into a young healthy body. But monetary gain is not my major objective. The advancement of science is my goal. And you, fine sir, will have the honor of being the subject of my grand experiment."

"What grand experiment? What are you going to do to me?"

Sivana moved Winterbottom so that he could see a large man on another operating table. Electrical wires were also attached to this person. The other man seemed unconscious.

Sivana patted the man's chest. "See this fellow. Do you have any idea what he is?"

"Not a clue."

"He's an artificial man that I created with my own hands from parts of cadavers."

"It's a corpse then?"

"At the present moment, he is, but soon he will live. Your life force will be in him. So, you see, I'm doing you a favor. The body I'm giving you will be larger, stronger, younger and healthier than the one you have now."

"But my body is perfectly fine. Except for an occasional head cold, I'm almost never ill. I like the body I'm in." Tears welled up in Winterbottom's eyes at the thought that the handsome face and well-toned body that he admired every morning in the mirror would no longer be his. "Don't do this."

"You'll feel differently once you're him. Lycan, turn on the power."

Thrope flipped the switch that turned on the electrical equipment. Winterbottom felt a jolt of electricity course through his body. It was as though a thousand insects were stinging him. The lights flickered for an instance, but remained on. The machinery buzzed and whirled. Electrical current crackled between two poles. Liquids boiled and bubbled in an elaborate chemical apparatus. Pungent vapors rose. Dials and meters flicked back and forth or rose steadily toward the red. Strange wave forms appeared on an oscilloscope. The stench of ozone permeated the air.

Sivana watched the corpse on the other table for signs of life. Suddenly, he cried, "He breathes. My creation lives. He lives." He jumped around like a madman screaming, "He lives. He lives."

Winterbottom felt his essence draining out of him.

At that moment the door to the laboratory opened, and Varga burst in. He pointed a pistol at Thrope in Robert's body. "Tepes, turn off the power." Thrope knew who he meant, took a look at the pistol and switched off power to the equipment.

"No," cried Sivana. "The transfer is incomplete. Turn power back on immediately."

Varga said, "Don't do it." He approached Sivana. "Doctor Sivana, you're under arrest." He brought out handcuffs and placed one on the mad scientist's wrist and attached the other end to a table. He turned to Robert's body. "You had better leave now, or I'll charge you with aiding and abetting."

Thrope in Robert's body ran from the room. Varga went over by Winterbottom. He unloosened the straps that held him on the table. "Are you alright? I may as well tell you. I'm with Interpol. This man ..." He pointed at Sivana. "... is wanted by various governments for various crimes such as organ legging, grave robbery, kidnapping and murder."

Winterbottom rose to a sitting position. "I'm a bit woozy. Somehow I feel as though something inside of me was missing. It couldn't be anything important though. Otherwise, I'm okay. Quick Vargas, we've got to find Vlad Tepes. He's got Ilona. He plans to do something awful to her. He's really a vampire, the famous Dracula."

"I thought as much. Well, there are laws against vampirism. We Romanians know how to deal with the undead." He dug in his pockets and pulled a large crucifix, a wooden stake and a hammer. "I also have garlic and a hand mirror. My gun is loaded with silver bullets."

"Let's go then."

"Where? Do you know where he brought her?"

"Not exactly. We'll search the castle."

They went up to the main floor. As they entered the foyer, Winterbottom heard piano music from a room halfway down the hall. They entered a well furnished parlor. Szilagy was at the piano playing Beethoven's *Moonlight Sonata*. Her eyes were glazed as though in a trance. Vlad stood next to the piano also with a rapturous look on his face. "Beautifully played, my dear. You make a father proud. The *Moonlight Sonata* is my favorite piece. It speaks of the beauty of the night."

She turned her face toward him and smiled. "It's mine too. Thanks, dad."

When she finished, Winterbottom and Vargas applauded. Winterbottom said, "Are you alright? I was afraid that Vlad was going to harm you."

"Just a family quarrel. We've patched things up. I'm going to live here from now on. How is Robert?"

"Not good. I'm afraid Doctor Sivana has transferred his soul to Lycan Thrope's, the werewolf's, body."

"Oh no. Where is he? I must go to him."

"He's in a dungeon cell. I'll take you to him."

They went down to the dungeon. Tepes, in Thrope's body, was just morphing from his werewolf form to a human one. Vlad opened the cage, and Szilagy rushed in. She took Tepes in her arms. "Oh, my darling. What you had to endure because of that evil man, Boris Sivana."

Robert said, "I'm afraid our love affair is over. You cannot want a man who turns into a wolf periodically."

She chuckled. "Why wouldn't I? Most men become wolves every time a lovely woman passes by. We'll simply lock you up on full moon nights."

While this tender scene was occurring, Vlad had stared into Varga's eyes. The Hungarian inspector turned away. He said, "I must turn Doctor Sivana over to my superiors now. It has been nice meeting you folks." He walked away in a semi-trance.

"Aren't you going to arrest Vlad Tepes?" asked Winterbottom.

"For what? He's done nothing wrong. I'm sure he knew nothing of Sivana's criminal activities." He left the dungeon area.

Soon after, Winterbottom, Szilagy, Robert and Vlad returned to the main floor. Robert thanked him for all his help and paid him his fee with a large bonus. Vlad asked whether he needed transportation.

"Just as far as the village. I can make my way from there." Winterbottom planned to call on the beautiful gypsy woman, Esmeralda. Perhaps he might find her home at a time when her husband was not around.

CPSIA information can be obtained at www.ICGtesting.com
Printed in the USA
LVOW08s1601201016

509596LV00002B/292/P